-24-43-1-10-6-83-67-14-4-
-3-3-43-0-66-0-0-0-6-
-0-7-11-2-1-27-
-9-33-5-0-0-80-1-

CORPORATE HIGH SCHOOL

BENJAMIN GORMAN

Copyright © 2015 by Benjamin Gorman

Published in the United States by Not a Pipe Publishing, Independence, Oregon.
www.NotAPipePublishing.com

Hardcover Edition

ISBN-13: 978-0-9983880-8-3

Cover design by Benjamin Gorman

The names of corporations "Walmart," "Hobby Lobby," "McDonalds," "Starbucks," and "Google," and the use of their associated imagery are registered trademarks of the corporations and are used in this novel as parody and criticism, uses which are specifically protected under 15 U.S.C. § 1125 (3) (ii). The author, Benjamin Gorman, and the publishing company, Not a Pipe Publishing, are not affiliated with the aforementioned corporations. The use of these corporate names and logos are not intended to cause confusion, or to cause mistake, or to deceive as to the affiliation, connection, or association of the aforementioned corporations with the author, the publishing company, or their products, or as to the origin, sponsorship, or approval of his or their goods, services, or commercial activities.

The names of public figures such as Sam Walton, David Green, William Henry Gates III, and David H. Koch, are used as forms of commentary protected by 15 U.S.C. § 1125 (3) (ii and B)

This is a work of fiction. Names, characters, places, and incidents either are products of the writer's imagination or are used fictitiously. Any resemblance to actual persons, living or dead, events, or locales is entirely coincidental with the exception of names of historical and/or public figures like Sam Walton and David Green who are subjects of statements of fact and opinion. Corporations such as Wal-Mart and Hobby Lobby are referenced as a parody and as a criticism of corporate personhood. They are not people.

First Edition published in 2015

ALSO BY BENJAMIN GORMAN

Novels

The Sum of Our Gods

The Digital Storm
A Science Fiction Reimagining of William Shakespeare's The Tempest

Don't Read This Book
A Novel About a Book You Shouldn't Read

Poetry Collection

When She Leaves Me
A Story Told in Poems

Anthologies

Shout
An Anthology of Resistance Poetry and Short Fiction

Worth 1000 Words

pán|dé|mïk|2020
An Anthology of Pandemic Poems by OPA Members

Denial Kills
An Anthology of Poetry and Short Fiction

Corporate High School

To All Teachers and Students
Who Think Real Schools Are Worth Fighting For

23-24-43-1-10-6-83-67-14-4-
1-5 0-3-3-43-0-66-0-0-0-6-
15-12-0-7-11-2-1-27-
19-33-5-0-0-80-1-

PROLOGUE

Sunday, January 6th, 2115

If you are reading this, it means somebody told you about the code. Please don't share it with just anybody. Eventually, The Corporation will crack the code and this record will disappear from the net.

We have to get the word out to as many people as we can first.

People have to know the truth if they are going to fight back.

1-23-24-43-1-10-6-83-67-14-4-
1-5-0-3-3-43-0-66-0-0-0-6-
15-12-0-7-11-2-1-27-
23-23-5-0-0-80-1-

CHAPTER 1

Sunday, September 16th, 2114

Mom is in jail. The Corporation put her there. That's why we had to move, and that's why I have to start at a new high school tomorrow.

That sounds terrible. It sounds like I'm mostly mad because I have to start at a new school. Of course I'm a lot angrier that Mom is in jail. That sucks so bad I don't have words for it. Dad has words for it. Lots of four-letter words. He's super-pissed at The Corporation. He remembers the time before The Corporation ran everything, so, to him, it's this big giant enemy. Me, I can't get that mad at The Corporation. Getting mad at The Corporation is like getting mad at the ocean or at air or at God or something.

Dad is always talking about how things don't have to be this way because they didn't used to be this way. I guess that makes sense, but it's hard for me to imagine it. Like, when he was young, if somebody was charged with a crime, they were arrested by the police.

Then they went to court. If they were poor, they were appointed a lawyer who would fight for them. Dad says those lawyers were often inferior or unmotivated, but at least poor people had someone on their side.

That's not the way it works now. Or, at least, that's not how it worked for Mom. Mom committed the crime of being too poor. When Dad lost his job (that's another story), we couldn't pay the bills. Dad says there used to be something called bankruptcy protection, but that's been gone for a long time. So there was nothing we could do. We thought they would toss us out of our house, take our car, that kind of thing. Instead, The Corporation charged Mom with fraud for using her Corporation credit card to buy food and clothes at one of their CorpMarts, then not paying the bill. They said that was like making a promise and then breaking it. So guys came to our house and took her away, but since our town had privatized the police force, it was Corporation Security Guards (everybody in my old town called 'em CSGs, or just Geez for short) who came to get her. Then, when it came time for the trial, the only attorney who would defend her was the one provided by the government. Only, because The Corporation started those corporate law schools a few years ago and then couldn't find placements for all their grads, they'd contracted with the government to get all the public defender jobs, so they were offering her a Corporation lawyer to defend her from a Corporation charge. So of course that wouldn't work. When she told the judge she was refusing counsel because of the conflict of interests, I think it made him mad, like she was

3

accusing him of running a sham courtroom where people couldn't get real justice (which she basically was), but she sounded very respectful when she said it. Her respectful tone didn't make any difference, though, because he sentenced her to three years in a minimum security prison where she could work off the debts. Guess who runs the prison? Yeah, you guessed it.

At the sentencing, Mom cried and begged the court not to take her away from her husband and her "beautiful little girl." That's what she said. She even repeated it; she pointed at me and made the judge look at me and said, "You see her? That's my beautiful little girl, Harriet. You are taking her mother away, sending her off to debtor's prison. It's 2114, not 1814! You know that isn't right. Don't do this, please." She was crying. I was crying. My dad was even crying, and he's not a crying kind of guy. He's more of a ranting and lecturing kind of guy. But in court, he just cried.

Maybe it would have made a difference if my name had been something more generic like Faith or Grace. Weird names are a sign that somebody is trashy. That's why I hate my name. Nobody names their kid Harriet anymore. My parents picked it because they like Harriet Tubman, this bad-ass abolitionist and suffragist who freed slaves with a pistol in her hand and then fought for women's rights. My parents are both big history buffs. I'll bet the judge didn't even know who Harriet Tubman was, let alone make the connection, but he probably thought my weird name was just one more sign that Mom was a deadbeat.

In retrospect, I like the "beautiful" part of "beautiful little girl." I don't really think it's true, but it was nice of her to say it. I guess I was a beautiful baby, back when I was just soft brown skin and ticklish giggles. Mom probably still sees that baby when she looks at me. That's why I have mixed feelings about the "little girl" part. I know I'll always be her "little girl," and I know that probably would have received more sympathy than "young woman," but I'm 16. I'm not a little girl anymore. I know it. The Corporation sure-as-hell knows it. So I'm pretty sure the Corporation fake court knew it, too. Maybe she would have been better off if she'd told them that I get my clothes in the "Young Women" section of CorpMart, go to a corporate school, text my friends on a CorpMart pre-paid handcom. Maybe then they would have cared about me. I know my mom loves her little girl. The Corporation doesn't.

So we moved here to Oregon because that's where the prison is. Dad wants to be able to visit Mom every chance he can. I want that part, too, but I'm really going to miss my friends in Illinois. Dad knows this is tough for me, so he's trying really hard to be on my side about everything. But, to him, being on my side means being against The Corporation. I don't really care about the politics that much. Ranting about The Corporation doesn't get me any closer to my friends. But I appreciate his effort and the situation we're in, so I'm playing along.

That's why I agreed to keep this journal. Dad wants me to write in it every day after I come home from the new school. I think he wants me to get used to slamming The Corporation all the time the way he does. He's making me write it out on paper, which is weird. I told him it would be much easier as a vlog but that I could type it out as a blog if he wanted, and then people could read it and see what it's like for us out here. That way my friends in Illinois could read it, too. But he said The Corporation would read it and shut it down, and he's probably right. They own all the Internet service providers, so even though you can say whatever you want online, they can control the speed that any page loads, and if they don't like what you are saying they can technically honor your free speech rights but slow down the page so much that nobody can read it. They're allowed to do that. Also, anything bad I write about The Corporation will hurt my future career opportunities. (By the way, I do know that it's not actually called "The Corporation." That nickname has become so common, many people have forgotten the company has an actual, legal name. But really, "The International Chamber of Commerce Global Holding Company and Church of Jesus Christ of the Free Market Utopia, LLC." is way to long two long to write out, especially by hand, and the acronym "I.C.o.C.G.H.C.a.C.o.J.C.o.t.F.M.U. - L.L.C." is just stupid and doesn't spell anything. So I'm going to call it The Corporation like everybody else does.) My dad says that it will be better if I write the whole journal out on paper first, then decide if I want to upload it later. A year ago I would have said he was being paranoid, but I think he's probably right. Only, I doubt I'll ever upload it. I mean, who cares what I have to say about going to school each day?

For example, who will care about how I'm feeling right now? I'm so nervous I can hardly write this down without my hands getting shaky, but who would care about that? It's a predictable kind of nervousness. Tomorrow is my first day at a new school, so of course I'm nervous. I'm a wreck. It affects everything I do. Like, I want to eat, but when I think about grabbing one of the cookies we bought on the train, then I think about not fitting into my jeans for the first day, and I walk around the kitchen in a little circle three time like a nervous dog. Then I give up on the cookies, come back to my suitcase, and try to pick out my clothes again. And that's a whole other nightmare. But I've taken a break from that task for too long now, so I'm diving in again.

Okay, I think I've got my outfit picked out. I think it's a lot harder for girls than for guys. It's 2114, so you'd think we'd be past that kind of sexism, but it's still there. When guys go clothes shopping, CorpMart basically gives them three choices of looks. They can get sports clothes, hunting clothes, and rock'n'roll clothes. The sports clothes are sweat pants or athletic shorts and t-shirts with the logos of sports teams on them. The hunting clothes are camo jeans and camo shirts or t-shirts with pictures of animals on them. The rock'n'roll clothes are black or blue jeans and t-shirts with the logos of bands on them. Those are the options. Guys can be jocks or hunters or musicians. If they want to be interesting, they can mix and match. Their outfits can say, "I like this band, but my camo pants tell you I'm a really aggressive fan." Or, "These sweatpants tell you I like sports, but the animals on

7

my shirt tell you I mostly play hunting video games."
Or, "I'm wearing this team's shirt because I like to
watch football on TV, but these baggy jeans tell you
I'm a cool, casual fan." There are maybe 9 other
combinations, but that's basically it.

Girls' clothes are so much more difficult because,
even though The Corporation wants to put us into
three groups, they all get complicated by the sizes we
can buy. The young women's department has clothes
for girls who want to look sexy-fashionable, sexy-
athletic, and not-sexy-religious. But if you mix and
match those, there are millions of messages you can
send. Plus, it's totally okay for a girl to buy stuff in the
Young Men's department, but if a guy does that, even
in 2114 people are not cool with that. I don't think it's
homophobia as much as a kind of horrified reaction
that a guy doesn't want to fit in. But if a girl goes into
the Young Men's department, it's like she's just
looking for a new way to fit in, and people are okay
with that. Which is unfair. It also means girls have
even more choices to make when they are trying to
decide what kind of messages to send. Like, if I got
boys' jeans that were really loose, that could mean I'm
really casual about things, or it could mean I'm trying
to rebel against gender stereotypes, or maybe that I
like video games and don't play sports. If I paired
them with a tight athletic top over a sports bra, it
could mean I'm athletic but also really conservative
and I'm hiding some tight athletic shorts underneath.
Or it could mean that I'm athletic but I'm interested in
guys who aren't. Or a dozen other things. Or I could
get really tight white jeans in the sexy-fashionable

part of the Young Women's section, and then pair them with a loose rock'n'roll t-shirt from the Young Men's section, and that could mean I'm on the cutting edge of fashion and I'm artistic, or that I'm a band groupie turbo-slut, or, if it's a Christian band, that I'm one of those sexy-for-Jesus girls and the white is a sign of purity and the tight is a sign of sexy. Of course, white jeans would also send the message that I'm the kind of girl who never spills anything and doesn't ever feel nervous about getting her period, and that is definitely not me because I'm anxious about everything all the time which is why I don't own any white jeans.

So here's what I picked: for a top, I'm going to wear a t-shirt from a band from Illinois. The band is called Go Go Dr. Claw, a reference to a cartoon show from last century that I've never seen before, but the shirt is black and tight-but-not-too-tight with a little cut at the neckline that's long-but-not-too-long so it hints at the cleavage I don't really have but doesn't actually show that I don't have any. Besides the cut, I like the shirt because it's rock'n'roll but they don't have it at CorpMart, which pretty much sums up my taste in music.

For pants, I'm wearing these black and gray camo cargos that are too big for me. I'm skinny, so they ride low on my hips, showing off my best feature (my waistline), and hiding the fact that I don't have much in the way of hips or ass. Plus, because they're so loose, it might look like I'm the kind of person who doesn't really care what she wears and just grabbed something crumpled up next to the bed she rolled out

9

of in the morning. I would like to pretend to be her, rather than the person who spent more than an hour trying to figure out what to wear tomorrow. Come to think of it, I'm going to go throw them in a pile next to my bed right now so they have the right wrinkles and not the ones from the suitcase. Probably no one would notice that, but I would spend all day imagining that they were all noticing.

Done. Balled up and crumpled on the far side of one of the hotel room's beds. I have to share a room with my dad until he gets us an apartment, and that could take a few days. He wouldn't like me tossing my clothes on the floor. He'd probably accept it if I explained why, or he'd grumble about how crazy teenage girls are and let me leave them there, but it's not worth trying to explain it. It's better if he just doesn't notice them.

The most important part of the outfit is the part no one will see. It's the necklace that Selina gave me. She's my best friend in Illinois. They have a machine at CorpMart that will print military-style dog tags with whatever you want on them. She got me one that says, "Love you, *Hermanita Negrita*. —Selina." That's what she has called me since we became friends in 1st grade because I have dark skin and she speaks Spanish. Selina is fourth generation American, or, as she likes to say, "My people came here as illegal immigrants back when Americans were treating illegals like shit, back before Americans were illegal immigrants in Canada." That's how she talks. I miss her. It's only been a couple of days, but I wish she were here so bad. I wish she could go to the new school with me tomorrow. She'd protect me. She's shorter than I am now, but she's so ballsy that if anybody looked at me sideways, she'd get right up in their face and use every word on the Corporate Schools Forbidden Word List in two languages. And it's a long list of words.

Instead, if anybody looks at me sideways, I'll just touch the necklace and know she's got my back. Maybe that will give me a little bit of courage.

Right now, I need it.

-24-43-1-10-6-83-67-14-4-
-3-3-43-0-66-0-0-0-6-
-0-7-11-2-1-27-
-5-0-0-80-1-

CHAPTER 2

Monday, September 17th, 2114

I survived. Actually, it wasn't all bad. Some parts were pretty cool. I have really mixed feelings about my first day. That's what I told Dad when he picked me up in the new rental car.

He said, "Having mixed feelings is the perfect sign that you're a teenager."

"Why? 'Cause adults don't have mixed feelings anymore?"

"No, because little kids don't have mixed feelings. Grown-ups do. Trust me, seeing my little girl come out of that school looking brave and grown up, but also knowing it's a corporate school and I have to send her back there tomorrow morning— I know a thing or two about mixed feelings."

I repeated my offer to go to the public school. I really don't want to go there, so I would hate it if he took me up on the offer, but I'm not really that worried about him accepting. Nobody wants to send their kids to public schools anymore, no matter how much they hate The Corporation. Public schools might be free, but you get what you pay for. Corporate schools cost money, but you get it all back in vouchers at tax time, so as long as you sign a contract saying you'll turn the voucher coupons over to The Corporation, they don't really charge you. Meanwhile, the public schools have all the kids who can't get into corporate schools. Like, if you have a disability or you don't speak English or you misbehave and get kicked out of a corporate school. Because corporate schools are technically private, they don't have to accept everybody, so they don't have to take anybody who has any special needs that would cost the company money. So the public schools are a nightmare, because they get the same amount of money per kid as the corporate schools but have to deal with the hardest kids.

Dad knows that. "No, Baby, that wouldn't be right. It's tempting, though. Just because I hate those Corporation mother...." His voice trailed off because he knows he's not supposed to use that kind of language around a kid, but he still said the bad words just loudly enough for me to hear them all because he knows I'm not really a kid anymore. That, more than mixed feelings, is the perfect sign that you're a teenager: Grown-ups don't know how to talk to you anymore.

Speaking of things grown-ups don't know, that brings me back to the beginning of the day. I woke up to find that Dad had found my pants lying on the floor. Noticing they were wrinkled up, he'd ironed them for me. And he'd done it funny, like they were men's formal slacks, ironing these long, crisp pleats in the front that went halfway down to the knees. Only, I had to wear them because he'd gone to all the trouble. At that point, I thought the whole day and probably the rest of my high school career was ruined. We didn't have a car yet because Dad hadn't had a chance to rent one, so we had to take a taxi, and Dad kept asking me if I was nervous and then telling me it would be fine, and that showed me that he was really nervous which then made me more nervous. When the cab pulled up in front of the school, I thought I would throw up.

"Think you can find your way? I don't want to embarrass you," Dad said.

I assured him that I could find my way just fine (which I was not at all certain about) but that I wouldn't be embarrassed to be seen with him (a bald-faced lie). I gave him a hug and got out of the cab.

That's when I was reminded of the absolute best thing about corporate schools: They're all basically the same. Back home in Illinois, I'd gone to Samuel Robson Walton Corporate High School #5491 (named after Sam Walton's oldest son). My new high school has Alice Louise Walton Corporate High School #7348 (named after Sam Walton's only daughter) in big letters next to the CorpMart smiley face, but otherwise it looks the same. It has a big, mostly empty parking lot in front just like my old school because most kids don't drive. It's mainly there for football games and choir concerts and stuff. Near the main doors, there's a wide entrance to the subway station underneath the school. All the corporate schools are built over subway stops (or the subway stops are built under them), and kids were streaming out of the tunnel and up the short flight of stairs into the first building. Like my old school, there are actually four buildings but only one entrance. The buildings are large, two-story boxes covered in beige stucco with no windows on the first floor and only a few windows on the second floor in the managers' offices and the associates' breakrooms on the corners of each building. Building A houses the main office, the counseling office, and a bunch of classrooms. Building B is all classrooms. Building C is vocational and technical ed. classrooms. Building D looks just the same as the other three, but inside it's mostly open from the floor to the second story ceiling around a big enclosed gym, with other PE rooms around it. Even though I couldn't see them, I knew right where the baseball, soccer, and football fields would be in the back: Just like old SRWCHS#5491.

It's hard to describe what a relief it is just to know where to go. I think, at some level, that's the key to The Corporation's success. It tells us where we belong and guides us there so we never have to think twice about where we're going.

Even though ALWCHS#7348 is designed just like my old school, I later learned that it has way fewer students. My old school had almost 5000. My new one has just over 3000. So the lines for the metal detectors were a lot shorter, and, when I looked beyond the machines, the halls seemed eerily empty.

As I neared the front of the line, the two security guards and the greeter seemed to know I was new and nervous. The security guards were around my dad's age. The one waving the wand over everybody was a huge Hispanic guy, easily 6'5", with a very serious expression and a thin, severe mustache. He smiled at me and nodded as I stepped up to the machine, though. The woman watching the X-rays machine's images of the backpacks was chubby and very dark skinned. I think maybe she was glad to see a black student coming into the building, because all the other kids were white or Hispanic. She smiled at me, a big, warm, welcoming smile, and shout-whispered over the machine's humming, "It's gonna be fine." I tried to smile back, but, even though she sounded sincere, the welcome sounded like a warning to me.

The greeter was much older than the security guards. In fact, he was the oldest guy I've ever seen, like somebody had unwrapped a mummy and dropped him on a stool as an advertisement for history classes. The creases in his forehead were so deep he could have been using them to file things. He was thin and hunched over, and his jowls hung down below his chin like a droopy dog's. But when I stepped through the metal detector, he smiled at me so warmly that it felt like his crow's feet were giving me a hug.

"Welcome to Alice Louise Walton Corporate High," he said and then waited to see if I wanted anything. When I mumbled thanks he just nodded and let me pass.

I went down to the office, filled out an online form that pulled up all the records from my old school, and had my schedule transferred to my tablet. The schedule gives you a map to your classes that's GPSed to guide you to where you're going from the exact spot where you're standing, but after a quick glance I knew that all my classes were right about where they'd been in my old school, so I put the tablet in my backpack and headed to my first class, Science Test Prep, Grade 11, Executive Track. Dad says they used to call the highest levels of classes "Advanced" or "Honors," but that seems kind-of vague to me. The Corporation's levels, Executive, Management, and Associates, are far more straightforward. I've always been pretty good at taking tests, so I've always been in the Executive Track. As much as Dad hates the name, he's glad I get into those, because that's the only way to get accepted to one of the universities that aren't owned or operated by The Corporation. Not that it matters, since we'd never be able to afford one of them anyway, but if I keep my test scores up I can start at the Executive Track at one of the state universities that are run by The Corporation, and I should be in good enough shape after that.

When I got to the class, I was one of the first students, and that was a good thing. I would have been embarrassed if I'd had to pull out my tablet with everybody watching in order to find my seat in the seating chart, but since there were only a couple student in there, I didn't mind them seeing me do the search. In a couple of clicks, I found my seat in the middle of the sixth row. There, I fiddled around on the web, looking for funny articles that got through the Corporation Speed Scrubbers, but, really, I was watching as all the kids came in.

The first thing I noticed was that there were no other black kids. That got my attention, but I guess that's because I'm overly-sensitive about my skin color. Lots of the kids were Asian or Hispanic, so it wasn't like the school was all white, but it was pretty different from my school in Illinois. I decided it wouldn't be a big deal and to pretend that I hadn't even noticed. That's the way we do it, now. We notice that all the models in all the CorpMart ads are in groups that are perfectly mixed to include as many races as possible, and then we politely pretend that we didn't notice. My dad is the first to point out that we haven't graduated to perfect racial equality as long as almost all the executives and politicians and 1%ers are white, but we're polite enough not to talk about that in public, and that's an improvement over a time when people enslaved or hanged one another, I suppose.

The next thing I noticed was that, beyond some slight differences in racial demographics, everybody was the same as they had been at Samuel Robson Walton Corporate High School. They wore the same clothes they each carefully selected from the same sections of CorpMart. The little buzzing sounds that escaped from their earpieces were produced by the same bands on all the Corporation Music Video channels. The backpacks they wore were one of three designs you could find at CorpMart (sporty, hunter, and rock'n'roll, of course). They all carried tablets that were only differentiated by their colors: Pastels were from last year's models, earth tones from the year before that, neon for the latest models. Next year it would probably be back to bright primary colors, and then we'd start the cycle all over. It made sure that we all wanted the newest model, but the technology didn't change much. My dad once explained that CorpMart had figured out that cosmetic improvements were good for business, but significant improvements might lead to decreases in sales of old models and all their stock of add-ons. It was just more efficient to make us want computers that already worked with all the stuff they already had.

I was thinking these anti-Corporation, cynical thoughts of my dad's and barely noticing the kids who kept coming into the room. After maybe 60 of them had walked by me, somebody actually caught my eye. Suddenly, all those complaints about sameness disappeared.

He wore the same kinds of signals everyone else did, all sporty clothes, a sporty backpack, a new neon green tablet with a football logo on the back and another glowing on the wallpaper. But, somehow, he transcended the brands. Clearly he was a jock. He was a good six inches taller than everyone else and made of muscles. But then, the guys with him were all no-necks, too, and my eyes could barely focus on them. It was as though everyone else in the room was suddenly being filmed with those old, fuzzy cameras that used film on reels, the ones they show us clips from in history class to show us scenes from way back, but he was in Mega-Optimized-Super-Retinal-HD. Maybe the other guys in the class were out of focus because they were all trying to grow mustaches that just made them look fuzzy and gross. He looked like he'd shaved right before walking into the room and the aftershave hadn't dried yet. In fact, that's exactly what he looked like: a model for razors or shaving cream, with really thick, straight, brown hair that made you think he probably needed to shave all the time, but without a single hair on his face, even in the perfect cleft in his chin. Have I mentioned that I really don't like facial hair of any kind? I might have failed to mention that.

Like those models, he also looked like he didn't care at all about his perfect appearance. For example, he looked like his eyebrows were sculpted, but he also radiated such coolness that I was absolutely sure he didn't have to sculpt them. It was like a giant block of marble fell out of the sky, hit the floor right in front of Michelangelo, and before Michelangelo could even put a chisel on it and hit it with a hammer, all the excess marble fell away and this guy was just standing there shrugging, saying, "No big deal."

I felt such a strong urge to run my fingers through his hair that I involuntarily spread my hands out on my desk just to keep them under control.

A soft voice behind me said, "If you drool on your first day, that impression will last forever."

I turned around way too fast, almost spinning and spilling myself out of my chair. "What? I didn't—I don't know—"

The girl was dressed in the wildest get-up I have ever seen. Her shirt was old, like maybe a hundred years old. It had been a white shirt with a simple yellow smiley face on it, but she'd dyed it all these colors radiating out from the face in waves. Her hair was blond and straight and very long. It trailed down her back while two big earrings escaped into the light in the front. They were silver rings with little shimmering decorations hanging from them. I stopped talking (finally) because I was trying to figure out what they were.

She pointed at them. "Dolphins. I know. Crazy."

"Oh," I said. At the time, that seemed like a perfectly intelligent response. "And I wasn't going to drool or anything."

"I exaggerate. For fun. I'm sure no one noticed you were staring. And who wouldn't, right? But he's taken, so, you know, hands off the merch."

"Oh, is he your—" I started.

"No way. Ken's a god among boys, and I'm a freak-a-zoid among drones, so we're not at all compatible. No, he's dating Kimberly."

"Super popular mean girl?"

"Worse. Super popular girl who is so nice that everybody loves her."

"Fake?"

"Nope. The real deal. I would say that we used to be best friends, but then it sounds like we had a falling out or I'm just jealous that now she's everybody's best friend. Which I'm not but I am just a little. By the way, what's your name?"

She said this all so fast that I almost forgot the answer to her question, but I felt like I had to spit it out before I lost a game show. "Harriet."

"Catch me at lunch, Harriet. I'll tell you all about everybody who is worth knowing." She pointed at the ceiling. "Bell."

And, a millisecond after she said it, the bell rang.

21

The screen at the front of the room lit up and the lights slowly dimmed. Everybody had their tablets out, so the room was a field of glowing screens planted in neat rows.

The teacher on the screen wore the usual white shirt, dark tie, and blue vest with a nametag. It said, "Mr. George." He flashed a smile that was clearly the product of a reminder on the teleprompter.

"[Big Smile!]" it must have said.

"Welcome to Science Test Prep, Grade 11, Executive Track, Day 20. Please log in on your tablets so I can take attendance."

We all tapped a few times. When a hundred kids tap gently on glass screens at the same time, it makes this barely-audible drumming, the sound of bones hiding under skin.

"Good." Mr. George looked at his own tablet. "It looks like all 186 schools are present in real time. Excellent." He said "excellent" as though acknowledging the least important event in the history of the world. "Today we're going to review the portion of the test that covers the water cycle...."

I leaned over toward the girl with the dolphin earrings and whispered, "How will I find you at lunch? What's your name?"

"Sky. Well, my parents named me Scarlet, but I renamed myself Sky."

"Sailor's delight," I said.

"Huh?"

Just then, both our tablets vibrated and little pink rectangles with rounded corners popped up, informing us that we were being given a warning from the Discipline System not to talk during class. You used to be able to cover the microphone on your tablet and get away with whispering during class, but since then The Corporation has installed cameras and mics in all four corners of every room and the system monitors all the students all the time. If you break the rules (talking during a lecture, using a word on the Corporate Schools Forbidden Word List, whatever) you are given a warning, and your parents get an email telling them how many warnings you have received. Too many warnings, and you're kicked out and have to go to the public schools. Now I had a warning on my very first day and Dad would hear about it before I even got home.

I sat stock-still, eyes focused on the screen in front of me, holding my breath so that I wouldn't get another one, but I guess Sky wasn't too phased by the warning. "Oh," she continued whispering, "and you won't have to look hard to find me at lunch. You won't even need the search map. Just use your ears."

I didn't look at her. I didn't want a second warning. But I nodded just enough to let her know I'd heard her. I also heard her tablet vibrate when the system gave her a second warning. Out of the corner of my eye, I saw her lean her tablet up, cover the camera with her thumb, and flip off the warning bubble with a shaking hand held close to her chest. I didn't turn, but I couldn't help but smile, and a little laugh tried to escape from my nose.

Sky, I decided, would make Alice Louise Walton Corporate High School #7348 bearable, at least until they kicked her out.

CHAPTER 3

Monday, September 17th, 2114, continued

After Science Test Prep, English Test Prep, P.E. Test Prep, and History Test Prep, it was finally lunch time. I resisted the urge to search for Sky on the Search Map. It identifies where everybody's tablet is in real time, so it would have been much easier to find her that way, but I took the bait and went on a Sky scavenger hunt.

In between the four buildings, there's a big courtyard. It looks similar to the one at my old school, but here I noticed an interesting difference. The one at my old school was completely covered with a Plexiglas ceiling that would bear the weight of the Illinois snow. The floor had carpet. The tables were made of pressboard and chairs had fabric cushions. Clearly, it was an indoor space that just happened to allow sunlight in through the transparent ceiling. The one here has a concrete and brick floor. Metal tables and benches line the sides of the courtyard. In the middle of the courtyard, there are these round stone planter boxes with real flowers and bushes growing in them. When I first looked up, I thought the ceiling was made of the same rectangular Plexiglas tiles, but when I looked more closely, I realized the tiles were actually flat screen TVs sharing a single image of a blue, sunny sky dotted with a few puffy clouds. This courtyard is designed to create the illusion that we're really outside. It makes me wonder, do the corporate schools in Arizona and California do this, too? Do they have the same planter boxes but with sand and cacti? Do the courtyards in Minnesota and North Dakota have courtyards at all? Maybe all the corporate schools aren't quite as identical as I thought.

Of course, none of them can really have outdoor courtyards. There may be regional differences, more snow in Illinois but more blue sky days to show off, more gray, overcast days here in Oregon to hide behind a fake, projecting image on the ceiling, but the weather is broken everywhere. The people who design the schools are from an older generation that is still surprised by this fact. They think we need to see blue skies so we can be fooled into thinking everything is okay. My generation, we've grown up indoors. Almost every day is too hot to go outside in the middle of the afternoon. We hide out in our apartments, ride the underground subways, hide out in air conditioned schools, even eat under fake TV skies at lunch. We're used to everything being record breaking. Record breaking high temperatures on random winter days. Record breaking lows during storms in the summers. Every summer is the hottest on record. It seems like each super-storm has record breaking wind speeds or dumps the largest amount of water ever recorded. And then there's the coastal flooding and the inland droughts. The Corporation might want us to think about the local weather, but they can't fix the global climate. And since every town has the same CorpMart grocery store, the same CorpMart mall, the same corporate restaurants, they should just give up on making each high school feel slightly different....

I was contemplating this when I heard the guitar. I couldn't see where it was coming from at first, but the sound echoed gently between the stone rings and the concrete walls. I walked around the big planter boxes until I saw her.

Sky sat on the edge of one of the planter boxes with a guitar on her lap. The body of the guitar was light blue (sky blue, I realized), and she was picking a complex melody made by plucking individual strings, but when she saw me, the song suddenly changed. Now she played chords that formed a simple tune, and she started to sing in a powerful, clear, beautiful voice:

"Oh Harriet,
"I wondered how long it would take
"But you sought me and now you have found me
"Sitting here by the side of a—"

She stopped, resting her palm against the strings so that all the music died, and she looked around in an exaggerated way, then shrugged and started again.

"...a lake
"Made of bushes and flowers and plants.
"Oh Harriet,
"I want to compliment you on your well-pressed pants."

26

I felt my face flush at the mention of my dad's ironing job, but I laughed with her as I sat down.

"My dad was nervous for my first day," I explained, "so he ironed my pants before I woke up."

"Okay, one: Your dad sounds adorable. And two, the pants look great."

"Thanks," I said, looking down at the creases that had mostly disappeared when I shoved the pants roughly into my gym locker. "He did this weird thing with the creases."

"He made them into Mom Pants. 'Cause he's a guy, and that's how they think all pants should be ironed."

"Exactly."

"Like I said, he's adorable."

"That is not the word I would use to describe him, but I would love to see his reaction if you called him that to his face."

"We'll make that happen," she said, and I felt like I'd been accepted 100%. I mean, who just meets you and promises to come over to your house to make fun of your parents?

I changed the subject. "So, you said you'd tell me about everybody who is worth knowing."

"Yes, well, we should divide everybody into groups. First, there are the people worth knowing. Then there are the people worth knowing about. Which do you want to know first?"

"Um, I guess the people worth knowing?"

She smiled. "Good call. As of right now, I would say the people worth knowing at Alice Louise are one Sky Leibowitz and one Harriet Washington." She

27

leaned closer to me and said, "I googled you. I hope you don't mind."

"Google" wasn't quite on the Corporate School Forbidden Word List, but it was still a little subversive. The Corporation bought out Google in a hostile take-over like 50 years ago, but no matter how much they try to kill the verb "googled," encouraging us to use the generic term "searched" or the inexplicable verb "bing-ed," the word "google" hangs on.

"No problem. Wish I'd thought to google you. But then, if you're the only other person worth getting to know, that shouldn't take long," I said. I tried to have a jokey tone, but I think she could hear a bit of disappointment in my voice. If Sky had zero friends and I had zero friends, adding one another probably meant we were doomed to have one friend each until graduation.

She elbowed me like we'd been chums forever. "I'm just being a snot. Let's see. You'll need to be introduced to Lucas, Gina, and Juan as soon as humanly possible. They're all in the play and they have play practice during lunch and after school, so I'm a drama widow for a while. That's why the timing of your arrival is so perfect. Anyway, Lucas is the funniest person I know. He's gay and out and flamingly fabulous. Juan is his best friend, so everybody thinks they have a thing together, but Juan is straight and secretly in love with Gina. Gina is straight and secretly in love with Lucas."

"So is Lucas in love with Juan?"

"Alas, the triangle of misery is broken, because Lucas loves to have everybody give him attention but he can't really be in a relationship with anybody. His parents disapprove of his sexuality, so he plays up how flamboyant he is just to make them mad, but they've also made him secretly hate his own sexuality so he doesn't ever want a relationship. He's complicated."

"So, if Gina knows Lucas is gay — and complicated — why doesn't she take the hint and notice Juan?"

"My dear Harriet, the heart wants what the heart wants. Plus, Gina is hyper-sexual but doesn't want to be a slut, so being in love with Lucas is the safest thing for her right now. That's my amateur psychologist professional opinion."

I nodded. "It's good. You're good at that."

"I'll go one better. Juan loves Gina because he has low self-esteem and loving her reinforces his belief that he's not worthy of love."

"Ah," I said. "But you recognize that he is worthy and secretly love him, right?"

I was totally kidding. But Sky, who talked faster than anyone I'd ever met and didn't seem to need to breathe, suddenly sat up and sniffed in two big, gasping lungs full of air, like I'd punched her and knocked the wind out of her, or like she'd been crying and was trying to hide a sob.

"Holy fl—" she started.

"Just kidding!" I shouted, cutting her off before she could say any words that were on the Corporate School Forbidden Word List and get in trouble for the third time in one day because of me.

29

"I never thought about it like that," she said, looking out into the courtyard and speaking to no one in particular. "Do I love him? Like, love, love? Or even a crush? Do I have a crush on Juan?" Then she looked at me, hard. "Do I have a crush on Juan? Do I love him?"

I held up my hands to defend myself. "I've never met the guy. Is he cute?"

"Well, yeah. I mean, yeah, I guess he really is."

"Is he smart?"

"Yeah."

"Funny?"

"Big checkmark. Really funny. That's a huge deal to me."

I shrugged. "I don't know anything about love, but that sounds like a crush to me."

"Well look at you, Miss Love Connection! First day!"

"Beginner's luck," I said.

"So, are you going to tell him?"

"Absolutely, positively not! I think I mentioned that he's secretly in love with Gina? Wait until you meet Gina."

I couldn't really respond to that, not having enough knowledge of the parties to argue against Sky's appraisal of Gina's unbeatable status.

Instead, I took the opportunity to pull my lunch out of my backpack, open the can of Diet Coke and the pre-packaged cheddar-ham-crackers-and-candy-bar Lunchable, and make myself my first mini-sandwich, washed down with the soda. It tasted like refrigerated plastic mixed with the grease from factory machinery.

I couldn't wait until my dad got us an apartment so I would have a kitchen to make real lunches in.

"So," I said, my mouth still half-full, "what about the people worth knowing about?"

"You mean Ken?"

My face felt hot again. "No," I said too soon and choked a little, breathing in some cracker crumbs and carbonation. I coughed a few times while Sky smiled knowingly.

"You know my secret, and now I know yours. So we're even and can't tell a soul until the other one dies. Classified. Redacted from all documents." She mimed zipping her lips shut, turning a key, and throwing it over her shoulder. When you think about it, that makes no sense. Zippers don't lock with keys. Still, I knew what she meant.

"Seriously, I don't have a crush on this Ken person."

She did a very bad impression of me, dropping her voice way down. "'This Ken person.' Right. Methinks she doth protest too much. You know, those are lies you're choking on, not crackers."

I laughed, then coughed some more.

I was rising up out of this coughing fit when I noticed this group of guys walking by us, and when I looked up, this tall, kind-of skinny giant shadow loomed over me.

"Hey, Sky," Ken said. And then he was looking at me. "Hey."

"Hi," I said. That was it. Anything else and I would have coughed some more. Or barfed up pre-process

31

slices of cheese and crackers on his very, very white shoes.

Sky swooped in for the assist. "This is Harriet. She just moved here from Indiana."

"Illinois," I corrected.

"Right," Sky continued. "That's what I meant. I have officially decided she is cool."

"Cool," he repeated. "Well, welcome to Oregon and Alice Louise Walton Corporate High."

"Thanks," I said.

I thought about what to say next.

He thought about what to say next.

Mostly, we just looked at each other's faces. It should have been painfully awkward, and I'm sure it was for Sky, and it obviously was for his friends because one of them put a meaty hand on his shoulder and said, "Yeah, welcome, Harriet," and started guiding Ken away.

But it wasn't awkward. It didn't even seem strange that Ken mumbled, "Yeah. Harriet," as he walked away, or that I just kept looking up at the place where his face had been. I can't even remember if I was looking up at the fake sky or at a patch of the stucco walls of Building 2 because all I could see was his face.

"Holy ...flooding ...flood!" Sky squealed.

Her tablet vibrated in her backpack as two more warnings for using forbidden words popped up, but she was too excited to care.

CHAPTER 4

Monday, September 17th, 2114, continued

Okay, so I guess I should make this clear for anybody who is ever reading this from another country, just in case I ever do decide to post it online. Of course, it would take you about three seconds to figure out the "flood" reference if that's not a curse word where you're from. Still, I'll write about it because it actually explains a lot more of my life right now than just what Sky got in trouble for.

Different countries have different swear words, and different people take different words more seriously than others, right? Well, we used to be the most puritanical country about sex and bodily functions, so, while the Brits got their panties in a bunch every time somebody said "Bloody" because it was a reference to the blood of Jesus, they could toss around the C-word like it was no big deal. But our body-part dirty words were off limits, like the D-word and the C-word, and bodily function related words like the S-word. Then we had the mother of all bad

33

words, the F-word, because that was a word related to sex, and that was something we just didn't talk about way back when. But then we caught up with the Europeans, thanks to the Internet and all the porn, and none of that bodily function/sex stuff was off-limits anymore. Only, it turns out, people really like having some words that are off-limits because then they can break the rules to show that they are upset or excited. So we desperately needed a bad word and we had played those old ones out. Basically, we needed a new F-word.

At the same time, the sea levels were rising and there were all these horrible storms and refugee crises. Whole states, like Florida, disappeared. I know that's old news because it happened like 40 years ago, but it relates, so bear with me. So people didn't want to think about all the horrible devastation that came with the sea level rising, but they needed a thing they weren't allowed to say, and it was like "Ta-da!" So people started using "Flood" instead of the old F-word.

And then there were the pandemics that spread all over the world because people were living more and more closely together as the waters rose, so "Plague" became a bad word, too. Lots of insults use words like "Pox" and "Scab" and "Puss." But none of them is as bad as "Flood."

Of course, the old bad words are on the Corporate Schools Forbidden Word List, even though they are old-fashioned now, but the big one that most students get in trouble for is the new F-word. You're allowed to say it if you're actually talking about a flood. You just

34

can't use it as an expletive, and the computers can detect that from context in a blink. Bam. There's your warning point, your email to your parents, your possible expulsion to the public schools. One day into getting to know me, and Sky was looking down the barrel of that.

But here's why it really connects to my life: This town, just like my old city in Illinois, exists because of the flooding. We used to live in a town that came into being when all the people had to move out of cities like Chicago and St. Louis because the Mississippi turned into a lake and Lake Michigan basically washed Chicago away. My parents met at the University of Illinois, which was in this twin city called Urbana-Champaign, but it was in this really flat part of the state and became a swamp. So they moved to this new, artificially elevated town, basically an island in the swamp north of where St. Louis used to be, and that's where I was born. It's called New Rockbridge which is funny because it has tons of bridges but none of them are made of rock, unless you count concrete.

See? Flooding determined where I was born. And then it determined where I'd move, because this city where we live now is called Mt. Hood. Obviously, it used to just be a mountain, but the people had to move to it and build a city.

Oh wait. It gets better. When my dad picked me up in the rental car at the end of the first day, he was super-excited because he'd found a job, and it even comes with an apartment that we'll be able to move into next weekend. Guess what he'll be doing?

Construction. For people and businesses displaced by the flooding.

Dad was so happy about the job and the apartment that he took me out to a restaurant that isn't owned by The Corporation or located inside one. That's a big deal for us. We can't really afford places that make their own food in their own kitchens after you order it. Those are for special occasions or for Corporation Specialists (you know, like doctors and dentists). It was really hard for me to sit there and pretend to be happy for him. I ordered a salad because it was the cheapest thing on the menu, but I told Dad I was just so excited for him that I didn't have much of an appetite. Really, I was in agony, so mad at the whole situation and then hungry as well because the salad wasn't very filling.

I should have been happy. I didn't tell Dad about Ken, of course, but I told him about Sky and how she was going to introduce me to her friends. Talking about that made me feel a little better for a while, and that brief bit of real joy helped me hide my true feelings. I think, because he was happy, he wanted to see the bright side of my day, too. He didn't even mention the warning points I'd received during first period, though I'm sure he got the email. I'm not sure if all adults are that way, or just all parents, or just my dad, but it seems to be a pretty common thing; older people can't handle the strength of young people's feelings, so they decide what we should be feeling and then pretend that's all they see. Or they just dismiss our feelings as hormones or something, shake their heads, and grumble about "teens."

But I have every right to be mad. Sure, I made a friend, and a cute boy talked to me, but c'mon! I'm not one of those ditzy girlie-girls who gets so sucked into that kind of thing that she forgets about the rest of the world. I sat there wearing a plastic smile, but my eyes and brain still worked. I mentioned that my parents met in graduate school, right? My dad has a Ph.D. in history. He's smarter than every Corporation executive in this whole town. And he's happy because he has a job in construction and we'll have a tiny apartment? Oh, and let's not forget that Mom is in jail just down the road!

The whole situation is so thoroughly flooded-up!

Dad is asleep now. We came home, watched some shows online, and he sacked out pretty quick. I can hear him snoring softly. That used to be a good sound because it helped me to feel that he was close. Right now, while I sit here writing this under the light of the little lamp on the hotel-room desk, it's a good sound because it lets me know that I can hide these hot, angry tears that are falling down my face. He won't hear me sniffing and ask me what's wrong. Even the comfort of the sound of his snoring is twisted up and ruined here.

I hate this place.

-24-43-1-10-6-83-67-14-4-
-3-3-43-0-66-0-0-0-6-
-0-7-11-2-1-27-
-5-0-0-80-1-

CHAPTER 5

Friday, September 21ˢᵗ, 2114

The last week has been crazy-busy. Sure, there's the exact same amount of homework as there was in Illinois, but that's not really a big deal. Some take-home, practice multiple choice tests. I fill in bubbles pretty quickly. But on top of that, we had to move in to our new apartment and get it all set up. We went to see Mom for the first time. I don't think I'm quite ready to write about that yet. And I started hanging out with Sky's friends. That was the best part. They seem really cool, and they might just make this place livable.

On my second day at Alice Louise Corporate High, Sky introduced me to her friends. Instead of eating in the courtyard, she grabbed me by the arm and led me down to the auditorium. She walked in as if she owned the place, dragging me like a sacrificial animal or a convict being led to the gallows, right down the middle aisle between rows and rows of empty chairs while the cast of the play tried to pretend we weren't interrupting while shooting suspicious glances in our direction. She basically pushed me into a seat in the front row, plopped down beside me, and stared up at the annoyed actors on the stage.

I didn't even know the play. Sky had told me that it was about pioneers in Nebraska, an adaptation of a novel from 1910 or 1915 or something. Sky said that Gina read the book when she heard they were going to be doing the play, and Gina assured everybody that it was really good, but once they had the script, they all admitted this particular version was pretty terrible. Gina had wanted to play the lead, Alexandra, but instead she'd been given a small part, Mrs. Hiller, a character described in the cast list as "a neighbor." Juan wanted to play Carl because he was Alexandra's lover, but instead he got the part of Frank, a guy who kills some of the main characters in a fit of rage.

"He's totally wrong for the part," Sky said, "but he does a pretty good job anyway."

Lucas, in an effort to shock everyone, tried out for the part of Marie, a girl who is the love interest of two of the male characters. Instead, he got the part of the priest, and Sky assured me the director was having a hard time keeping Lucas from playing him like the most out, flamboyant gay priest in history.

Because the three had small parts, Sky got their attention and motioned for them to come down and join us in the front row. Juan and Gina stood just off stage, and they shook their heads, obviously afraid to break the rules during rehearsal. Sky just kept waving them over, and she wasn't particularly subtle about her hand gestures. Finally the director stopped the actors on stage and said, "I'm sorry, but this is a closed rehearsal." He was a senior who wore a black turtleneck and brought his own director's chair to sit in.

"Oh," Sky said, almost succeeding in sounding like she had no idea she was doing anything wrong. "Okay. Well, I just need Gina, Juan, and Lucas for a minute, and since they aren't in this scene, we'll just step out into the hall."

The director rolled his eyes and waved us all out of the room.

In the hallway, Gina tried to scold Sky as soon as the door closed. "Sky, you can't just pull us out of—"

"Guys, this is like a thousand times more important than a rehearsal." She took my arm again and pulled me in front of them. "This is Harriet. She's new here. She has my official seal of approval so you all need to befriend her right now before she replaces you."

There was a weird moment where no one knew what to do. I think I shrugged and waved. Gina waved and said, "Hi." Juan hesitated, then reached out and shook my hand.

Lucas rolled his eyes. "Oh my gaawd, guys. You have no idea how to be civilized, sociable creatures, do you?" Then he looked at me. "Hmm. I think you should be greeted in a Parisian style, don't you?" He looked at Sky. "She looks like an exotic Parisian runway model type, don't you think?"

Sky didn't even hesitate. "Exactly."

I was frowning, confused, when Lucas grabbed my upper arms like he was going to pull me into a hug, then leaned towards me and kissed the air on either side of my face. After the second kiss, he got even closer and whispered, "*Enchanté, ma chérie.*"

I must have looked pretty funny when I said, "Um, *¿Hola, mi amigo?*" I take Spanish as my foreign language test prep., so I wasn't even sure what he'd said.

It didn't matter, because Juan and Gina cracked up, but not in a mean way, and then they started asking me all these questions about myself as though I was a part of the group who had been away for a long time and they had to catch up on all the details of my life.

That afternoon, I told my dad my friends wanted to get together for some ice cream at night. He wanted to drive me, but I assured him I could take the subway to the CorpMart Mall just as easily as I could take it to school, and they'd given me directions even though I wouldn't really need them, so I was fine. He agreed to let me go, but I could tell he was pretty nervous about it.

Everything went fine, though. I took the subway there, got out at the stop that is right under the mall, and went up to the ice cream place on the third floor. I found Sky, Gina, Juan, and Lucas at a table by the railing overlooking the whole mall, and we ate ice cream and drank Coke and shot spit wads at the people below us and laughed so loudly that eventually one of the security guards came over and told us we had to knock it off or she'd have to kick us out. So it was basically the best night I've had a long, long time.

That was Tuesday. On Wednesday, after school, Dad and I went to the prison to see Mom....I'm still not ready to write about that yet.

On Thursday, Gina, Juan, and Lucas had rehearsal after school, so Sky and I went to the library. It's an empty, closed-down building made of brick with concrete pillars in the front, built way back when people from Portland first started moving up here to Mt. Hood to get away from the rising floodwaters of the Willamette and Columbia rivers. Back then, people would check old-fashioned paper books out of places like that, but once everybody got used to reading everything on their tablets, it just couldn't be sustained, and The Corporation didn't like libraries because they kept people from buying books at the The CorpMart online store, so it went the way of the dinosaurs like so many other kinds of places. But the building is still there, and Sky likes to sit on the steps and play her guitar for the people walking by. She puts out a hat like people should drop coins in even though she knows no one carries coins, so instead they mostly take pictures of her with their handcoms like she's a statue representing all the street musicians who ever lived. Sky loves that.

I just sat next to her, criss-cross-applesauce style like they taught us when we were little, but I didn't sing at first because I don't have a musical bone in my body. Eventually she got me to be the rhythm section by tapping out a beat on the side of her guitar while she played, then tricked me into singing a little bit. Pretty soon we were singing together, mostly old bluegrass-emo-fusion songs from way back in the

2050s and 60s. And I can't express how good it felt to just sing like there was nothing wrong with the world, but also to sing like all the pain is as real as breath and you can push it out if you find just the right note. When I'd think about that, about my mom and my dad and my upside-down life, I'd forget that we were sitting out in front of a closed library in front of everybody, just two girls messing around. I'd sing like I really meant it, because I did, and then I'd stop being all nervous about my singing and we sounded really good. Sky noticed, too, and she said we were a great little band, but she didn't ask why I was suddenly singing that way because she could tell that I wasn't ready to explain. I loved her for not asking.

So that was Thursday. Which brings us to today.

Our varsity football game was a home game, so we all went. My dad drove me because all the parents come out to the games, too. He didn't go to the games in Illinois, and I didn't either, and that was no big deal there, but I guess he learned about the games from the people at his work because he was the one who told me we had to go.

I was nervous about telling him that I wanted to sit with my friends, but after he finally found a spot and parked the rental in the high school's packed parking lot, while we walked with the crowd toward the football field behind Alice Louise Corporate High, I worked up the courage.

He stopped all of a sudden, and I thought I'd hurt his feelings. Instead, he did this thing my mom taught me how to do when I was two years old. He bobbed his head from side to side, sliding it back and forth on

43

a horizontal plane, popping it to punctuate his words. Mom has always said this is the key to showing a little attitude, and that attitude is a black girl's form of martial arts. But my dad actually does it even better than she does. Whenever he gets any attitude from her, he does it back to her in this really exaggerated way and sometimes snaps a "Z" in the air to really make fun of her. She always laughs when he does that, and that laugh is the best "I love you" in the whole world. So when he did that to me while he said, "Maybe I want to sit with my own friends. Did you think of that, Miss Thang?" I felt so happy I wanted to cry.

And he wasn't only kidding. He found some guys from his work that he wanted to sit with, and I could see them all having a good time because Sky just happened to be sitting ten rows behind him and slightly off to one side.

After I found her and sat down, the others found us, and that was when the weird love dynamics of the group became completely obvious to me. When Gina arrived, she sat down on the other side of Sky, but there were some other people down the row, so Juan couldn't sit next to her. He sat by me at first, not too close and not too far. Then Lucas showed up and just wedged himself in between Juan and me like that was perfectly normal behavior. So, while we watched the game in front of us, we had to lean forward whenever we wanted to talk to one another. Of course, we mostly wanted to talk because none of us are huge football fans. I was in the middle, so I had the perfect position to witness the weirdness. Whenever Gina would lean forward to say something, Juan would lean forward to make sure he could hear every word. When Juan would talk, Gina would lean back and Sky would lean forward to listen to him. Gina would lean in to laugh loudly at all of Lucas' jokes. Lucas, for his part, didn't lean toward anybody in particular, because he wanted to make his jokes so loudly that everybody around us could hear, so he would just stare straight forward and make these big pronouncements.

"This sport is perfect!" he'd announce. "Men in tight pants piling onto one another for my entertainment. It's beautiful. This has to be the gayest sport."

Juan frowned. "No way. The two-man bobsled. Ice dancing."

"Winter Olympics don't happen often enough to satisfy my needs."

Sky leaned forward. "Juan's right, though. Men's competitive diving? Greco-Roman wrestling? Beach volleyball?"

Lucas rolled his eyes. "Clearly you just like to see a bunch of nudity, you skank. I am a chaste young gentlemen. The tight pants are sufficient. In dog-pile formations."

Gina was leaning forward to stare around me at Lucas. She rocked back, laughing a little too loudly at his joke.

"See?" Lucas continued. "Gina knows what I'm talking about. Minx."

Sky and I shared a look.

"Dude, this game is all about hetero aggression," Juan said. "Those guys are venting all their sexual energy into trying to kill each other, but they aren't doing it for you. They're doing it for the cheerleaders down there."

Lucas sighed loudly. "That's probably true. But the cheerleaders don't really care how many skulls they crush, do they? They aren't even watching the game. The cheerleaders are looking up here. And you, my boring hetero friend, are looking at the cheerleaders. So really, the boys might as well be playing for Gina, Sky, and me."

Juan shrugged. "I can't argue with that." Then he looked at Gina to make sure he was in the clear. She was looking at Lucas. Sky looked down at the ground. I saw it all.

"Besides," Lucas continued, "I know one player who isn't playing for the cheerleaders." Suddenly, he stood up and shouted, "Hey, Ken! Score a touchdown! Harriet is watching!"

He wasn't loud enough that Ken could hear him, but I grabbed him and pulled him back down anyway. "Shut up," I said, trying to sound nonchalant and unembarrassed.

"But you should feel flattered. He's trying to commit multiple homicides to win your favor."

"No, he's not. His girlfriend is right down there." I pointed at her with my head, too afraid to even aim a finger in Kimberly's direction.

"I hear he's got his eye on you." Lucas nodded like this was a simple fact.

Juan shrugged. "That is the word on the street."

"Shut up," I said. "Sky exaggerates everything."

Sky suddenly went pale. I'm guessing she thought I was about to spill the beans about her crush on Juan, which I swear I would never do.

"It's not just Sky," Gina said. "His own friends are talking about it, too."

"What?" I was shocked. "Kimberly is going to hate me, and I didn't do anything. I swear."

"The heart wants what the heart wants," Lucas said.

Now, I am not kidding or exaggerating when I write this: When Lucas said that, Sky, Gina, and Juan all looked down and nodded in agreement. I would have laughed if I hadn't just learned that I had accidentally made enemies with the most popular girl in school.

But I couldn't focus on my friends' love issues because my eyes wouldn't stop flicking back and forth between the back of Kimberly's blond head in the front row and the number 26 on the back of Ken's jersey down on the field.

Since all the corporate schools have the same four names, in order to be identified when they play sports, they have to have unique mascots. In Mt. Hood, athletes for Alice Louise Corporate High were the Abominables. It wasn't because their teams were abominable. It was a reference to the fact that there was still snow on the top of Mt. Hood each winter. Also, I guess there used to be lots of Sasquatch stories in Oregon. Their uniforms were white with navy blue numbers and trim, and the emblem on the side of their helmets looked like an angry, screaming, albino

47

ape with sharp teeth outlined in dark blue. It was so over-the-top agro that it was just funny. The mascot, Abominable, was even funnier. Some student ran around the sidelines dressed in an albino ape costume with big, floppy blue feet. The mascot did a good job of hamming it up. He posed with little kids on the sidelines, jumped into the line with the cheerleaders and half-participated/half-mocked their routines, and led the crowd in the wave by running back and forth in front of the bleachers, giant feet flopping with each step.

"Who's in there?" I asked.

"That's Graham Davidson," Gina said.

"He's good," I said.

"He is. Which is weird, because outside of the suit he's this shy, kind-of mopey guy. They call him 'the high school hermit.' He hardly ever talks. I don't like him much when he's out of the suit. He just ignores everybody and reads pretentious, old-fashioned paper books. Kind of stuck-up, if you ask me." Gina shrugged. "But you're right. Once he's Abominable, he's great."

Lucas leaned over in my direction and shout-whispered, "Gina doesn't like him because he embarrassed her in class one time."

"He was a jerk," she explained.

"I really don't think it was personal, Gina," Sky said. "He just disagreed with a point you were making, and he made a full-throated argument."

"He called me a Corporation robot."

48

"No, he called us all Corporation robots. Actually, he didn't even say that. He said The Corporation treats us all like robots and we all tolerate it."

Juan leaned forward. "If I remember right, his exact phrase was 'Stupid plastic Corporation animatronic mannequins.'" He looked right at Gina. "I was offended, too."

Sky looked at me. "I think he felt bad. He didn't talk to anybody for like two weeks after that. That made everyone think he was being smug, but I think he felt guilty for hurting our feelings."

"Maybe," Gina said. "Or maybe he's just a jerk. Either way, I like him better when he's in the suit and can't talk."

Sky sat back to make it clear that she didn't want to argue about it, but the look on her face told me she didn't approve of Gina's opinion of this Graham guy.

Throughout the conversation, I continued to watch Abominable. At that point he was teasing some members of the team by standing behind them and mimicking their poses on the sidelines. They took it well, laughing and pushing him away gently when they caught him. At that point I noticed that, although he occasionally led us in some sort of cheer, Abominable wasn't paying any attention to the game itself. In some backwards way, that drew my eyes to the action on the field.

I'm actually a pretty good football fan. My dad and I used to watch a lot of games on the computer and he taught me all about it because he loves the sport and used to play it in high school. He says he was pretty good when he was a freshman, but then all the other guys kept getting bigger and faster and stronger, so he had to give up on that and rely on his brain. I guess that's how he became the overly educated construction worker he is today.

I know enough to identify all the positions and most of the kinds of defenses. I also know that a quarterback shouldn't throw a short pass to a wide receiver in the middle of the field unless he wants the receiver to get clocked. That was why I gasped when the quarterback threw the dangerous pass, not because he was throwing it to Ken. As soon as I saw the quarterback aim that bullet straight over the middle, I thought, "Uh-oh." Then I saw this long, skinny shape leaping for the ball. I didn't even register the number 26 on the jersey before he'd caught it and tucked it, and then he was landing and taking his first step when they hit him.

The safety caught him in a good, fair tackle, slamming his shoulder into Ken's chest. Ken was rocked back by the force of the hit. The DB was a half-step behind, and he'd launched himself when he saw Ken catch the ball. He caught Ken, helmet to helmet, right in the back of the head. While the first hit made a crunching sound, the second made a clap like a shotgun blast. As though it was part of the hit itself, the entire crowd groaned in unison, so it was like one sound that went ker-chunk-BAM-ooooooh.

Then Ken, the DB, and the safety all fell down, and everybody was looking to see if Ken had held onto the ball. The ref whistled the play dead and declared it a completion for a short gain, and a few people cheered, but we couldn't really see through the pile of bodies and the players who'd gathered around it.

I looked to Kimberly. I could only see the back of her head down in the front row, but something about her posture and the way her hands were pressed to the sides of her face, pushing out her blond hair into this strange shape, made me feel as scared for her as I was for Ken down on the field. It was like sitting behind someone in a movie theater who thought she was going to see a romantic comedy, someone who has never seen a real horror movie before, and who is suddenly realizing she's seeing the scariest movie of all time. No, that's not right. That sounds like it could be funny. But this wasn't a movie.

Then I looked over to my dad. The other guys around him were leaning from side to side, trying to see between the players to figure out what was going on down on the field, but my dad was completely still, transfixed. His face was a mask I couldn't read. Horrified? Angry? Shocked? Pitying? I couldn't tell.

And that's when I started crying. Sky, Gina, Lucas, and Juan all think I was crying about Ken. I'm sure they do. But I wasn't. I wasn't sitting on those hard bleachers anymore. I wasn't sitting under that dark, starless sky and those blinding stadium lights. I'd been transported.

Suddenly, I was sitting in that wooden chair in the bright prison visiting room. My dad was sitting next to me. The guard opened the door and my mom came in wearing a prison jumpsuit. And I looked at my dad, and I watched all these different feelings trying to fight to push through his shifting expressions. He

51

smiled, a big, real smile, and then it was a sour, fake smile, and then it was an angry scowl, and then it was that pinched face you make right before you cry, and then it smoothed out into that same mask he wore when Ken got hit.

I burst into tears in that visiting room, too. Twice in one week, and I'm not a big crier. I just didn't know what to do with my feelings. I still don't. But I guess I'm ready to write about that now.

-24-43-1-10-6-83-67-14-4-
-3-3-43-0-66-0-0-0-6-
-0-7-11-2-1-27-
-5-0-0-80-1-

CHAPTER 6

Friday, September 21st, 2114 continued

We couldn't take the subway out to the prison. It doesn't go there. That's a big part of the reason Dad wanted to rent a car instead of just taking cabs until we got situated in our new apartment; he knew we'd need a car even after we were into our new place so that we could go visit Mom.

The real estate is more valuable the higher up you go (because people are scared of flooding during the superstorms, of course), so they built the prison farther down the mountain near the shores of Lake Columbia. That's dumb, because they'll just have to move it when the waters rise, but I guess they did the math and decided it was a better idea to build it twice on cheap land rather than once on expensive land. As you drive down the mountain, the houses get worse and worse, older, made with cheaper materials, crumbling from the weather. It's hard not to feel depressed as you pass by them, sinking through time toward the world that's under water. Then you make this sharp turn and there it is, hiding among the tall trees that are all that's left of the forests that used to stand around the foot of the mountain. Unlike the houses, the building is big and modern, but somehow it's the most depressing of all.

Unlike my high school or the Mt. Hood CorpMart Mall, the building is rounded, like a giant igloo. That makes more sense, practically speaking, since it has to withstand the freak snowstorms and gale-force winds. They will probably build all the buildings this way someday, but for now they are holding on to the classic Corporation design for all the places they want the public to visit. This place is certainly not something they want anyone to like. The solar panels on the roof are bright and clean because they wouldn't work otherwise, but the concrete sides of the dome are dirty. Moss grows out of the spaces between the blocks, and patches of slimy algae are cut by lines where the dirty rain carved them away. The parking lot is barely paved, with muddy holes in the cracked asphalt and blackberry bushes encroaching from every side. Of course, there isn't a lot of traffic. Just the Corporation guards and staff, and it doesn't take a lot of people to manage a minimum-security prison.

As we walked toward the dome, I noticed that there were only a few windows in the front near the main entrance (only entrance?). I realized there would be no real sunlight inside. My mom loves to work in her garden or sit and read books on the back porch of our house. The house we left in Illinois, I mean. The one we'll never go back to. She loves to soak up the sunlight. I'm not sure how she'll handle years indoors.

We found the front doors unlocked. Inside, a receptionist greeted us with an absurdly warm smile and directed us down a hallway past the offices where the staff works. We passed through a metal detector/drug sniffer machine. Then a guard patted us down just to be sure. Finally we made it to a waiting room where we sat and read a few news articles on some outdated tablets that were tethered to the coffee table on rubber-coated wires. Eventually, a third guard leaned halfway through the door on the far end, called our names, and motioned for us.

The visiting room was smaller than I'd expected. It was divided in half by a Plexiglas wall. That was split by four partitions so that visitors could speak with some measure of privacy to one of four prisoners at a time, but there were no other visitors or prisoners when we came in. The guard motioned vaguely toward the chairs, so I guess it didn't matter which of the four stations we picked. As we found a pair of chairs in one of the partitioned sections, the guard on the other side of the glass opened the door and said, "Madison Washington."

Nobody ever calls my mom "Madison," even though it is her name. She went by Maddy even before she married my dad, but her full name sounds ridiculous because it's the name of two presidents. The guard didn't shout her name or even say it rudely, but hearing her full name made me cringe, like she was being scolded the way I know I'm in trouble when my parents say, "Harriet Alexandra Washington." Even if they sound completely calm, I know I'm in trouble when they use my middle name, and that's what it sounded like to me when the guard said my mom's full name, like she was in trouble.

She wasn't in leg chains or handcuffs when she came into the room, but the one-piece prison jumpsuit was almost as bad. It was gray with bright orange reflective stripes on the shoulders, sleeves, and down the legs. I guess that's so that if a prisoner ran they would be easy to spot with a searchlight. Also, orange is the opposite of Corporation blue, and I couldn't help but think that was intentional, like the company was saying, "The prisoners are *not* with us, okay?"

Everything about her seemed different. Besides the horrible jumpsuit, she'd changed her hair. Mom usually straightens her hair or braids it, but she was either letting it grow into an afro or dreadlocks. I couldn't tell, because it was at that in-between stage. Her skin looked ashen, but that might have just been the bad fluorescent lighting. There were rings under her eyes, the kind she gets when she hasn't been sleeping enough. Also, Mom usually has great fingernails, but they weren't painted. None of those things probably sound like a big deal, but all together they felt weird, like she was almost my mom, like someone had tried to clone her but hadn't committed to the job with any great attention to detail.

Dad put out a hand and pressed it to the Plexiglas, and that's why I turned and saw his expressions change. First, he smiled. It was one of those big smiles he used to flash when I was little, and he got back from a conference, and I ran to give him a hug. Then the smile changed to a scowl, like he was angry and holding it in. Then I thought he might cry. His face twisted and his lower lip quivered. He closed his eyes tightly to hold in tears. After that, he tried to put on a smile again, but now he wore it like clothes that didn't fit. And then he just went cold.

Mom made it into the chair on the other side of the glass. She put her hand up and pressed it against the glass, matching his. "Oh, Eli, Baby, I'm okay," she said. I thought that might cause him to break down, but I guess it was the thing he needed to hear, because he let out a rushed sigh and composed himself some more. Then she looked at me.

"Harriet, my beautiful baby girl, you are a sight for sore eyes," she said.

"Mom, I've missed you so much," I told her.

"I miss you too, honey. Every hour of every day. How are you? How is your new school?"

"Pretty much the same as the last one," I said. Then I laughed. The laugh felt all wrong, but I had to let it out.

"You making friends?"

"Yeah," I said. "Some surprisingly good ones, actually."

"Good. That's really good to hear."

Then we sat in silence for a second while she looked deep into my dad's eyes. I couldn't read everything that passed between them. It was like they were exchanging telepathic messages, and I could only pick up a little bit between the static. She was asking him if he was okay, and he was telling her that he was, but that he missed her. She was saying that she loved him and missed him, but there was something else, too. Something about a secret.

"Dad got a job," I said. My voice came out like a chipper cheerleader's, and I hated the sound of it.

"That's great," she said. "Eli, what'd you find?"

"Construction," Dad said. "Working for a contractor who builds apartments on big contracts." Then he looked down at the ground. "Big Corporation contracts."

"That's great," she said. "Really, Honey, that's good. That's better than you think."

He looked up at her. Some more of that telepathy passed between them.

I didn't want to interrupt, but I couldn't handle the silence. "The company gave us an apartment and a rental car."

"Good," she said, but she was still looking at him, like she was finishing the message. Then she seemed to remember me. "That's good. Is it a nice place?"

"Small but fine. Cozy, I guess you could say. Oh, and Dad ironed my pants for the first day of school."

Mom smiled at that. "Oh, he didn't."

"It was sweet," I said.

"Was I not supposed to do that?" he asked us both.

Mom laughed. It was a full, real laugh. Then she told me, "Harriet, you need to tell him when you want things to be wrinkled. Otherwise he will iron them or fold them or hang them up. He's a history professor in his soul. He likes things to be archived neatly."

Mom got her Ph.D. in sociology. She is more comfortable with messes than my dad.

"I'm sorry," Dad said. "I didn't—"

"It's okay, Dad," I said. "I thought it was very nice of you."

"You two need to take care of each other, okay. Harriet, that means that if your father needs to go off on one of his rants, you have to say, 'Mm-hmm,' and nod like you are listening. Promise?"

"I promise to pretend to listen, Dad."

"That's all I ask," he said.

"And Eli, you've got to get more food into this girl. She's too skinny."

He threw up his hands. "She eats three squares a day and then goes out and has ice cream with her friends. It just makes her grow taller. I don't know what to do."

Mom nodded. "Just keep her away from the boys who like their girls too skinny." She looked at me. "Any particular boys he needs to watch out for?"

"No!" I said. "Mom!"

"Good," they both said at the same time. Then Mom laughed but Dad didn't.

"So," Dad said, "what do they have you doing here?"

"Product assembly. Sometimes it's textiles. Whatever comes down the line. Simple, light factory work. Nothing interesting."

"Working conditions?" he asked. I could tell he was angry but not with her.

"Ten-hour shifts. Three breaks. Could be worse. There's not a lot to do in the off hours. Very restricted network access."

"I'll bet," he said.

"I can send you letters. And they have real, old-fashioned paper books in the library. Between those two, I'll stay busy."

She shot him another look I couldn't quite read, but it seemed to be important. "I got a copy of *The Complete Works of Shakespeare* out of the library. I've never read them all straight through. I'm starting with *Troilus and Cressida*." Then she said something that didn't make any sense to me. "I'm starting at the beginning and I think I'll read by fives. I'll tell you how that goes in my letters."

"Okay," Dad said, as though this made perfect sense.

Behind us, the guard cleared his throat. We turned to look at him.

"I'm sorry," the guard said, "but the time is almost up."

"Thank you," Dad said. I wonder how hard it was for him to say that to the Corporation guard. I'll bet it wasn't easy.

We turned back to Mom. "Harriet," she said, "I'll write to you, too. I won't have much in the way of news from in here, so my letters might be short, but I want you to tell me all about what you are up to, okay. And I don't want to hear about you getting into any trouble." She shot Dad another one of those meaningful but indecipherable glances. Then she looked back at me. "They will read all my mail, after all."

"Of course," I said, not really understanding.

"I'll make sure she does," Dad said, "and I'll respond to whatever you send me."

That seemed like a strange way to say he would write her back.

"I love you, Honey," she told me. "You are my pride and joy."

That's when I started to cry. I didn't want to, and I tried to hold it all in, but it just came out in a rush. "I miss you, Mom," I said. I may have even said, "Mama," like a little kid.

"I miss you, too, Baby. We'll see each other soon."

"I love you, Maddy," Dad said. "We love you so much."

She kissed her fingers and then pressed them to the glass. He did the same thing. That just made me cry harder. Pretty soon I could barely see through my tears. Dad put his arm around my shoulders, pulled me up out of the chair and into his chest, and then led me back out to the car.

Once we were on the road, I blew my nose like 50 times until I was under control. Then I frowned and looked at him. "What was all that about the play she was reading?"

"Oh, I think she just wants me to read the same play so we can discuss it."

"Yeah, but—"

"Harriet, will you find me that notepad in the back seat? And a pen?"

"Sure, but I meant—"

This time he silenced me with a look.

I turned back and found a notepad and pen in his messenger bag. As I turned back around, I realized he was slowing the car down. He pulled the rental over to the side of the road, took the pen and paper, and started writing. When he was done, he tore it off the spiral wire and handed it to me. I read it while he pulled back onto the highway and accelerated.

It said, "The car listens just like your tablet. The play is a code so she can write private messages to me. Do not talk about it out loud." He'd underlined "not."

I looked up at him. He was staring straight down the road, his face completely controlled again.

"Does that sound good?" he asked.

"Yes," I said.

He took the paper out of my hand, crumpled it up into a ball, and pushed it down into the trashcan full of used tissues.

"So I hear there's a football game on Friday," he said.

He didn't explain anything else about the code when we got home. I tried to hint about it yesterday, and then again today before the game. But I guess he can't talk about it in the apartment, either. Now I see that was what Mom meant when she said she didn't want me to get into any trouble. She didn't want me to be involved in these secret messages.

So what kind of trouble are they writing about?

-24-43-1-10-6-83-67-14-4-
-3-3-43-0-66-0-0-0-6-
-0-7-11-2-1-27-
-5-0-0-80-1-

CHAPTER 7

Monday, September 24th, 2114

So, it's only Monday, and I can already tell this is going to be a week filled with stupid drama. First, I got in trouble in class. Then I found out I might be in much bigger trouble.

I guess the in-class thing wasn't that big a deal, but I never get in trouble in school, so this took me by surprise. It was in my History Test Prep class. The teacher was reviewing the timeline that might be on the test. They give you some historical events, and you have to drag and drop them into place on the line in roughly the right places to show that you have a general sense of when things happened. We've all seen those kinds of questions before. They could be really hard if you didn't know what events they would ask about, but we always do.

My dad has explained how The Corporation always knows exactly what to teach us to get us ready for the tests. See, the federal government used to contract out to the test making companies to make their national tests. It was very contentious. Politicians had to weigh in the specific wording of different questions. It was a mess. Then The Corporation bought up all the big test makers. The politicians loved it, because it took this whole situation off of their hands, and who can really speak out against The Corporation now without fear of some very serious repercussions? The Corporation had to make sure their students did better on the tests than the kids in public schools in order to justify having their own schools, so they just made sure they had the answers sooner than everybody else by being the ones to make the tests. Then the teachers teach us exactly what will be on the test, and guess what! We always outscore the public schools and the other private schools. Smart system, eh?

So the teacher was walking us through the list of items we'd have to learn for the timeline question this year, and I noticed something weird. In between President McKinley's assassination in 1890 and the U.S. entering World War I in 1917, there's only one fact, The Danbury Hatters' Case in which the Supreme Court ruled against unions using the Sherman Antitrust Act as a justification for their decision, claiming the union unlawfully "combined" to unfairly restrain trade. I mean, fine, they can choose whatever historical events they want for their test, but the Sherman Antitrust Act wasn't something on the list, so how was anybody supposed to make sense of this case.

Now, I know about the major events of the Progressive Era because of my dad, but I never wanted to embarrass myself by bringing up all the stuff he talks about at home. I mean, just because my dad is a history nerd doesn't mean I want to be seen that way. I normally just quietly get my A on the annual test and bite my tongue when they skip major things or get stuff wrong. But today I broke my own rule.

We have a button on the tablet's classroom home screen that lets the teacher know we have a question, and before I'd even thought through exactly what I would say, I tapped it hard. The teacher on the screen in front of the room, Miss Davis, a nice lady with a big, toothy smile and blond hair pulled back tightly against her head, must have seen a light or heard some secret notification because she looked up from her notes and said, "Oh, it looks like we have a question from Alice Louise Walton Corporate High School #7348. Yes?"

Suddenly I remembered that, whenever anybody from any other schools asked a question, we'd see an image of that person in a pop-up next to the teacher's head. So, I realized, there were now a gajillion other students looking at me on their screens in their classrooms. I panicked for a second.

"Um, well, uh, I just... It's just that, well, the timeline includes the Danbury Hatter case in 1908 and says that we're supposed to understand that the court ruled that the Sherman Antitrust Act could be used against unions because unions are anticompetitive. Only there's no mention of the actual Sherman Antitrust Act on the timeline, so how are we supposed to know what that means?"

Of course, I know about the Sherman Antitrust Act. It was the law that said that monopolies were illegal. It's true that it was used against unions at first, but then it was used against trusts and corporations until The Corporation had the whole thing repealed and replaced with Free Market Protection Act of 2028 which made it illegal for the government to limit corporations' abilities to merge or control whole sectors of the economy. I knew that, so I know that it doesn't really matter that for over a hundred years it was illegal for a single company to take over a whole industry. I mean, that ended almost a century ago, so who cares, right? But I guess a little bit of my dad's rants have seeped into my brain, because it just bugged me that the timeline skipped the whole point of the Sherman Antitrust Act and tried to make it sound like unions were these evil, anticompetitive things. It even stated that in the present tense, like it was some indisputable fact: "...because unions are anticompetitive."

I guess the teacher knew I'd put her on the hot seat, because she started flicking her tablet, looking furiously through her notes. "Um, well, that's a good point. I mean, if the test makes reference to the law, you should know what the law was about, but...." She fell silent and we all waited while she flipped through her notes some more. "I can't actually find it here in my notes," she muttered under her breath. "Must be some obscure law."

I raised my hand but didn't wait to be called on. "Actually, it was a very important law, a turning point in the relationship between the robber barons and the government. It basically said that companies couldn't have monopolies because monopolies are anticompetitive and restrain trade. It's true that it was initially used against unions, but that was never its intent, and Congress later amended the Sherman Antitrust Act with the Clayton Antitrust Act in 1914, another major law that's not on the timeline, which carved out an exemption for labor unions because, and I quote, 'the labor of a human being is not a commodity or article of commerce.'"

"Well," the teacher said, "you certainly know more about these laws than most people, but, as you said, they aren't on the timeline, so we shouldn't waste our time with them because they won't be on the test."

I should have just shut up right then. I don't know why I didn't. Maybe I didn't want to let her escape like that. Maybe I thought I would be more embarrassed if I backed down than if I got the last word in. Maybe I let my dad speak through me. Or maybe I secretly hate The Corporation more than I think I do. Whatever the reason, I opened my big mouth again.

"Well, of course it's not on the test. The Corporation's not going to put that on their test. I'll bet they don't mention the time The Corporation's mercenaries were sent in to slaughter 6,000 protesting workers at a factory in China, either! Let's just skip ahead and look!" I made a dramatic show of tapping and sliding on my tablet. "Here we are! 2063. The Massacre in Tianjin. Not on the timeline. Not on the test. Shocking."

I looked around the room. I guess I'd hoped for a little laugh or some nods of approval. Instead, I saw sixty faces staring at me like I was a Martian with scales and tentacles and five big, bug eyes. Then I did some quick mental math; there were probably 10,000 eyes popping out of 5,000 heads, staring at me on tablets spread across the country, and, if my classroom was any clue, there were probably 5,000 mouths hanging open, too.

What the flood am I doing? I thought. Luckily, I didn't say that out loud.

The teacher looked really angry. Between her blue apron, her white blouse, and her beet-red face, she kind of resembled a French flag. "Yes, well, Miss..." She looked at her tablet. "...Miss Washington, if you're finished we have a lot of material that we actually have to cover for the test you don't seem to care about, so, whether you respect the test or not, if you could at least respect everyone else's time, that would be just great." She took an angry breath through her nose, stared at her tablet, and rediscovered her place. "Anyway, back to the Spanish-American War...."

At that point, I was pretty sure the day couldn't get any worse. So it had to.

After class, I went out to the courtyard to find Sky. I beat her out there, so I found the bench where we normally sit. When she showed up, I started to tell her what happened in History Test Prep. I was so frustrated that I was completely absorbed in my own complaining, and I was only a little way into it, so I wasn't paying any attention when somebody walked right up to us and stood there. She didn't cough or tap her foot. She just stood there, waiting patiently. I cupped a hand over my eyes so I could see her against the sunlight coming into the courtyard, and my heart dropped into my stomach.

It was Kimberly Moore, Ken Ford's girlfriend.

"Oh," I said, "Hi, um—"

"Hi, Harriet," Kimberly said. "I'm Kimberly. I'm sorry I'm meeting you like this. I know you're new here and I'm not accusing you of anything. I just want to warn you: Stay away from Ken, okay?"

I felt like she'd slapped me. Or like I wanted to slap her. "I didn't—"

"I know." Her hand shot out, and I flinched like she was going to hit me, but she saw that, hesitated, and then brushed her fingertips against my shoulder very gently. Then she pulled her hand away really fast like I'd burned her or something. "I'm saying this for your own good. Just... just stay away from him, okay?"

Then she turned and walked away so fast I thought she would take off and run through the courtyard.

I turned to Sky. "Did that just happen?"

"I think she was starting to cry," Sky said.

"She was threatening me. She was gearing up to punch me in the face!"

Sky shook her head. "No. Not Kimberly. She was really upset, but not with you."

"Right. Because she's the genuinely nice girl who just told me to keep my hands off her man or else."

"I'm worried about her," Sky said.

"Her!" I was about to let Sky get a glimpse of my Clayton Antitrust Act insane side when we were interrupted again.

"Harriet Washington?"

I almost snapped, "What?" when I registered the voice: Old. Not just adult-old. Old-old.

I shielded my eyes and looked at the speaker. It was the ancient security guard.

"Yessir?" I guess I called him "sir" because he looked like he might have sat at King Arthur's round table when he was young.

"Will you come with me, please? Mr. Robb, the school senior manager, would like to speak with you."

I rolled my head around like I was stiff and sighed loudly. I know I looked bratty, but I couldn't help it. "Fine." I gathered up my lunch and shoved it into my backpack.

"Hey, Harriet," Sky said, "let's hang out after school so I can get all the details, okay?"

"Sure," I said, but I still sounded angry because she'd taken Kimberly's side and I hadn't quite forgiven her for that yet.

I followed the old guy toward the entrance to Building A. He walked so slowly that I was worried he'd choose the stairs and then I'd miss my next two classes, but he took me to the elevator.

Inside, he pushed the button for the third floor.

"So, what does Mr. Robb want to see me about?" I asked in the nicest voice I could manage.

He pointed at the cameras in the corners above us and didn't say anything. Instead, he took his handcom out of his pocket and started tapping on it. I assumed he was checking his mail.

The doors opened, and I followed him out, but he stopped just a few feet down the empty hall and held out an arm like he was protecting me from imaginary traffic. Then he tapped on his handcom again. A strange, buzzing static came out of it, loud enough to cover up the sound of his shoes when he turned around and stepped back toward me. He raised his hand, curled it around his face, and scratched the opposite side of his nose, hiding his mouth from the cameras.

"Mr. Robb seems like a nice man. He isn't. Don't say anything to him that you wouldn't say to the CEO of The Corporation."

I nodded, but just a short nod. Just enough.

The old man tapped on his handcom again, and the sound stopped. Then he led me down the hall and knocked on a door marked "Senior Manager."

"C'mon in!" The voice sounded happy. The old man looked at me sideways, shook his head a little, and then opened the door.

"I brought Harriet Washington to see you, sir," the old man said.

"Oh, good. Thank you, Mr. Rorty. Come in, Miss Washington. Have a seat."

I stepped into the office. The senior manager, Mr. Robb, was standing behind his desk. He is broad-shouldered and a little on the short side, built like a wrestler. His blond hair is cut short and gelled back but with a very straight, neat part on one side. He sat down at his desk, and, as I walked toward the open seat in front of him, I noticed that his hands are really large. He folded them, leaned forward, and flashed a kind-looking smile, but I was suspicious because of what the old security guard, Mr. Rorty, had said.

We sat there in silence for a second.

"Miss Washington, do you know why I've called you up here today?"

"I think I do." I didn't elaborate.

"Yes, well, what are we going to do about this situation?"

"Mr. Robb, I think it was a valid question. How can they ask us to reference the Sherman Antitrust Act but not tell us what that was."

"But you know what the..." He glanced down at the tablet on his desk. "...Sherman Antitrust Act was, don't you? So you aren't really concerned with your ability to answer the test question. You were trying to make a point, weren't you?"

"I guess. I just don't think it's fair."

"Fair? How is it unfair? Everyone has access to the same information. Everyone gets a random sampling of the same questions. What about that is unfair?"

I decided not to point out that only students at corporate schools had access to exactly what information would be on the test. I presumed that, by "everyone," he meant only the students at corporate schools. "That's not what I mean, Sir. I mean that it's unfair that the test deceives everyone into believing a skewed version of history. It might do that to everyone equally, but it's not fair that it does it."

"I see." He leaned back in his big chair. 'So it's not really about equality. It's about being fair to your version of history."

I wanted to shout that it wasn't just my version, it was the truth, but I know better than that. Of course everybody picks and chooses what parts of history they think are important. I just find The Corporation's version to be particularly deceptive. "I guess that's right."

"I'm worried about you, Miss Washington," Mr. Robb said. "I'm worried about this version of history that you find so important. Actually, to be more accurate, I worry about where you're getting your 'facts' from." He made air-quotes with those giant hands when he said "facts." "Would you like to tell me who has been feeding you all this anti-Corporation propaganda? Is it a student at this school?"

"No," I said. "I mean, nobody has been feeding me propaganda. I just like to read about history."

"I see. And it says here that your mother is in prison and your father is a construction worker. Are they telling you these things, Miss Washington?"

I felt like laughing, but I held it in. It seems his tablet only had current information about my parents' professions. "They're a construction worker and a con, Sir. They aren't into reading about history."

"I suppose not. Well, just between you and me, there are some dangerous people spreading a lot of falsehoods and dangerous propaganda about The Corporation right now. Some of those people are right here in the city of Mt. Hood. The Corporation knows they are, because the information goes through The Corporation's servers, but these people have done a good job of hiding their identities. Eventually, they are going to be caught, and, if they've incited any violence or participated in any anti-business behaviors, they will be punished. I know I don't have to tell you about that, considering your mother's situation. So I'm just warning you to stay away from anybody who is trying to feed you this kind of information. Don't look for them online. Don't seek them out. And if you hear anything or if you are approached, you come to me immediately and let me know, okay? These are bad people we're talking about here, Miss Washington. Dangerous people. Terrorists and terrorist sympathizers. Do you understand how serious that kind of thing can get, Miss Washington? The consequences get severe extremely quick."

Without thinking, I mumbled, "Quickly."

"Hmm?"

"Nothing. I mean, I understand."

"Then you can probably also imagine how outbursts in class like the one you exhibited today will attract these people like flies. It will also make the authorities suspect you are already one of these terrorists. So I will expect you to be more careful in the future. This will count as a warning, of course. And so I will have to send an email to your father. You understand that, right?"

"Yessir." I made sure I sounded like I really regretted it.

"All right. You can go back to class."

I stood up and started toward the door.

"Oh, and Miss Washington, I want you to know I'm on your side. I'll be watching out for you, keeping track of your email, looking out for these people, okay? If you do your part, avoid any more outbursts and let me know about any unwanted attention, I'll make sure you aren't falsely accused of anything."

So I guess it was National Threaten-Harriet-but-in-a-nice-way Day.

"Thank you, Mr. Robb," I said. And I left.

After school, I told Sky that I was in trouble and that I couldn't hang out because I had to go home so my dad could yell at me when he got the letter from the senior manager. I didn't really think my dad would be mad, of course. I was still just a little mad at Sky because she'd taken Kim's side earlier.

But when my dad got home, he called me over to the table, pointed at his tablet, and said, "I got a letter from your school principal today." He refused to call the senior manager by his title.

"Yeah, I know. But—"

"Just don't say anything and listen to me," he said. It was not like my dad to cut me off. I was stunned.

"You cannot behave that way in school, Harriet. You're going to get yourself in trouble and we have enough of that already." His voice was rising toward a shout, but, as he spoke, he started scribbling on a pad of old-fashioned paper with a real, wooden pencil. It was one of those wide ones they use at his work to mark off wood before they cut it. I almost never see pencils anymore, so the flashing yellow caught my eye.

"You are grounded!" He was shouting now. "You will come home straight after school for the rest of the week. You will not email your friends about this or anything else. I am so mad right now I don't even know what else you punishment will be...."

He held up the pad of paper and looked both directions out of the corners of his eyes. He barely missed a beat in his rant. "I know you probably don't think this was a big deal, but it's a big deal to me," he was shouting.

But the paper said, "They are probably listening. I am very proud of you. I love you. I am not angry with you. But you have to be more careful, okay? For Mom."

"Do you hear me, young lady?" he finished.

I nodded. "I read you loud and clear, Dad."

"Good," he said sternly, but he put his hand on the side of my face, the way he did when I was a little girl, and then he kissed me on the forehead. Quietly.

-24-43-1-10-6-83-67-14-4-
-3-3-43-0-66-0-0-0-6-
-0-7-11-2-1-27-
-5-0-0-80-1-

CHAPTER 8

Tuesday, October 2nd, 2114

It turns out that being pretend-grounded is basically the same as being for-real-grounded. I had to tell my friends I was busted. I did it via my tablet on the school's servers so that The Corporation would intercept it and record that Dad is on their side when it comes to my bad behavior. Then, after school each day this week, I had to come straight home. So that sucked.

In the evening, I mostly just watched shows on the computer. Dad is obsessed with this new project he won't explain to me. I can't even ask about it or he shushes me, frowns dramatically, and points at the walls. I would think he was losing his mind, but if he is, I'm guessing my mom is, too, because she's in on it. I figured that out last weekend on my own.

Last Saturday we went to the flea market. He told me he wanted to get some furniture for the apartment and thought he could get good deals. Flea markets are technically illegal, because it's against the law to resell anything purchased at CorpMart. It's a violation of their copyrights, because you could theoretically steal their designs when you buy their stuff second hand. I know that's dumb. First of all, what's to stop someone from stealing the designs when they buy something first-hand at CorpMart? Second, who buys a used dresser just to take it apart to learn how The Corporation designed a dresser? Who buys a cheap TV just to take it apart to learn how to make a much more expensive TV? It's stupid, but it's the law. Really, it's a way to avoid competing with anybody, but even The Corporation can't stop people from re-selling their old junk. There's lots of old junk to be sold, too, because everybody has had to move to higher ground over the last few decades, so they have lots of stuff from their big, underwater houses that they want to profit from as they move into the new apartments in the hills.

Mt. Hood's not-so-secret flea market meets in a parking lot outside of town behind the weedy ruins of an old bottling plant. One of Dad's new friends, a guy from his work named Manuel, went with us to show us where it was and help lift furniture into the car. He's a little older than my dad, with a thick beard that was probably black and straight once but is now speckled with long, curly, gray hairs that stick out all over. He liked to tell goofy dad-jokes, the kind all my friends' dads tell and that make my dad smile but which he never tells. Manuel has a friendly smile, but his teeth are yellow and he smells like the fat cigars he's always chewing on. He didn't smoke in the car, thank God, but he lit his cigar as soon as we got to the flea market and I had to walk in his smoke trail. Still, he seems like a nice guy.

I looked through the old clothes and jewelry, but I didn't find much. I think I would have had a lot more fun if Sky had been there. She would have convinced me that a lot of the junk was actually really cool.

At one point my dad went off on one of his dad lectures. "Look around at this whole market, Harriet. This is what capitalism should look like. People buying and selling real goods that they need. The pro-corporatists, they say that anyone who doesn't support The Corporation is a communist. But look at these people, all trying to get ahead. Do they look like communists to you?"

I sighed. "No, Dad."

He ignored my attitude. "See, I believe in free enterprise. I just know that we need to have regulations to make it fair." He looked at one of the vendors, a woman selling sunglasses in Tupperware containers and clothing folded into neat little piles on card tables. "Ma'am, help me illustrate a point for my daughter. If you could afford to buy one of the other booths here and employ its current owner, then take a cut of the guy's profits, you would, right? You'd start a franchise?"

The woman shrugged. "Sure, I guess."

"And then, if you could use that money to buy three more stalls, you would, right?"

"Yep."

He turned to me. "And that would be right. That's capitalism. And she should be allowed to do that. But what if she is so successful she buys the whole market.

79

And then she can drive up the prices, fire as many of the workers as she wants, and keep them from starting up their own businesses because there is no other market. That could happen in an unrestrained free market. And it would be a disaster. And it would eventually collapse."

The woman shook her head. "People would just start another black market somewhere else. That's what I would do if someone bought this one."

"Exactly!" Dad said. He turned back to me. "Or the people would rise up and beat her up if there weren't rules against that. Or they would steal from her because she couldn't watch all the booths at once."

The woman nodded at that.

"We need capitalism, but we also need rules. Rules that keep markets open and fair and that prevent one company run by one family from taking over a whole industry." He lowered his voice, but I could tell that the lady was still listening in. "See," he said, "people are afraid of too many rules coming from the government. They think it's tyranny. They call it communism. And people are right to be afraid of repressive governments. But corporation used that fear to push people in the other direction, to get them to be so afraid of government control that they were willing to turn all their power over to corporations, then, ultimately, to the one corporation that bought all the others. At least, in a democracy, they had the power, albeit very little power, to affect that government. But they don't get to vote on what The Corporation does. Only the shareholders have a say in that, and only the richest have enough shares to have any real say. So they gave up a little bit of power in exchange for no power at all."

The woman leaned over her table. "But why? Why did they do that?"

Dad loved that. I rolled my eyes.

"For thousands of years, governments controlled people with swords and bullets. But some very smart people figured out that a more efficient way was to trick people into thinking that everything was simple, black and white, right or wrong, with us or against us. They reduced long political speeches to sound bites and cut citizens' responses down to bumper stickers and 140-character microblog posts. They bought the schools, the churches, any place where people might learn that human society is complicated, and that freedom and security are maximized when we are all engaged in that complex discussion. They convinced us that 'government' equals 'bad,' that 'business' equals 'good,' and that the next shiny plastic toy is more important than people coming together to solve society's problems. And it goes all the way back to your school, Harriet, where they said that the only things that mattered were the things they could measure easily, so they taught whole generations that the most complicated problems in life could be solved by filling in the right bubble. They said, 'Let us supply the questions, let us tell you the possible answers, and let us tell you which answer is right.' Once people let them do that, those people were more controlled than anybody living under the rule of a tyrannical government."

Manuel stepped up behind me. Or maybe he'd been standing there for a while. I didn't hear him coming, and I jumped a little. He moves very quietly.

"Elijah, we should keep shopping."

Dad looked at his watch, then dropped his lecturing professor face and went back to his normal absent-minded-professor look. "Sure, sure." As we walked away, he said to Manuel, "Sorry about that. I just thought it was a good illustration for Harriet."

"Well, it was loud enough that it was also a good illustration for The Corporation of just who their enemies are."

Dad nodded. "You're right. I'll be more careful."

"Just remember," Manuel said, "you never know when they are watching or listening. Every handcom is a microphone and a camera for them. And most of these people would sell you out in a heartbeat if The Corporation paid them to. Loyalty is a luxury item these people can't afford."

That struck me more than Dad's lecture. My first thought was that The Corporation really benefits from keeping its own customer base poor and desperate. My second thought was, What secret do my Dad and Manuel have to worry so much about?

Here's where things got fishy. Dad and Manuel made a big show of asking me what I thought of the pieces of old furniture there. Our apartment came furnished with the basics, and the stuff at the flea market wasn't really any better. I would say so, and they would move on just a little too quickly. It didn't take me long to figure out that they really didn't care about the furniture. They were looking for something else. Books. Every time they would find some plastic crates full of old, waterlogged books, they would pretend like they didn't really care, but they would go through them all. I got curious, so I pretended to be interested in the books, but I kept an eye out for their purchases. By the end of the day, Dad had his own milk crate full of books. They were all classics; Dickens, Tolstoy, Hemingway, Márquez, Dostoevsky, Faulkner, Kafka, a Bible, and every copy of Shakespeare's plays they could find. Some of the plays were in their own books. There were a couple of Complete Works, too. And some old anthologies, these big fat books called Norton's that had lots of shorter classic works in them. Dad also got excited when Manuel found some blank notebooks.

The only actual furniture we bought was a medium-sized bookshelf and an old, metal trashcan. Fishy, right?

It irritated me that this Manuel guy, this person my dad had only known for a few weeks, knew more about this mysterious project than I did. I know I shouldn't make assumptions. I feel guilty. But, even though my dad is a Ph.D. who works construction, I found it highly unlikely that he's starting a book club with his construction buddies, and that they are all into reading 200-year-old novels and 600-year-old plays. So I watched him carefully when we got home. As soon as Manuel left and Dad thought I was sucked into a TV show, he populated his new bookshelf, then grabbed a book and a notebook. He started scribbling away with a pencil, mostly writing in the notebook but also writing in the book itself.

He caught me looking.

I raised an eyebrow to ask what he was doing.

He frowned, shook his head, and nodded toward the walls.

Glad we could have this little talk, Dad.

So, anyway, while things at home are getting more and more mysterious, things at school are getting clearer. The big Homecoming dance is coming up, and people are pairing off or breaking up as they prepare to present themselves for this official couplehood ritual. Sky and I have decided that we are going to go together unless one of is asked. We'll have to make it clear that we aren't a couple, just a pair of losers without dates, but we both like dancing, so it's worth a little awkwardness. The plan gives us an excuse to get ready for the dance so that we're all set if someone does decide to ask.

Sky is holding out hope that Juan will wake up and ask her. This is one of those mysteries that is resolving itself; this will not happen. Juan has asked us to help him plan this elaborate act where he'll ask Gina to the dance. That's killing Sky, but she plays along just to have an excuse to hang out with Juan. It's painful to watch. Juan is so dense. When he asked us for our help, I couldn't believe he couldn't get a clue.

We were in the courtyard, eating lunch, and he comes up to us, bouncing on the balls of his feet. "Guys!" he shouted.

"Yeah?"

"I need your help!"

"What are friends for?" Sky says. And the word "friends" sounded like poison in her mouth.

"Awesome!" He was totally oblivious. "I'm going to ask Gina to the dance. Since we're both theater geeks, I thought I should write up a sketch, and we could perform it, and it will end with me asking her at the end. But I can't use the normal theater geeks because they will tell her. But I know you guys can keep a secret. So, will you help me?"

I looked at Sky, hard, encouraging her to say something.

"Sure!" she said. "We'll help."

I chose my words carefully, pausing long enough that anybody with half a brain would know I was saying more than I was saying. "If Sky can keep a secret, I can too, I guess," I said.

She looked at me, her wide eyes broadcasting "Shut up!" in infrared.

But Juan didn't notice. "That's great. But we'll have to act fast. Pardon the pun."

Sky laughed too loudly and too hard. I rolled my eyes.

Juan barreled on. "Okay, if I write the script tonight, can we meet after school tomorrow at my house to rehearse?"

"I can't," I said. "I'm grounded."

Juan hit himself in the forehead. "I forgot."

"It's okay," Sky said. "I'll come over today and we'll write it together. Then we'll rehearse tomorrow at lunch with Harriet, then again after school without her. Have you asked Lucas if he'll help?"

"I'm going to ask him right now. I just ran into you two first. Thank you a million times." He was back to bouncing, and he looked like he was about to bounce

85

away. "So, Sky, I'll see you at my house at, what, four? Cool. Okay, I'm going to go find Lucas. Thanks!" And then he ran away, drawing the attention of a bunch of other people who were eating peacefully.

I spun on Sky. "What the hell?" I nearly shouted. My tablet vibrated in my backpack, that familiar warning about swearing popping up inside. I didn't care. I was already pretend-grounded.

"I know. I'm sorry. I'm pathetic," she said, covering her face with both hands, then running her hands back over her hair. She stared up at the clouds, afraid to look at me. "I just thought that, maybe, if I can spend more one-on-one time... Also, if I can get Lucas into it, he'll see how Gina looks at Lucas... And maybe there will be something in the script that will tip Juan off."

"Or you could just tell him. Today. When you're at his house."

She kept looking up. "I could." Then she looked down at her feet. "I can't."

"Sky!"

"I know!"

Sky's hopelessness turned out to be lucky the next day. If we'd been eating in the courtyard on Tuesday, things could have been really awful. But Sky had gone to Juan's house where she'd found Lucas already helping, and the three of them wrote this stupid little sketch. The next day we were practicing in an empty classroom, so we didn't hear about the big blow-up until later.

Here's what we pieced together. People were eating lunch in the courtyard and everything was normal. Then this little kid, a freshman who's maybe 4' 10", named Samuel but who everybody calls "Squeaky," because he is socially awkward and obnoxious, came running into the courtyard and shouted, "Kimberly and Ken were having a full-on screaming match out in the bleachers, and now they're coming this way!" Then he went running into the halls of Building 2, shouting his news to anyone who would listen.

Everyone was primed and listening when the doors to Building 3 swung open and Kimberly burst into the courtyard by herself, tears streaming down her face and snot dripping out of her nose. (I'm not positive about the snot part of the rumor, but the girl got in my face and told me to stay away from her man, so I choose to believe in the snot.) She was walking really fast, but not running, so she only made it about halfway through the courtyard when the double doors were banged open again and Ken stormed through like an angry bull.

"Kimberly!" he shouted.

She stopped right in the middle of the courtyard, but she didn't turn around.

Ken tried to lower his voice, but everybody was listening too closely for anything to cover the sound. "Will you just talk with me for a second?"

Everybody agrees about the next part. She spun around and pointed a finger at him, jabbing it like she wanted to stab him with it if he got too close. "Oh, now you want to talk! Now!"

"I just... I just think...."

"I know what you think. You said it. You're dumping me."

He put his hands up, defending himself. "I didn't say that. I said I wasn't sure about us right now. And can we talk about this somewhere else—"

"No! You said you have been thinking and you don't want to be with me right now. After everything I've put up with. I've stood by you, Ken. Through every concussion, the doctors, the coaches giving you a hard time, Mr. Robb, the weeks of silence, all of it. I stood by you! And now you don't know about us right now. I hear you. I'm the one who listens, remember? I hear you. So what do you still want to talk about?"

He put his head in his hands and stood in silence for a minute. And then everybody says he started shouting like some kind of wild animal. "I don't know, okay? I don't know! I just want you to stop crying! And stop yelling at me!" And then he brought both his fists down on the table so hard it jumped against the bolts that held it into the concrete, and it made a sound like a gunshot. "Flood!" he shouted.

Suddenly Kimberly became very quiet. "Okay, Ken," she said. "Okay. Calm down. I'll stop yelling. I'll try to stop crying. But there's nothing to talk about, okay?"

He pressed his palms into his eye sockets. "I just think...I don't know—"

"No," she said, calm, cold. "No, Ken. No more. Just let me go." And then she turned and high-tailed it out of there.

Ken looked around at everybody. The freshmen and sophomores looked away, embarrassed to be watching, but the juniors and seniors just gaped at him, shocked and entertained by the show.

He turned around and went back toward Building 3 and the bleachers beyond, but the double doors only open one way, so he slammed his palms into them and they didn't budge. People sniggered. He grabbed the handle of one of the doors and swung it so hard that it smashed into the doorstop and dented the door, making another of those gunshots. "Flood!" he yelled again as he stepped into the building.

Like I said, we weren't there when all this went down. When we'd finally pieced the whole story together, Lucas looked right at me.

"So what are you going to do now?"

"Me?" I shouted. "What are you talking about?"

Sky sighed. "Harriet, you can't deny that this changes the landscape for you a little bit."

"I have no idea what you guys are talking about," I lied.

"Well," Lucas said, rolling his eyes in a huge arc from me to Sky, "I'll bet if Ken asks Harriet to Homecoming, she'll figure out what we're talking about real fast."

I guess I hadn't considered that possibility. I still don't know how I feel about it. Even now, imagining what I'd say if he walked up to me in the hall and asked me to the dance, I'm not exactly sure what I'd do. Blush? Hyperventilate? Giggle like a middle-schooler?

There is no point in lying to a diary. I would say yes.

-24-43-1-10-6-83-67-14-4-
-3-3-43-0-66-0-0-0-6-
-0-7-11-2-1-27-
-5-0-0-80-1-

CHAPTER 9

Saturday, October 6th, 2114

As Sky would say, "Oh my god, oh my god, oh my flooding gawd!"

Okay, I'll back up. But holy flooding cow, it's been an amazing week.

Last weekend, I got together with Sky and Lucas at Juan's to work on Juan's play. Juan lives with both his parents, something that's increasingly rare, and they both have jobs, so they live in a house instead of an apartment. It's a little house, but it has a window in the living room that looks out on their backyard, where Juan's dad keeps a carefully manicured flower garden. I kept looking out at the flowers just so I wouldn't have to watch Sky stare at Juan. At first, Lucas didn't know that Sky was secretly crushing on Juan, but it was so uncomfortable watching Sky try to help Juan prepare to ask Gina to homecoming that eventually Lucas, one of the most self-involved people I've ever met, could feel my discomfort. When we took a break, he motioned me over and stepped through the sliding door onto Juan's back porch.

"What is going on with you two?" he shout-whispered.

"Nothing." I traced my foot across the edge of the concrete slab porch while examining Juan's dad's flowers.

"Nothing like really-nothing, or nothing like you-don't-like-Ken-nothing? Because it feels like there's a lot of meaningful nothing going on in there."

"Nothing like nothing I'm allowed to tell anyone about it or someone will kill me," I said.

He got very excited. Lucas is good at getting excited quickly. He bounced up and down and shook his fists in front of his chest. "Who?"

"I can't tell you that! She would bash me over the head with her blue guitar!"

"Sky?"

I looked at him sideways.

He cocked his head. "So Sky has a big, meaningful nothing that's making it, like, super-duper awkward in there, because...? Oh. Sky likes Juan. Wait, she likes Juan?"

"I did not say that," I said while nodding my head vigorously.

"And she is helping him ask Gina to Homecoming." He sighed. "That is the most tragic thing I have ever heard. Like Romeo and Juliet-tragic."

I frowned. "Actually, it's more Cyrano de Bergerac-tragic."

"Um, true. And, um, geek."

I conceded that point. I felt guilty comparing Sky to Cyrano. She's not the ugly guy giving the handsome Christian the words to woo his Roxanne. Sky is beautiful and shouldn't feel any need to hide her interest in Juan like Cyrano did. I feel compelled to help her speak for herself, but you can't make someone speak up for herself. You can't push someone to do something alone.

"She doesn't want to say anything to him," I told Lucas, "and we have to honor that."

"So we have to participate in this tragedy, helping Sky break her own heart?"

"Yep. I guess so."

"That sucks." Now Lucas stared out at the flowers.

We stood in silence for a second.

"Look," Lucas said, "I'll tell you what. We'll go along with this travesty. But when it crashes and burns because Gina watches our play and then tells Juan that she'll go to the dance with him but she only likes him as a friend, because that's exactly what's going to happen, then you have to let this Sky thing die. Deal?"

I shook my head. "No guarantees. Until she's ready to say something, I made a promise. But I think she should say something. And you can't say anything because you don't know anything about this."

"Fine," Lucas said, "but if she told him, it could be a much bigger disaster than you think, so don't say anything to make that happen, okay?"

"Fine," I said, even though I really don't understand this big disaster he's worried about. "And you don't say anything, either."

"I promise. You won't get bashed over the head with a guitar."

We went back in and finished the rehearsal.

The big production was on Monday. Juan wanted us to perform in the courtyard, and I'm sure he would have done it there if it had been a monologue, but he agreed to do it in an empty classroom at lunch. Sky was the one who got Gina and brought her in.

The plot of the play was simple and silly. Lucas played the part of the medieval bard, and he told Gina the story of the dashing knight who traveled the world, searching for the princess upon whom he sought to bestow his favor. He entered into a great tournament where he faced the fearsome Black Knight. That was my part.

"I am the fearsome Black Knight," I announced in this big voice. Then I leaned toward Gina. "Get it? Because I'm black. That's why they made me the black knight. Racists."

That got a big laugh from Gina. I nailed it.

Then Juan and I pretended to joust. He and I galloped toward one another, miming lances and shields. We missed the first time, I hit him with a glancing blow the second, and he knocked me off and defeated me the third time.

Then the bard explained that the brave knight volunteered to fight the evil dragon who had been forcing the townsfolk to provide it with a virgin to eat. Sky stood on a chair, flapping her arms like wings, and then she grabbed a Barbie doll, bit its hair, and popped its head off. She spit the head away and shouted, "Nice try, villagers! I said 'virgins'!"

Gina got a big kick out of that, too.

"No more virgins for you, monster!" Juan said, and charged at Sky, stabbing her in the stomach with his imaginary sword. She died dramatically.

"Having finished his great test of strength and valor, the knight in shining armor returned to the princess to seek her favor," Lucas said.

Juan galloped over to Gina and said, "Princess Gina, will you go to Homecoming with me?"

Silence.

It was agonizing. Suddenly the air in the room was Jell-O and we were all choking.

"Juan, I can't," Gina said. "I'm sorry." She looked at each of us, and I tried to read her expression. Does she know about Sky's feelings? Was she trying to send a message to Lucas? The only thing that was clear was her wretchedness as she apologized to Juan. She knew she was breaking his heart. It made me want to give her a hug. Which was weird, because I think Juan and Sky both deserved one more, but in that moment I felt the worst for her. Love is stupid.

"I'm sorry," she mumbled again, and then she turned and left.

"Wait, Gina," Juan said. He took off after her, and we could hear his voice coming through the doorway. "It's not a big deal. I...."

I turned around very slowly, just in time to see Sky burst into tears, bolt out of the room, and go running down the hall the other way.

Lucas and I just stood there in shock. Finally he said, "Well, that didn't go down the way I thought it would. Worst. Play. Ever."

I shrugged. "I thought you were good."

"Oh, I was amazing. And you were brilliant. But the play was a disaster." He frowned. "Maybe if we'd had a bigger budget for costumes."

"I'll go find Sky," I said.

"And I'll go find Juan. And Kleenex."

"Will he cry, too?"

"No way. He's super macho. But I'll cry for him. That's what gay friends are for."

"You're the best, Lucas."

"Oh, I'm well aware," he said, and walked off in a dignified way in the path of his undignified best friend.

I found Sky in the bathroom. We didn't have Kleenex, but she dabbed her eyes and blew her nose with a lot of toilet paper before we had to go back to class.

So that day sucked.

The cloud of despair was still hanging over all of us on Tuesday, and I thought the whole day would be terrible, but in my first period class, I got my first of many surprises. Ken always walks into the room with the other guys from the football team, but on Tuesday they all walked in without him, and every one of them looked at me, then looked away really fast. It was completely freaking me out, and, when I looked over at Sky, she shrugged because she'd noticed, so I knew everyone else had noticed, too.

Then Ken came in right before the bell. He made his way down the aisle that led to my desk, which was weird for him, and when he passed me he barely slowed down. He set a single carnation on my desk, flashed me a quick smile, and kept going.

"Oh. My. God," Sky started, but I shushed her before she earned herself a handful of warnings for cussing.

I admit that I didn't pay any attention to Science Test Prep that morning. While Mr. George talked about the crests and troughs of waves, I stared at my single flower. It's amazing how much a flower can mean. Why a carnation? Why just one? This one was a simple hot house bloom, white and pink petals with shocking red edges. Had he picked it out with any particular attention to the colors? Did they mean something?

I think I spent the last five minutes of class trying to decide if it would be better to hide the flower in my backpack or carry it through the halls. If I shoved it in my backpack, not only would it get battered by my tablet and lunch bag, but he would see that I'd hidden it, and that might look like I didn't want it. If I walked down the hall holding it like a candle in front of me, people would think I was showing it off and word would get back to Kimberly. As much as I was irritated at her warning, I didn't want to rub this in.

I decided to hold it causally at my side, flower up, and try not to call attention to it. The upperclassmen didn't seem to notice, but it felt like every freshmen and sophomore in the building walked by me and took note of the flower while I made my way to my second-period class. Weirder, it seemed like all the football players, even the upperclassmen, looked at it and smiled.

Then, in second period, a different football player whose name I don't even know walked up to me, set another carnation on my desk, and said, "That's from Ken," in this soft, deep voice.

This one was a little more pink than white, and the edges of the petals didn't have that bright red edge. Did that mean something? I made a mental note to ask Sky, then remembered that she was probably not in a mood to discuss Ken's choices of flowers.

In third period, a different football player brought me another carnation.

Another in fourth.

I couldn't wait to talk to Sky (and I was afraid she wouldn't want to talk about it) so I sent an email to Selina in Illinois. I've written her a handful of times since I moved here, so she knows about my new friends here, but I hadn't told her much about Ken except to say that there is at least one hot guy here.

After my normal pleasantries, I wrote, "Remember that cute guy, Ken, that I wrote about before? Well, he's asking me to Homecoming. He gave me a carnation in first period, and he's had another delivered to me each period throughout the day. I bet he'll ask me at lunch. So excited! And nervous. Kinda' freaking out. Needed to tell you about it and get your verdict."

With the time difference, she must have been in her seventh-period class, but she wrote me back right away. Her email said, "Aaaaaaaaaaaaaaaaaaaaaaagh! You go, *Hermanita*! As for a verdict, the romantic flowers are promising, but I can't really decide until I see a picture of him. Be sure to have him take his shirt off and flex for me. Then I'll decide."

I replied, "Okay, I will...never, ever do that. But thank you for your support, Big Sis'."

"You know I always got your back!" she wrote.

I tapped the dog tag under my shirt. It was good to have her here with me.

To my surprise, Ken didn't ask me to Homecoming at lunch. I found my usual place in the courtyard, set my flowers down carefully beside me, got out my lunch, and ate while I waited. Sky found me and asked about the flowers right away. She didn't seem to be bothered by the fact that I was getting asked while she was in mourning for Juan, or maybe she wanted the distraction.

"Oh. My. Fl—"

"Careful!"

She skipped to "Gawd!" She made a hilarious face of exaggerated shock, her eyes popping out and her mouth hanging open, and she didn't say a word for ten seconds, which was probably a record. "Okay, so tell me everything. Every detail. Did he come to all your classes? Did everyone see? Everyone is talking about it. Kim knows, you know. But she hasn't said anything to anybody about it, even though everyone and their mom is asking her what she thinks. Are you nervous? I would be so nervous. He could ask you any minute, you know. Will you say yes? You should totally say 'Yes.' It's fine with me, by the way, because I'm going to go with Lucas just as friends of course."

"Well—"

"Oh, you have to say 'Yes.' This is your big shot, and he's totally hot and, really, it's cool with me."

"You're sure?" I asked.

But before she could answer, a big shadow loomed over us. I was sure it was going to be Ken, so my breath caught in my throat and I coughed out this weird choking noise as I looked up and shaded my eyes, but it was another of Ken's friends with a fifth carnation.

"This is from Ken," was all he said, and then he just walked off.

Sky and I talked about it for the rest of lunch, and she even let me answer most of her questions, but I still couldn't quite describe all the feelings I was feeling.

In sixth period, another football player brought another carnation.

Ken is in my seventh period class, so I was scared to even walk in there, but when I arrived he wasn't there. Then he slipped in just before the bell rang, and as he walked by my desk, he set another flower down again. By now everybody had heard about it, and they were all watching for it, so there was an embarrassing chorus of "Ooooo," as he walked beyond me and took a seat in the back of the room. During the whole class, I could feel him watching me. Every few minutes I'd pretend like I needed something out of my backpack so that I could turn around, and then I'd find him staring at me, but everybody else behind me would look at me, too, so I'd spin back around and face forward.

White people think black people don't blush. That's not true. We're just blushing ninjas. My face burned so much I thought my cheeks would set my eyebrows on fire, but nobody could see the difference in the color of my skin, so I tried to act cool about the whole thing and resisted the temptation to put my hands on my face just to feel how hot it was.

At the end of class, I moved slowly so that he had time to catch up with me. Ken came up to me and stood by my desk, waiting silently while I gathered my things, but other people were lingering to see the show, so he didn't say anything. Once I got up, he led me to the door, his hand touching my forearm just briefly as he guided me out of the room, or skin touching just long enough for some energy to pass between us. I didn't feel a shock, but a chill ran up my spine and the hairs on the back of my neck stood up.

He walked with me through the halls of Building 2 (the length of the building, then down a flight of stairs, then all the way across it again, so almost a third of the school watched us walking together). We stepped out into the courtyard, and he had another friend positioned near the door who handed him the rest of the flowers. We made our way through the planter boxes to a spot where no one was standing or sitting right beside us, and then he turned to face me.

He held out the four remaining flowers. "These are for you, too," he said.

I took them and held them with the others in both hands in front of me. I stared at the dozen. "They're beautiful."

"You're beautiful," he said.

I blushed again, ninja-style.

I didn't know what to say to that. I still don't. Do you say, "Thank you"? That sounds like you're saying, "I know I'm beautiful, but thanks for noticing." Do you say, "You, too"? Guys don't want to be beautiful, even if they look like Ken and they undeniably are. Do you say "No, I'm not"? That just makes it sound like you're fishing for compliments or have low self-esteem. I could have said something joke-y like, "Well, beauty is in the eye of the beholder, but I guess if you like this look, that's cool for me." As tense as the situation was, I didn't want to try and burst it with humor, because the moment was also perfect. I am pretty. Not as pretty as some girls. I'd reserve the term "beautiful" for women like my mom. She's beautiful, even in a prison jumpsuit. I know I'm supposed to lie and say that I don't think I'm pretty, even in a diary, because it makes me sound stuck up, but something about that social rule makes me uncomfortable. Why aren't girls allowed to have an accurate sense of their own attractiveness? I'm probably a seven, maybe a six. Ken was talking about me like I'm a nine or a ten. And that felt really good. Why do I have to argue with him about that?

So I didn't say anything. I just let the sun fall on the flowers he gave me and on the face he finds beautiful and I tried to soak in his gaze as much as I soaked in the heat and the light and it felt so, so good.

"Will you go to Homecoming with me?" he asked.

"Yes," I said, a little too seriously, like I was agreeing to a big contract.

He smiled a really big smile. Not relieved. I could tell that he knew I'd say yes, and his confidence didn't bother me. He just smiled like he was really happy, and that was great, too. The smile reached all the way to his eyes, and they were staring at me like everybody in the world wants to be stared at, like my face produced that smile. He just said, "Good," and then repeated it softly a few times. "Good. Good." Then he woke up a bit. "Okay, well, I, um...." He motioned toward the football field through Building 3.

"Yeah," I said. Not my most eloquent moment.

"Okay, so, I'll send you all the details and stuff."

"Okay," I called after him as he started off.

"Good, good," he said, looking away from me, then turning back to smile again, then repeating the turn as he made his way to the door.

I watched him go, and when he left through Building 3, I noticed that the door had been replaced with one that hadn't been painted yet. The big dent he had put in it was gone. I was surprised that the school had acted so quickly; minor damage like that usually lingers for a lot longer, like years longer. I took it as a good sign. His big, public falling-out with Kim was passed, and the evidence was disappearing, too.

He was going to Homecoming with me.

I'm going with him.

It hasn't fully sunk in yet.

What am I going to do with my hair?

3-3-43-0-66-0-0-0-6-
0-7-11-2-1-27-
5-0-0-80-1-

CHAPTER 10

Friday, October 26th, 2114

If you want my opinion (and you're a diary, so you
have to), Homecoming Week is a very strange
tradition to bring into a corporate school. First, lots of
people from my dad and mom's generation still went
to public schools, so they aren't coming back their old
stomping grounds when they come to our school or
our Homecoming football game. Our school, Alice
Louise Walton Corporate High School #7348, is only
nine years old. How many former graduates are really
coming back? Second, because everyone has had to
move due to the flooding, hardly anybody lives where
they used to once upon a time, so no one is really
coming home to anything. And third, all the corporate
schools are basically the same, so there aren't any
unique traditions for anybody to look back on. So
what's the point? I guess somebody at the corporate
headquarters in New Little Rock ran the numbers and
decided it was a very cheap way to make corporate

schools feel like the old public schools and sell some extra clothes. Fine. But I think it's kind of stupid.

I've obviously given this more though than it's worth, but, if I'm totally honest, I had another agenda; I wanted to plan this whole rant about how dumb Homecoming Week is so I could blab about it to Sky and make her think that I wasn't crazy-excited about the dance tomorrow. Which I totally am. Also, I wanted her to think the whole thing isn't a big deal so that she'll feel a little better about Juan's botched attempt to ask Gina to the dance.

When I spend all this time in my head trying to plot and plan the perfect things to say, it almost always ends up being a waste of time. Generally, people don't say what I want them to say, so they accidentally block my best planned lines. In the worst cases, something just comes up and prevents the whole conversation from taking place, so if you ever see me scowling for no apparent reason, it's probably because I'm mourning the death of the perfect one-liner that didn't magically fit into a conversation the way I wanted it to.

This was one of those worst cases. I was early to school, and I ran into Sky in the line for the metal detectors.

"Sky," I started, "have you ever thought about how—"

"Harriet! I'm glad I caught you!"

She didn't catch me. I found her. I couldn't decide if I should point this out or continue with my rant about Homecoming, so I hesitated too long and she plowed ahead.

"Yesterday, after school, I was getting my stuff together, and I found a note inside my guitar case, tucked into the strings. It's got your name on it. I really wanted to read it. Like, all night I thought about it and tried to decide if I had the right to read it because it was put in my guitar case, but I promise I didn't read it. So you have to read it right now and then tell me what it says. I have a whole list of guesses about who it's from and what it says, but I won't tell you what they are until after you read it. Here." She pulled a carefully folded note out of her backpack and pushed it at me.

I couldn't read it right away because we were at the machines. When I put my watch and house key in the little basket, I dropped the note in, too, and I flashed Sky an impish smile. Then I looked at the security guards quickly to make sure that was okay while I loaded my backpack on the conveyor belt. The giant guy with the wand, Mr. Chavez, didn't seem to care, but he motioned me through the machine, impatient. The lady watching the X-ray machine's display, Rosa, looked up and smiled at me, but I don't think that had anything to do with the letter. She's the only black person on staff, so she always smiled at me because I think she's just glad I'm here, and I always smile at her because she's nice. Once I stepped through the machine, I looked over at the really old security guard, Mr. Rorty, the one who escorted me up to the principal's office. He gave me a strange look which might have been an expression of concern or maybe of disapproval. I couldn't tell. Of course, he's so old, it might just have been a look of confusion; for all I know, he might have decided I was his daughter or his first girlfriend from 200 years ago. I smiled at him anyway and took the note out of the bucket with my other metal doo-dads.

Sky caught up as soon as she was through the machine and gave me a little push on the shoulder. "C'mon, c'mon. Read it!"

"I don't know," I said. "It is only addressed to me. Maybe the writer wants me to go off and find a quiet, private place to read it by myself."

Sky looked thoughtful, then guilty. "Yeah, you're probably right. I'm sorry I pressured you. I'll give you some space, and we can talk about it at lunch if you feel like-"

I pushed her back. "I'm totally kidding, you..." I couldn't think of a good, gentle insult, so I just let the sentence fade away. See? That's the kind of situation I could have prepared for if I'd known it would come up. I resolved to think of a great line for the next time that exact situation appears, which, of course, never will.

The outside of the envelope just said, "Harriet," on the outside in rough, quick handwriting. I thought it might have been Ken's, but I realized I'd never seen his handwriting. There were no notes with all those carnations. I opened the note. It turned out that the envelope was the note itself, cleverly folded out of a single sheet of typing paper. The message inside was typed, then printed out of one of those old printers people used to connect to those computers that didn't move. Before I even read it, I found myself wondering where someone would even find a machine like that now. I was too curious about the note to contemplate that question for long, though. Not that Sky would have let me, anyway. She was standing very close to me and making a big show of staring up at the ceiling or at the other people walking past us in the hallway.

The note said:

> *Ken is not himself. Be careful, and don't*
> *judge him too harshly. It's not his fault.*
> *—A Stranger Who Is On Your Side*

I handed the note to Sky.

"You sure?" she said, but she was already reading it and had finished it before I told her it was fine.

"So, those guesses?" I asked.

"Well, my first guess was Ken, but that's obviously wrong."

"Right. Second guess?"

"It could be Kim," Sky said.

"I doubt it. I don't think she's on my side."

Sky shrugged. "Maybe her warning wasn't just trying to keep him for herself. Maybe she really was looking out for you."

"First of all, I think she would have signed her own name. Plus, not to be too sexist, but the handwriting on the other side doesn't look like a girl's."

Sky turned it over and examined my name closely. "Nope. Kim has beautiful handwriting."

"Are you sure you don't have a crush on Kim?" I asked.

She smiled a little at the joke, but I could tell that I'd reminded her of Juan.

"Sorry," I said. "Bad timing."

"S'okay."

I tried desperately to shorten the silence. "So, um, who else could it be? One of Ken's football buddies?"

"On your side? Like, not on his side? I don't think so."

"Okay, so we don't know who the secret stranger is, but what about the message itself? What do you think it means?"

"He's on the rebound?"

"Maybe," I said, but that didn't feel right. We didn't have any better guesses, but that didn't stop us from speculating all through lunch. We got Juan and Gina in on it, though Lucas wouldn't play along.

"I say there's insufficient information in the note." He waved the whole thing away with one expressive, flapping hand. "The person is playing with your head on purpose. Don't play their game. Just enjoy your date with Ken."

That seemed like good advice, but I wanted a second opinion. Luckily, it was Wednesday, my day to go visit my mom, so I took the note with me. After we'd exchanged the normal "I love you"s and "I miss you"s, I asked my dad to let us talk privately real quick. I know that was a big sacrifice for my dad, because he wants to get every second with her that he can, so I really appreciated it when he nodded and rose.

My mom caught my dad before he left the room. "Eli? I think I'll write you three letters this week. I know my letters are all much ado about nothing, but I think I can fill at least three with that much ado."

He nodded. "I don't mind. I love your much ado about nothing. I'm sure I'll love all three. I love you, Baby."

As he left the room, I frowned at my mom. "What's up with all that Shakespeare stuff?"

"Oh, it's nothing, like I said. Don't worry about it. So, what did you want to talk to me about?"

I told her about my date with Ken. She could tell I was excited about it.

"The popular football player? And a senior? A little cliché, don't you think?" But she was smiling at me.

"Somebody's got to go out with the perfect guy, right?" I said.

"Oh, he's perfect? The carnations thing was good, but I think you can make him do better next time. Men need to be trained. Did you know your father once gave me a book of 18th century poems about death for Valentine's Day?"

"That's terrible!" I said.

"No, it was perfect. You see, when we were first dating, he didn't know anything about poetry, but I told him I liked it, so he would find these corny love poems to send to me. Slowly, carefully, I trained him to read better poetry. Then he gave me that book and said, 'When you read these, I want you to see me in them. Because I am going to love you until I die and forever after.'"

I smiled. "Okay, that's pretty good, but it's still not a great gift."

"Harriet, you'd better be glad he gave me that book. Some women want diamonds and some women want flowers, but I wasn't going to let anybody into my heart or into my bed without a lot of poetry first."

"Mom!" I did my ninja-blushing, but my mom can see it.

"I'm just saying, this boy may seem perfect now, but you should make him a lot more perfect for you before you do anything you'll regret."

"I know, Mom. Wow, not what I wanted to talk about."

"Sorry, Baby. What did you want to talk about?"

So I told her about the letter.

She frowned. "And you don't know who this stranger is?"

"No. At first, Sky thought it might be his ex, but I don't think so."

"No, it doesn't sound like an angry ex's letter. Or even a genuinely caring ex's. No other guesses?"

"M-mmm."

"Well, regardless, I think you should take this seriously, Harriet."

"You think I shouldn't go with him to the dance?"

"No, that's not what I mean. Go with him. Get to know him better. But keep this in mind. Not so much that it keeps you from having fun. But enough that you remember what I said about not doing anything you regret."

"Mom!"

She didn't smile this time. "I'm serious. And it's nice to be forgiving and accept this mysterious person's opinion that it's not Ken's fault, whatever that means. But, to me, that implies that it is someone's fault. My advice: Figure out whose fault it is, but don't let it be any kind of excuse if this Ken fellow doesn't treat you the way you ought to be treated, okay? You don't owe him anything, and he's not your project. It sounds like there are other people who are interested in taking care of him. You take care of you first, okay?"

"But you are always talking about putting others first."

"And you should. But while I'm in here, you take care of yourself. That's how you can help me. When I'm out, we'll save the world together, but I can't save you from the wrong kind of man from here."

"Yes, you can, Mom, because I'll keep coming to you for advice."

That made her cry a little. "Thank you, sweetheart. That means a lot to me. I love you so much, Harriet. You and your dad keep me going, you know?"

"I know, Mama. And we keep going for you."

Then our time was up. The guard came into the room on Mom's side of the glass and led her away, and I stepped out into the hall and met up with my dad.

When we got back into the car, he just said, "Anything you need to tell me about? I can pull over if you need me to."

"You already know I'm going with Ken to the Homecoming dance." I leaned forward and yelled at the dashboard. "You hear that, Corporation? I'm going with Ken to the Homecoming dance." Then I turned back to my dad. "I just wanted to get Mom's opinion about how I should handle that."

"I wish I could give you the kind of advice you need," he said. I think he was a little hurt.

"She said exactly what you would have said. Be careful and make sure he treats me right."

"Good."

"And something about a book of poetry about death. You're a weirdo, Dad."

Nothing much happened on Thursday at school, since we still couldn't figure out who the stranger was, and on Friday all anybody could talk about was the Homecoming game. I guess there's a big rivalry with William Henry Gates III Corporate High #3724 over in New Beaverton. That's southwest of here, across the Lake Willamette estuary in the Coast Range archipelago. Their mascot is the Bill the Beaver, so you can imagine the kinds of jokes people come up with, especially considering the ridge of islands are surrounded by stinky swamps filled with mosquitoes that carry West Nile virus. Yeah. Stinky, moldy, diseased beavers. Doesn't take a whole lot of imagination. So everybody was amusing themselves making these sexist and gross vagina jokes about their football team. I guess that's how we get psyched-up for the big game here at Alice Louise Walton #7348. Personally, I didn't really care about the game, but I'm smart enough not to say that out loud. All I could think about was tomorrow's dance. After school, when Dad made a joke about how we were going to go watch my date play football, it took me by surprise. Ken's football fame isn't why I like him, so I'd basically forgotten all about that part of his life. I think that's how I make myself feel better about the cliché my mom mentioned, but as we drove over to the school, picking up Manuel and another friend of Dad's from work, I thought about how I was being selfish. Just because I didn't want to be the girl who obsessed about dating a big-deal football player didn't mean I should ignore that part of Ken. It's obviously important to him. So I decided to pay closer attention and then talk to him about it tomorrow at the dance. It's not like there's anything that interesting in my life we could talk about. What, I like to sing silly songs on the steps of the old library with Sky? I try really hard in school? My dad is a construction worker who is suddenly obsessed with Shakespeare? I keep a secret diary so my dad can build a case against The Corporation? My mom is in jail on a Failure to Repay conviction? Fun conversation.

I left my dad and his friends at their usual spot, then found my way over to my friends. It was hard because the stadium was packed; lots of the people from New Beaverton had come over on the ferries, and they were getting rowdy before the game even started, shouting at the Sasquatch and cheering their Beavers players who were just standing on the sidelines. I made my way through the hyped crowd and found that my friends had all beaten me there, and they were sitting in a different order this time. I sat down on the aisle next to Sky. Gina sat between Sky and Juan. Lucas sat on the other side of Juan. Because they aren't a football crowd, they didn't pay very close attention to the game, and because I'm not a huge fan either, I thought the stuff they wanted to talk about was way more interesting than what was going on down on the field. That made it hard to concentrate. I followed our first drive down the field and tried to cheer loudly enough for Ken to recognize my voice. He wasn't the one who scored, but he had a good catch for 15 yards on the drive, so I already had something to compliment him about. Then I thought I could ignore the game, and I admit I didn't pay any attention while we were on defense, but they had to punt and I found myself watching to see if Ken would score again. He didn't have any catches on that drive or the next, and I was starting to get mad at our quarterback. I thought Ken looked pretty open a handful of times, but the QB wasn't seeing him. Then, near the end of the first half, the QB threw this long pass and Ken caught it on the 20-yard line, then juked his guy with one quick head-fake and ran it in for a touchdown.

We all went bonkers, launching to our feet and screaming our heads off. Instead of doing a dance or spiking the ball, Ken pointed it right at me. People in front of me turned to look around, so I suddenly felt completely self-conscious, but also really happy...I don't know, honored, I guess. When the scoreboard chimed for halftime, Ken pointed at me again as he walked off the field. We were only up 7 to nothing, but it felt like we would win it in a landslide.

My friends teased me at halftime, saying I should go out for cheerleading (something I would never do in a million years) or get a job as the equipment manager so I could towel Ken off when he came back to the sidelines after scoring a touchdown.

Lucas got so excited he clapped his hands together in these tiny little patty-cake claps. "Wait, that's a job somebody gets to do? Could I do it professionally after I graduate?"

"Your parents would be so proud," Gina joked.

Lucas got quiet and looked away. I don't think he thought that was funny.

After halftime, it seemed I was right. We scored almost right away (not Ken, unfortunately), and then we intercepted it and a defensive player ran it all the way back for another touchdown. Because it was a blow-out, my friends stopped paying attention again, but now I was totally sucked into the game.

Then, at the end of the third quarter, the QB saw Ken down field and tossed him this high, slow, pop-up pass. Ken had to stop running his route and out-jump the guy covering him, but somehow he pulled it out of the air. When he came down, he took a single step and then he got hit by the Beaver's safety.

It was another of those terrible, thunderous hits, the kind that sends a crunching noise across the field and sets off a painful "Oooo" from the fans of both teams. Somehow Ken held onto the ball and didn't get knocked out. When he stood up, he held the ball up high over his head, and the crowd went nuts again, but I noticed the crack running down the side of his helmet before he did. One of the other guys on our team pointed it out to him, and he had to run over to the sidelines to get another one.

"What the hell?" I yelled to Juan, the biggest football fan of our group. "Aren't those made of metal? How'd it crack?"

He didn't look too bothered by it. "Corporation helmets. Cheapest materials possible. They crack all the time."

"Isn't that dangerous?"

He shrugged. "Sure. It's football, not checkers."

I did not find this reassuring.

Ken seemed fine, though. They sent him right back in, and he kept running his routes. Early in the fourth, he scored another touchdown, this one on a short pass and a long run, and everybody went crazy again. He pointed at me again, too, just to make sure everybody had seen him do it. Because so many people were turning to look at me, I waved to him, and the fans, especially the parents, found that somewhere between Satisfactory and Certifiably Adorable. A few even clapped in my direction, like I'd done something for the team.

After the game, two weird things happened. While we were making our way out of the bleachers and past the concessions stand, we passed the senior manager of our school, Mr. Robb. He shot me a glance that seemed to say, "I've still got my eye on you, trouble-maker," but maybe I was just being overly sensitive. Then he looked at Lucas and nodded.

"Lucas," he said.

Lucas nodded back. "Mr. Robb."

I was totally confused. Was Mr. Robb threatening Lucas? He must know that Lucas and I are friends. Was he telling Lucas to stay away from me? Or to spy on me? It could be either one, because after the strange exchange, Lucas hurried up ahead of us, like he didn't want to look me in the face.

I sped up so I could ask him, but right then our football team came running through the crowd, screaming and whooping. People slapped them on their shoulder pads as hard as they could, as though the quantity of pride they wanted to express was proportional to the pounds of pressure applied to the players' pads. A few people, all guys, I'm guessing dads, slapped players on their butts. I do not understand that gesture, either. Spanking as punishment for little kids and as encouragement of young men? What the flood is that about?

Ken came flying through the crowd, dodging the hand-shaking and butt-slapping well-wishers and only nodding at shouts of congratulations, but he stopped when he got to me, grabbed the back of my head, and planted a fast and forceful kiss right on my shocked lips. I didn't even have a chance to enjoy it because I was so surprised. Then he whooped again and took off after the rest of the players, running into Building 3 where they would go to the coach's room to debrief.

I stood there, most of the crowd parting to walk around me. I didn't even realize my friends were standing with me, staring at me like I was some kind of alien from a distant star, until Sky said, "Oh my gawd! Did that just happen right here in front of everybody? Was that the first time he's kissed you? It better be, because if he's kissed you before and you haven't told me.... Was that your first kiss ever? Like a real kiss from a boy who wasn't your parents or a boy in preschool or something, because that doesn't count. Well?"

"I guess," I said. I started walking, stumbling along at the speed of the crowd. "Wait, no, not my first kiss." Then I dropped to an angry hiss-whisper. "I've had boyfriends before. Back in Illinois. I'm seventeen years old for God's sake. But, no, Ken hasn't kissed me. I would have told you, probably texted you before I even got home and then called you right away. You know that. So, yes, it was my first kiss from Ken, I guess."

Gina was listening in. "Not great. Like, he basically smashed his face into yours. But that's a total ice-breaker for tomorrow night. You've essentially broken the seal. Now he knows you won't slap him or throw up on him if he kisses you tomorrow. That's actually a big deal for guys. They hate rejection." Then she caught herself and looked over at Juan. He was walking ahead of us, talking to Lucas, and if he heard her, he did a good job of pretending he hadn't. Gina dropped her voice to a whisper. "Ken is totally going to make out with you tomorrow after the dance. Trust me."

And I guessed she was right. I didn't have the courage to tell the prettiest, sexiest girl in our friend group that guys aren't the only ones who hate rejection, who fear that somebody will slap them or throw up on them to ward off an unwanted kiss. I don't think I ever would have had the courage to kiss Ken first, and certainly not in front of everybody in Mt. Hood and half the population of New Beaverton. But now that he's done it...well, tomorrow's dance will be a lot less nerve-wracking and a lot more fun!

-24-43-1-10-6-83-67-14-4-
-3-3-43-0-66-0-0-0-6-
-0-7-11-2-1-27-
-5-0-0-80-1-

CHAPTER 11

Saturday, October 26th, 2114

Okay, I'm not sure exactly how to tell the story of the dance tonight, so I'm just going to start at the beginning and tell it straight through to the end, because...well, you'll see.

First of all, it's Saturday (well, it's long after midnight now, so it's Sunday, but it was Saturday), so: No school. I woke up way too early for a Saturday morning because I was so excited. I watched videos and ate cereal and waited for a polite time to call Sky, but when she finally called me, she admitted she'd woken up early too, and we'd both just been waiting. We guessed Gina was awake, but we woke her up, then agreed to meet at the mall for lunch, but Sky and I were too excited, so she came over to my place.

This is going to sound really dumb, but we decided to get into our dresses and take some selfies so we'd have those to show the dresses to the hairdresser. Then we changed back to our regular clothes to go to the mall. I know that sounds ridiculous, but we were in an over-the-top kind of mood.

Neither of us had ever met Gina's date, some college guy her brother introduced her to. I learned that she was going to go with him, and then, after Juan's play, she thought about canceling. "But then," she explained, "I couldn't call Mike and tell him that a guy has a crush on me and I'm worried about hurting him because he's my friend, so I have to cancel. I know that sounds selfish, but it's really just cowardice. Mike is a freshman in college. I just couldn't tell him about my high school problems. Does that make me a horrible person?"

We assured her that it didn't, and I basically meant it, but I also think that a person can be generally good and decent and still do something that's wrong. It might be cowardice instead of selfishness, but that's not a whole lot better. I mean, if she had feelings for this Mike guy, it would be fine, but if she just likes him because he's older and that makes her too afraid to tell him about her real friends, that rubs me the wrong way. So he's in college. Big deal. There are lots of jerks in college, and if he really is so self-important that he can't be bothered with his high school date's high school problems, he's a jerk.

Sky assured Gina that it didn't matter because Juan wasn't going to come, so he wouldn't have to see her with Mike anyway. Juan was already planning to stay home and nurse his wounds by killing lots of zombies. He'd had recently purchased the newest video game console The Corporation makes, an E-Clipse 7, and he was really into this game where you played as a British super-soldier from the '30s, fighting the Neo-Soviets in Poland, only all the Neo-Soviets have been turned into zombies by a nano-tech infection, and you had to blast them with special EMP guns to turn them back into normal Neo-Soviets, then shoot them with normal bullets because, you know, Communists. As political allegories went, it was pretty obvious Corporation anti-communist propaganda, but I've played it at Juan's house, and the actual gameplay is incredible. Enough to make him forget that the girl he loved was going to the Homecoming dance with some college guy? Probably not, but the blood spatter was very realistic.

Lucas was taking Sky. She said she knew he was doing it out of pity, but Gina said Lucas wouldn't ever want to miss a chance to dance, so he really did need a date. That seemed to make Sky feel better.

When we finished lunch, Gina asked what we wanted to do all afternoon. I laughed. "I'm getting my hair done."

"That will take all afternoon?"

I shook my head. "Ah, the sound of straight-hair privilege talking." I pointed to my teased-out fro. "You have no idea how long this will take to do."

"How long?" Sky asked.

"Depends on what I decide to do. Could be all afternoon. You two need to come tell me what to get, and we should hurry."

Just the deciding part took about an hour. We showed the hairdresser, a nice lady named Stephanie, pictures of our dresses, and she had some good ideas, but she was obviously out of her depth when it came to my hair. She had to pull up directions and go to get chemicals from the back room that she'd never used before. My dress was this silver and purple number that went down to my ankles in a way that was pretty tame, but with a high slit on one leg so I could show off just a little skin. At the top, it was a little conservative, too. Not strapless or even spaghetti straps, the top went from mid-shoulder almost to my neck, but there was a deep enough neckline to be exciting. That wasn't my motive for the conservative shoulders, though. I liked that because it meant I didn't have to wear an uncomfortable strapless bra. I hate those.

Stephanie, the hairdresser, suggested that I dye my hair blond with purple highlights to match the purple in the dress. At first I thought that was as terrible idea, but she photoshopped a picture to show me what it would look like, and I thought it was actually pretty hot. It was also going to be really expensive, and I was hesitant to use Corporation credit because of what had happened to my Mom when we got behind on those bills, but Dad had given me enough money to mostly cover it, and I texted him and he said it was fine to put a little more on the card. I was embarrassed to have to ask in front of Sky and Gina, but then Sky had to turn down highlights because they were too expensive for her, and that made me feel better. I'm not glad that she's as poor as I am, but I'm glad that she's as poor as I am. Does that make sense?

Stephanie got to work on my hair first, because it would take the most time. While I sat in curlers and strong smelling chemicals, she dyed Gina's already short hair magenta and cut it into this 1980s mod style that swept over the right side of her face but fanned up into this wild, spiky fan on the left. It was cool. Then she dyed mine the first time. While it dried and set, she styled Sky's long, straight, blond hair into this fancy knot on the back of her head that turned into a wide braid running down her back. I thought it was very elegant, but I could tell Sky thought it was a little too boring and wished she'd been able to afford to put some blue highlights in to match her dress. I kept telling her that those never would have washed out of hair as light as hers, while I could just dye mine back to black in a heartbeat. Inside, I was getting very worried that Stephanie was going to burn all mine off with the straighteners and the dye. It turned out that she was worried about that, too, because she didn't dye it all the way. It ended up a light brown, and when she asked if I wanted to risk dying it more, I agreed to leave it there. Then she put in the purple highlights and shaped it into big ringlets that parted in the middle, and each had just a hint of purple. I was pretty pleased with it, but Stephanie felt badly that it hadn't gone all the way blond, so she cut me a deal, and I ended up not having to use credit, even after the tip.

Very happy with that outcome, I took the ladies back to my apartment. We nibbled at some dinner, too nervous to eat in our dresses and too excited to really eat before we put them on. We couldn't smother the butterflies in our stomachs, but we filled up enough that we wouldn't get sick from hunger at the dance, then got into our dresses and took more pictures.

Gina's dress was all about looking sexy. It was a little black cocktail dress with some plastic rubies that climbed from the hemline just above her knees, up her sides, and then danced along the low neckline. She had to wear a strapless bra, but she could fill it enough that she didn't have to yank it up every few minutes.

Sky's dress was light blue, of course. The skirt was flowy, with a solid layer covered by a gauzy layer that was so light it was almost white. White piping rose from the waist in a corset design. It had white, thin straps that allowed her to wear a normal bra, but the bra's straps wouldn't stay under the dress's, so we figured out a way to safety-pin them. I thought the dress was beautiful, but Sky lamented the fact that she didn't look as ravishing as Gina and I. I got the impression that she was throwing me in to be nice but really wanted to look like Gina. I understand she wanted to be the person Juan wanted, and I wasn't offended, but I thought it was a shame, because I thought Sky looked beautiful, while Gina looked like she was trying a bit too hard for this Mike guy. But, of course, I couldn't say that. I'd just spent too much money to get in a hair-pulling match with Gina, and it wasn't her fault that Sky was jealous of her. That didn't stop me from resenting her just a little bit, though.

Gina drove Sky home so they could both be at their own places to get picked up by their dates. I sat down on the couch in our little living room and waited for Ken. Dad was sitting at the kitchenette table with his

Complete Shakespeare, a notebook, a pen, and a highlighter. I'd look at him and wonder what he was doing. He'd look at me and smile, then look at the clock, then back to his work. Ken wasn't late, but he was getting close, and I was getting nervous. When the doorbell rang, I breathed out a huge sigh of relief, but my dad jumped up and beat me to the door.

"Ken? C'mon in."

"Thank you, Mr. Washington," Ken said. He stepped inside wearing his tux, and my first realization was that he was taller than my dad. That surprised me a little, even though I should have guessed it. I think my dad will probably always seem bigger in my mind than he is in real life. I didn't have time to think about that much, because my rational brain short-circuited a little. Ken wore a rented tux. His hair was combed with some kind of product that was supposed to make it very business-like, but this curl escaped onto his forehead like Superman's. In fact, he looked a lot like an actor I'd seen in an old movie playing Superman, as though Clark Kent had taken off his glasses and put on a tux instead of his cape and tights. That was good, because tights would have been very strange to wear to a school dance, and, if he'd been wearing anything skin tight at that moment, my knees would have gone so weak that I wouldn't have been able to get up off the couch. As it was, my mouth had gone so dry I couldn't talk right away.

"Okay, um, let me get some pictures, and then I'll let you two go to the dance," my dad said. He sounded both uncomfortable and amused, and I worried that he had hatched some plan to embarrass me, but he just got his handcom and took some pictures of Ken and me standing together. Ken put his hand on the small of my back very gently but didn't stand too close. I guess he didn't want to be too forward in front of my dad, but I leaned against him, feeling his chest against my shoulder. He took a deep breath that pressed him into me, and I thought I might faint.

We got into Ken's parents' car to go to the dance. He was nervous, squeezing the wheel with both hands. Neither of us knew what to say. We made some awkward small talk about the kind of music they would play at the dance. I told him I wished they would play some underground stuff, but when I said the names of the bands I like, he just nodded and said, "Yeah. Cool." I knew he had never heard of them, and that's fine, but it meant we couldn't really talk much about music. Instead, he told me a story about one of his friends who asked a girl to the dance and got shot down. I told him about Juan's play. He laughed really hard at first, then suddenly took Juan's side and looked mournful. "Man, that flooding sucks for him, pardon my language. I mean, I thought my flower thing was good, but I didn't write a play."

"The flowers were very sweet," I said.

"And, more important, you said 'Yes.'" Then he looked away from the road quickly and flashed a smile. "That's what matters to me. Tonight is going to be great."

I was completely, 100% positive that he was right about that.

When we got to the school, the parking lot wasn't as full as it is during football games, but there were more cars than on a school day. Most of the couples were coming up out of the tunnel from the subway. The sun was going down so the temperature was getting bearable, meaning the couples didn't have to rush into the building the way they normally did when it's too hot or cold. Instead, they hung out in front of the building, taking pictures of each other, finding their friends, grinning like dopes. It was a great scene. Ken offered me his arm like an old-fashioned gentleman and escorted me across the parking lot to the crowd outside the main entrance. He nodded and waved to some friends, and I guessed he wanted to go talk to them, but he stayed with me, and that meant a lot. Then I caught sight of Sky and Lucas, so I told Ken to go catch up with his friends while I caught up with mine, and that I'd meet him in line to go in. He looked relieved.

When Sky saw me, she tried to run over, but she wobbled on her heels and Lucas had to catch her arm so she wouldn't break a leg. Then she basically fell from him into my arms. "So? How is it going with Ken?"

"He's been a perfect gentleman. He let my dad take pictures. He's... he's great."

Lucas frowned, but he only said, "Hmm."

"What?" I asked.

He shook his head.

"What?"

"Nothing."

But it totally sounded like "Something."

Then Ken came over and introduced me to his friend, Jorge, and Jorge's date, Faith. I introduced them all to Sky and Lucas. We got into line to go into the building. Faith had on this great dress, and I told her so. She whispered thanks and then looked at the ground. Jorge wasn't quite as shy, but he only wanted to talk to Ken. Sky took over, talking to both of them and filling the silence. I stood between Lucas and Ken.

"So," Ken said, "Harriet told me about Juan's play. That really sucks for him." He shook his head.

Lucas nodded. "It was a flooding mess."

"Is he doing okay?"

"I checked in on him today. Killing communists seems to take his mind off of things."

"*Last Wall of Defense*? I love that game!" He turned to me quickly. "I mean, I'd rather be here with you, but if you'd said 'No,' I'd be at home drowning my sorrows in zombie blood, too." He paused. "Wow, that came out a lot grosser than I meant."

I laughed. Lucas shuffled his feet. I could tell something was up with him, but I wished he would try to hide it a little better.

We made our way inside. Just as we were getting in, we heard somebody shouting behind us. Gina skipped up the steps, holding hands with her date and dragging him along. Mike didn't look like anything special to me, but he seemed nice. Once Gina explained that he was a freshman at Northern Oregon U, Ken started asking about the football team there, and pretty soon they were deep in a discussion of Pac 16 football and the different schools' placements in the national tournament. I tried to participate, but the only comments that grabbed my interested were the times one of them would say, "Well, Stanford-at-Tahoe is a good school academically, but their team still sucks." I'd made a little mental note that said, "Look into Stanford-at-Tahoe."

The same security guards that greeted us each day were running the metal detector, but Mr. Rorty, the ancient greeter, wasn't there. Somehow that made me sad. You know that first time when you see one of the school janitors in the grocery section at CorpMart and realize they don't just live at school? Somehow, even at 17, I still imagined that Mr. Rorty lived at Alice Louise Walton Corporate High School #7348, and I was disappointed not to see his smile when I walked in. It made me wonder what it would be like if I ever met one of my teachers in real life outside of school. Of course, they all lived far away, mostly near Headquarters in Arkansas, but if I saw one of them on a vacation or something it would feel really weird.

The dance itself was in the gym. It was too packed to fit everybody, so there was an overflow space in the central courtyard where people could drink punch and stand around. The dance organizers had strung rows of Christmas lights in an uneven criss-cross net over the courtyard. It was a good thing, because the screens that broadcast the fake sky during the day don't show a night sky at night. They are just dark gray. The little lights reflected off of them faintly, creating a fake night sky with some depth, and in that yellow starlight, dozens of couples sat on the edges of the planter boxes or milled around the table with the punch bowls. Our group made our way over there,

Jorge leading the way to get punch for Faith. She was
so quiet, but she seemed really grateful for the punch.
I wondered if maybe she would start talking a bit
more once she'd had some, even though it was non-
alcoholic, like maybe her throat had just been dry or
she needed something to hold onto, but once she got
it, she stared down into the cup, smiling and leaning
on Jorge occasionally, so I decided she was just really
shy.

Sky, on the other hand, was never shy. "Hi, Mr.
Robb!" she said. I hadn't even noticed that the
school's senior manager was the one ladling out the
punch, but there he was. Standing next to him, Mr.
Rorty set out the plastic cups and the paper napkins. I
smiled at Mr. Rorty and he smiled back like always,
then looked over to Mr. Robb to make sure he hadn't
noticed the exchange.

"Hello, Sky," Mr. Robb said. "Lucas."

Lucas just nodded at him.

Mr. Robb looked over Lucas' shoulder and smiled.
"Ken! How are you feeling tonight?"

Ken made a motion like he was knocking on a
door, rapping his knuckles on the top of his head.
"Solid, Mr. Robb. Solid as a rock."

"Glad to hear it. And Miss Washington, you look
lovely tonight."

"Thanks," I said, taking the punch he offered.

As I walked away, Lucas leaned toward me and
whispered, "Careful. It might be poisoned."

"That would be yours, Lucas," Sky said.

Lucas nodded, but then his face fell.

Sky's eyes widened. "I'm sorry, Lucas. That wasn't funny."

"S'okay," he said, but he walked off. Sky followed. I just stood there, completely confused.

"Where are they off to?" Ken asked. He'd snuck up behind me, and I jumped a little.

"No idea." I saw that he'd finished his punch, so I drained my glass. "So, do you want to go dance?"

"Um, sure, I guess. If you want. I know it's not your type of music."

I took his hand. "I like dancing, though," I said.

I led him into the gym itself. When we passed through the doorway, it was like we crossed a membrane of sound, and when we pierced it, the space inside was packed with bodies and heat and a giant heartbeat I could feel in my chest. No, it wasn't the kind of music I like to listen to on my own, but it was catchy and danceable. There was not space to do anything that creative anyway. We were packed in like cargo containers on those big ships, locked together and swaying on the waves of sound in a giant group.

I don't know if Ken would have wanted to give me a little more space. I don't know if I wanted to give him more space. It didn't matter, because our bodies were pressed together by the crush of the crowd. I was extremely aware of my chest pressed against his, his arms wrapped around my shoulders, is hands locked together and resting on my lower back. I didn't know what to do with my arms. At first they were just folded in like squished little tyrannosaurs arms, but after two songs, I felt comfortable reaching up and putting them around his neck. And then, after a few more songs, my fingers were in his hair. Then his hands were climbing up my back. Then his fingers were in my hair. And then he was kissing me.

Looking back, I can't remember what song was playing. I can't remember that horrible moment when you're not sure if someone's about to kiss you, and you're not sure if you should lean into it because maybe they aren't, and it's just the absolute worst, and then...bam; everything is perfect. That moment just didn't exist. We were dancing, and then we were kissing, and it felt completely natural.

After a while, we were both too exhausted to keep dancing, and I guess that's when I started to remember that there was a world around me. I suddenly felt totally self-conscious, so when he pointed his head toward the gym doors, I nodded eagerly. We pressed through the bodies, back through that semi-solid layer of sound, and popped out into the quiet of the courtyard. Once we were out there, I didn't know what to say.

"So," Ken said, looking down at his shoes and shuffling his feet a little, "I was wondering if you want to go down and check out the lake maybe?"

Now I'm trying to remember how I felt about this at the time. Did it scare me? Was I relieved to not have to go back in and dance and kiss him in front of everybody in the school? Or not kiss him and ruin the evening? Maybe that's what worried me more than anything.

So I said, "Sure!"

Next thing you know, we were in his car and driving down toward the lake.

The brightly lit streets lined with high rise apartments whizzed by. We passed the huge CorpMart mall, then the smaller specialty Corporation stores, the Corporation car dealership, a CorpDonalds, a CorpBucks, a CorpMart Quickstop convenience store. The buildings got smaller and older and more run down as we descended through Mt. Hood toward the water. The asphalt disappeared. The sound of gravel under the tires surprised me and I started like someone who'd been shaken awake. I looked at Ken, and he smiled.

"The roads down here are wrecked, huh?"

We passed the turn off for the flea market, a privately owned You-Pull junk shop filled with broken down cars, a couple antique stores that may have been closed forever. Eventually there were just trees on the sides of the road. At first these were thick pines with ferns exploding underneath them creating a dense temperate jungle, but pretty quickly we got to the parts of the woods where the salt water had climbed up during the bad storms. Here the ferns were dead and the trees were dying. I stared out the window, watching a horror show, one of those old animated flip books where the pages turn and the image changes bit by bit. In this cartoon, a pine tree loses all its needles. Its root are more and more exposed by the erosion of the soil underneath it. It dries out. Beetles eat through its bark. It leans into its sisters and brothers, forming a spiderweb of rot. Some of them fall over completely, their roots sticking up and gasping like fish on dry land. And then they all shrink. There are fewer and fewer. And we reach the shore.

Ken turned onto an empty area that must have served as a parking lot when people came down to swim. It was covered in gravel just like the road, but clearly everybody knew about this place because there were a dozen other cars parked in the lot. People were standing around some of the cars, smoking, holding cups, talking. Other cars had couples in them. Ken drove past the little crowd toward the edge of the lot.

He parked and turned the car off.

We sat there in silence for a minute.

He said, "It's kinda' pretty at night, huh?"

At first, I thought he meant the beach. Some of the other students had started a few little bonfires down there. More cars were pulling in behind us. I realized this was just something that always happened after the dances. I thought Ken was talking about the fires, but when I looked at him, I saw that he was scanning the horizon, trying to take in the whole black lake under the black, cloudy night sky. I followed his gaze, but I couldn't see anything at first. Then the moon flashed through the clouds, on and off like a light, and when it was out, I could see the water clearly. Miles out, I could identify the tops of the empty skyscrapers that marked the place where Portland used to be. The walls they'd tried to build were way down below the surface, and most of the buildings were probably trashed underneath, too, but the skyscrapers had been built to withstand a lot of weather.

"What was that thing over there?" I asked.

"Used to be one of those aerial trams. It was like a bubble car that hung from a giant metal wire and took people up and down from a hospital or something.

When I was little, you could still see one of the cars connected to the wire, but it snapped during one of the storms when nobody was looking, and the next time we came out here, the car was gone and there was just that big arm that held up a part of the wire."

"That's sad," I said.

"Yeah." He put both hands on the wheel and pulled himself forward to the edge of his seat, then sat back, reached down, and unzipped his pants. "So, like, do you want to go down on me now?"

I leaned away from him so fast that my shoulder hit the car door. "Um, what?"

"Or, like, we could just have sex normal style at first, if you want. You won't get pregnant, I promise. Coach makes us all take the pill at practice every week."

"I..." I shook my head back and forth, trying to find the right words. No words came, but my eyes filled with tears.

"Aw man," he said. "I really flooded this up, huh? Aw, flood." His voice was very quiet. Then, suddenly, he started hitting his forehead with the heels of both his hands. Once. Twice. Three times. "Flood!" he shouted, so loud that it hurt my ears. Then he went back to hitting himself.

I grabbed the door handle, swung the door open, and climbed out. As I was going, I felt his hand try to grab onto my shoulder, and that just freaked me out even more.

"Wait," he called. Not a scary yell this time. Just a desperate yell. But I was too scared to slow down. I heard his door opening behind me. I was only walking, but I wanted to run.

"Harriet! I messed up. Come back!" I turned to look at him. "You don't have to go down on me on the first date. We can wait a couple dates for that, if you want."

"Just...just stay away from me," I said.

He started hitting his forehead again, this time with a closed fist. "Aw, man!" he kept muttering. I turned and began to walk away. I could hear him move behind me. His shoes ground against the gravel. I was walking, but he was running. I looked over my shoulder, and he was right behind me, reaching out for me.

I heard different footsteps, more crunching gravel, and that kept me from bolting at full speed. It stopped Ken, too, and he lowered his arms, looking into the darkness at the person who had appeared.

"Ken, c'mon back to the car," a voice said. "Let's talk. It's going to be okay."

I didn't recognize the voice, and it was hard to make out the owner. He must have been about our age, shorter than Ken, maybe a little taller than me. He was wearing a hooded sweatshirt, so I couldn't even identify him by his hair. His voice was soothing but also tense, like a person trying to sound calm when approaching a growling dog. I'd never heard the voice before.

He knew me, though. He turned toward me. "Harriet, just go down to the beach. Sky and Lucas are looking for you down there. They'll give you a ride. Everything will be all right."

Then he turned back to Ken and put an arm around him, guiding him back to Ken's car. "C'mon, buddy."

"I really flooded everything up, Graham," Ken said.

The guy's name was Graham. Where do I know him from?

"Just a mistake," Graham said in that same calming voice. "They happen. It could have been worse. C'mon. We'll talk about it in the car."

I stood there and watched. When they walked around to the driver's side of Ken's car, Graham guided Ken's head in like a cop trying to keep him from banging it on the doorframe. Then, in the glow from the car's interior lights, I saw his face inside the hood. I'd seen him before in class, but I'd never spoken to him, never even heard him speak. He wasn't one of Ken's football player friends. I didn't know him at all. How did he know my name?

When he looked at me over the top of Ken's car, he shrugged and shook his head a little, mouthing the words, "I'm sorry."

What. The. Flood.

For a second I just stood there in shock, but that shock slowly turned to anger. The night had been so perfect, and then it had turned sour so fast. At the very least, I'd suffered a gross come-on. I was almost sexually assaulted, maybe even raped. And then this guy comes out of the shadows, puts an arm around the guy who mistreated me, and consoles him like he was the victim! Of all the sexist, yeah-but-what-was-she-wearing, jerks, he is the worst! And mouthing "I'm sorry" does not make up for it.

137

I turned and started for the beach. Unfortunately, I was in heels, and even though they were pretty wide heels, walking down to the beach without breaking an ankle turned out to be tricky. I couldn't take my shoes off because the hill was rocky, but between the rocks there were these pockets of mud. The heels would sink right in and I'd nearly fall. Then I'd carefully pull the shoe up, trying not to let my foot slip out, only to have the other one sink in after a couple steps. Eventually I made it down the hill to the sand. I was just a tiny bit relieved. I took my shoes off and started walking toward the camp fires, and after a few steps I realized it wasn't sand at all. It was just mud. I was walking in bare feet in mud.

By the time I made it to the fires, I was so angry I thought I'd burst into flames myself. Then I heard Sky call my name. She came running over, lit up by the fire light, and I noticed that her feet were bare, too. She was walking in the mud barefoot looking for me. And then Lucas was behind her. He'd taken his shoes and socks off, and he was holding his pair in one hand and Sky's in the other. They were both walking in the mud for me.

And that's when I just lost it. I burst into tears. Sky wrapped her arms around me, and then Lucas put his arms around both of us, squishing Sky in between us. I cried until I was shaking, then stepped away and composed myself.

"Did he..." Sky hesitated. "Did he hurt you?"

I couldn't speak yet, but I shook my head. Finally I found my voice. "He.... He chased me when I wouldn't.... Then that guy Graham showed up—"

138

"Abominable?"

That's where I knew the name from!

"Yeah, that guy. Only it was like he was helping Ken and not me."

Sky frowned. "What a flooding plague-face!"

"I know," I mumbled. "Jerk."

"Well, he kept Ken from catching up to you. That's good at least," Lucas said. He took a pack of half-and-half cigarettes out of his tux's breast pocket, put one in his mouth, and lit it. "A terrible flooding ending to a terrible flooding night."

"But it wasn't terrible at first," I said. "It was kinda' perfect. Then, suddenly, it was a nightmare."

"Hmm. Well, then you have mine beat. Until the end. Here. Take a drag on this."

"I don't smoke," I said.

"Just a little. The marijuana will calm you down."

I took the cigarette and tried my first drag. It was hot and scratchy and tasted awful. I'd seen enough smokers to know I was supposed to hold the smoke in my lungs, but I coughed it right out again. "How'd you even get these? Don't you have to be 18?"

Lucas laughed. "Is a Corporation cop going to arrest a Corporation customer who is giving The Corporation money? I could buy heroin, needles, and rubber armbands at a CorpMart pharmacy if I wanted to."

"But you don't want to, right?" Sky asked. She sounded really concerned.

"No." Lucas grabbed the cigarette back from me, took a long drag, held it, and then blew it out slowly. "No," he continued, "I am enough of a disappointment as is, thank you very much." In the light of the fire, I could see that he had tears in his eyes.

Sky wrapped her arms around him. "I think you're wonderful, Lucas. Plus you carried my shoes. Certainly the best date of the night between Harriet and me, no offense Harriet."

"No, that's absolutely correct."

"Well, I don't think you'll have to worry about Ken anymore, Harriet. He'll be too ashamed to show his face for a while, and I have it on good authority that he'll be leaving Alice Louise Walton Corporate High School at the end of football season."

"Why?"

"They'll say he isn't cutting it academically. What that really means is that management won't have a use for him anymore. They have a way of throwing out the garbage once they've made use of something for a while. Trust me."

I was stunned. Again. And getting pretty sick of being stunned.

"How do you know this?"

Sky was still hugging Lucas, but she turned her head toward me and frowned. "Harriet, it's Lucas. Lucas Robb. Senior Manager Robb's son."

"Oh." Stunned again. And really not enjoying it. "I did not know that."

"Well, he would rather it were not the case as well," Lucas said. He took another big hit on his cigarette, then flicked what was left into the fire. "C'mon. I'll drive you both home."

We didn't speak in the car. I had more questions, but Lucas clearly wasn't in a speaking mood, and if

Sky could stay quiet for ten minutes, that was a sure sign that I should, too. Lucas dropped Sky off first, then took me to my apartment building. He made sure I got inside, waved at me, and drove off.

My dad was surprised when I came in so early. The first thing he said was, "Are you okay?"

I gave him a big hug and spoke into his shoulder. "It didn't end well."

"I'm so sorry, baby-girl. Are you all right? Do you want to talk about it?"

"No," I said. "I think I'll just write about it in my diary. Maybe then I'll know what I think."

"Okay," he said. "I hope that helps. I love you."

"I love you, too, Dad."

I came in here and got to work. Now it's all down on paper, and I still don't know quite what I feel. Am I still angry? Flood yeah! But I'm also scared, even though there's nothing to be scared of anymore. And I'm hurt. Hurt that Ken would think of me that way. Angry at myself for not seeing that he has some serious issues. Embarrassed that everybody at school saw me kissing him and probably thinks exactly what he thought. Afraid of going back to school Monday.

Oh, and maybe just a little bit excited to punch that Graham guy in the face the first chance I get.

-24-43-1-10-6-83-67-14-4-
-3-3-43-0-66-0-0-0-6-
-0-7-11-2-1-27-
-5-0-0-80-1-

CHAPTER 12

Monday, October 29th, 2114

I didn't sleep much this weekend. After the dance on Saturday, I was amped-up on adrenaline. I wrote in my room for a long time, then finally fell asleep around five in the morning. I was awakened by the storm alarms. The weather service has to let us know when one of the super-storms is rolling in. Back in the Midwest, those would be giant blizzards that can hit at almost any time of the year now, but out here they are typhoons that come in off the Pacific. Modern towns like Mt. Hood are well prepared for them. All the parking structures are built beneath the buildings so the cars don't fly away. Most building don't have much in the way of windows, and when they do, those are made of bulletproof Plexiglas. The apartment buildings and even the individual homes have underground access to the subway system, and the subways can still take people to school and work, so the storms don't shut life down completely. Still, when one of the storms is coming, they have to warn

142

everyone to get off the streets because the wind can pick a person right up off the ground and smash them into a building or toss them into a mountainside or way out to sea. The alarms are terribly loud. Even for those of us living on high ground, they remind us all that the climate is broken, that the water is still rising, that millions and millions of people were caught in flash floods when storms like these brought the ocean water over the dams back when people held on and tried to save their old cities. It's no wonder that "flood" is a swear word. It's the worst thing we can think of. And the alarms remind us all every time.

I guess that should have made me reflective, encouraged me to count my blessings or something, but when I woke up, I tried to text Sky and found that the storm had knocked out the local network. Not only was I cut off from my friends, but it meant I couldn't watch videos, couldn't do my homework for school, couldn't even access the books in my library.

Dad wasn't very sympathetic. "That's why we have real books, Harriet. They do not run out of power, and their network is never down."

I tried. I did. I found this old book Dad had picked up at the flea market. The pages were all wrinkled because the book had been soaked at some point, then dried out, but I could still read all the words. It was a book about gods from different religions all interacting. It was funny, but I wanted to research the different gods to see if the author got them right, and I couldn't log into Corp-i-pedia and search them, so I just had to read it through to the end. Then the end got kind-of freaky when a bunch of the gods went to

143

war against the half-formed monsters that predated the universe, and I think that contributed to my nightmares that night.

I don't remember all my dreams, but I know that Ken was chasing me in one of them. It was too dark to see him, but I could hear his feet crunching on the gravel. I kept running away and his footsteps kept getting closer until I finally woke up, sweaty and terrified.

In another one he had me in his arms on a crowded dance floor, only I wanted to get away, and then that Graham guy said it was all my fault, and everyone in the room started yelling at me. They were calling me names like "skank" and "whore." Even my friends were there shouting at me, Sky and Juan and Lucas. Then people in the crowd started throwing cups of punch on me. Warm punch. Warm, dark red, thick, sticky punch that tasted like salt and copper when it splashed on my face. I think that part came from the novel I'd been reading.

In another one, Ken was a giant monster with six arms, and he crawled toward me like a spider. Then he reared up and started groping me, his hands on my neck and my breasts and my crotch, but all the while the top pair of fists were banging into his forehead and he was roaring in this low, phlegmy, demonic voice, "Come back! It's just a flooding mistake! Flood!"

I couldn't go to sleep after that one. I decided to take a long, hot shower and then get ready for school, but when I came out of the shower my dad told me that school had been canceled until they got the network up. Even though the subways could get us all to school and the retractable tunnel could protect us right into the main doors, without the network there was no way to connect us with the teachers in Arkansas, so we wouldn't have anything to do there.

I was relieved that I wouldn't have to see Ken, but I needed to talk to my friends, and I was actually looking forward to confronting Graham. Instead, I was trapped in the apartment for another whole day.

I tried reading some more. While I was looking for a book, Dad came over and took three copies of *The Complete Works of Shakespeare* off the shelf and hid them in his room. I took the fourth copy and read *The Tempest* because my mom had mentioned that she was reading it.. No surprise; it was really good. Still, there were lots of words I didn't know, and I couldn't look them up. I got so frustrated that I couldn't start another one after lunch.

"Dad, I'm going stir crazy," I called into his room.

"Sorry, Baby. Don't know what to do for you."

"Can I go to the mall?"

"It might be closed, too. No network means no credit. No money to be made. How can The Corporation abuse its customers and exploit its workers when it can't take money from the former and refuse to give it to the latter?"

"Yeah, well, if it's cool with you, I'll go down there and ask the managers that very question, okay Dad? We'll call it field research."

He stepped out of his room, then leaned on the door frame and just smiled at me. "Okay, Honey. You go do some field research for your old man."

I grabbed my coat, then kissed him on the cheek. "Thanks, Dad."

I took the subway to the mall exit. Dad was right. The mall was closed. But, to my surprise, there were some other high school students on the platform. I got off the subway and walked through the groups of students, looking for my friends.

"Harriet!"

It was Juan. He was standing in the concrete stairway that led to the underground parking garage. He looked back into the darkness and shouted, "Hey, Sky! You don't have to go get Harriet. She's already here!"

I found my friends sitting in a small circle in a parking space in a corner of the parking garage. The floor was cold and clammy. The lights were running, luckily, but they were dim. The whole scene should have been terrible, but it turned out to be pretty great. We played cards and talked about people at school. Gina made me tell the whole story of my date with Ken because she hadn't heard about it at all. She seemed really interested at first, but when I got to the part where I made it down to the beach, everyone was sympathetic except Gina.

"Wow, yeah, that sucks. Okay, now let me tell you about my date!"

So it was just a ploy to not look selfish. Nice try, Gina. Anyway, she told us about her date, about how Mike was really cool at first, and then they went to a CorpCafe at the mall and tried to have a conversation, but they didn't know what to talk about.

"We don't know the same people. He's not into theater or music or fashion, and I'm not into college sports or politics. He wants to study poli-sci and become a lawyer, and I think that sounds like the most boring thing in the world. I told him I want to be a model and a stage actress and a movie actress, my whole triple threat dream, and he was like, 'Well, how do you become all those things?'

"And I explained that I'm going to move to New York City right after I graduate.

"And then he's like, 'And then what?'

"I told him I'll get an agent and some headshots, do some photo shoots while I audition for roles, the whole thing. But he kept grilling me for details about how to get an agent and how I plan to survive before I make any money. And when I finally explained that part of the whole thing is taking a huge risk and just going for it, he just shook his head like that was the dumbest thing he's ever heard."

Sky leaned forward. "So? Did you tell him off and make him take you home?"

"No. We went back to his dorm room to watch a movie and..." She looked at Juan, then down into her lap. "...and just hang out for a while."

We sat in silence for a moment. Then Lucas made a big show of standing up, groaning like an old man, stretching, sighing. "See? This is why I've decided to start smoking. It gives me an excuse to escape from awkward situations like this one. And I know it's super-addictive and bad for me and stupid, and I will just need to smoke more and more and more until it kills me, but I predict that my life is going to be increasingly filled with these uncomfortable moments, and I would rather be killed by nicotine and THC, thank you all very much." Then he spun on the ball of one foot like a dancer and stormed off. But he only went across the parking garage. Then he put one of those half-and-halfs in a long cigarette holder and made sure we were watching while he leaned on the wall and blew smoke up at the ceiling.

"What is going on with Lucas?" I asked. "He seems to be a lot more...Lucas than normal."

Sky leaned forward again. "Harriet didn't know that Lucas is Mr. Robb's son until last night. That was an oversight on my part. I should have mentioned it. Just never came up."

I waved that away. "Yeah, and he said his dad wishes Lucas wasn't his son. What's that all about?"

"It's complicated," Gina said.

"Nope," Juan cut her off, just sharply enough to be noticeable. "It's pretty simple. Mr. Robb doesn't want to be the senior manager of a corporate high school on Swamp Island on the edge of America. He wants to get promoted. Like everybody else, I guess. But he thinks the people in the head office in Arkansas won't promote him because he has a gay son."

"Is that really true?" I asked.

Juan shrugged.

"No way," Gina said. "The Corporation hires gay people and women and minorities. They're a modern company. Those attitudes are like a thousand years old."

Sky tilted her head to the side. "It's publicly traded, but the family is still the majority shareholders. They're all pretty Christian and conservative. Besides, it doesn't matter if they would really hold it against Mr. Robb. What matters is that Mr. Robb thinks they would, and he takes it out on Lucas."

"Like, how?"

Juan shook his head. "Nothing big and dramatic. In fact, Lucas sometimes wishes they would have big screaming matches. He's even tried to start them. But his dad just has the never-ending disapproval. Like Lucas disgusts him and can never do anything right. That's why Lucas can't date." He turned to Sky. "I mean date for real. Date guys."

"Yeah, I got that." She didn't sound sarcastic like I would have, and she smiled at him in this way that communicated that she was amused but not at all offended by his condescension.

"Sorry."

"No probs."

I realized she totally meant it. And she wasn't just being adorable because she has a crush on Juan. She was just being Sky. And I thought, why can't Juan fall in love with Sky just because she deserves it? Hell, if I were into girls I wouldn't give Gina a second look, but I'd be all over Sky. No, that's probably not true. I'd be drooling over Gina just like the dumb boys do, but then I'd have one conversation with her and get turned off by her self-absorption. Sky, on the other hand, makes everybody around her feel better just because she's happy and cool. A person like that deserves to have the guy of her dreams love her back, right?

I think I started to formulate a plan right then. No, that's an exaggeration. It wasn't even an idea yet. What comes before an idea? Is there even a word for that tiny little glimmer, that hint of a something? I think there should be a word for it. It's pretty important, when you think about it. All great ideas started out as something less than an idea, then became fleshed-out plans. But first they were this other thing. I'll call it a frictim. It's like a fraction of an idea, but a spark, like something caused by friction, but not even formal enough to have a -tion ending. Just a little frictim that can become an idea later.

My frictim was interrupted. I was spacing out a little, looking over Sky's shoulder, and I noticed another person in the parking garage with us who hadn't caught my eye before. He was sitting funny, legs crossed with one book in his lap but turned away from it and making a notation on the notepad next to him. It meant he was sideways to me, but I could only see the back of his head. In the dim light, I couldn't make him out clearly, but something about him seemed familiar. I leaned sideways and stared at him. Then he turned back to the book and started writing in it. That's when I caught his profile and recognized him. It was Graham!

Before I knew what I was doing, I was on my feet and walking toward him. He was concentrating so hard on his book that he didn't hear my footsteps, and while I was still crossing the parking lot, he turned away toward his notebook again. When I got to him, his back was twisted away from me, but he turned his head toward the sound at the last second.

Too late. I reached down, put both palms on his shoulder, and pushed. Leaned over like that, he had no chance of staying up, and fell hard on his other side as he tried to twist in my direction.

"What the flood!" I shouted.

The sound echoed through the whole floor of the parking structure, and probably to the floors above and below and out to the subway platform, too. Suddenly, I was aware that I'd made a scene, and everybody was watching. I ground my teeth but didn't look around at everybody else.

"What did I do?" he cried. It wasn't an aggressive shout or a wounded screech. If anything, he sounded amused as much as shocked.

I leaned closer and tried to lower my voice so everybody wouldn't hear me. "Your pervy friend was chasing me to do the-flood-knows-what, and you show up and rescued him!" I wasn't shouting. Just shout-whispering. But then I did shout. "Him?"

He closed his eyes very slowly, took a deep breath, and then said, "Can I sit up?"

I stepped back but didn't say anything.

He pushed himself back up until he was sitting cross-legged again, then reached out and picked up the book that had fallen out of his lap when he went sprawling. It was another copy of *The Complete Works of Shakespeare*. He carefully closed the book and set it down on top of the notebook he'd been writing in. Then he picked both up and started putting them in his backpack while he spoke.

"I can see why you would think that, and I'm sorry."

151

Oh, I hate those kinds of half-apologies. "I'm so sorry you are the one to blame for interpreting the situation incorrectly." Flood that!

He went on stuffing his stupid books in his stupid bag. "I'm sorry, because you're right. I didn't rescue you. I was rescuing Ken from himself, from what he might do to you. Now, that had the added bonus of preventing him from doing something to you, so I'd think you might appreciate that part. Maybe even be a little bit grateful. But I can understand why you wanted to be rescued in that situation, and why it bothers you that I focused my attention on a guy who has been my friend since he was four years old and not on the girl I have never even spoken to."

He stood up and threw the backpack on to his back, just one strap on one shoulder. Then he stuck out his hand. "I'm Graham. It's very nice to meet you."

I sneered at his sarcasm, but I shook his hand anyway. "I'm Harriet, the insignificant extra in your bromance."

"Do you even know what's going on with Ken?" he asked.

"Nope. Don't care. You just tell him to stay the flood away from me."

He nodded. "Won't be a problem. But if he dies on Friday, you might regret those words."

I stopped. "What do you mean?"

"I thought you didn't care."

"Don't be a jerk. What's going on?"

He looked around at the other people in the parking structure. That reminded me that they were there. "Let's maybe talk about it on the next floor up. It's...not a topic that will make us popular."

"I'm not trying to be popular," I said, but I turned and started walking up the slight slope toward the next floor.

We walked slowly, and he didn't say anything while we could see the other students hanging out on the subway level. Then we turned and I expected him to start, but he looked like he was trying to figure out what to say. He'd take these quick little breaths, like he was about to start, and then shake his head and keep walking. We walked the length of the next level, then turned again. I didn't realize it, but we'd reached the lowest entrance to the mall.

He stopped outside the glass doors. When he spoke, his voice was still quiet, like he was afraid the sound would carry all the way down to the others below. "Ken and I used to be best friends. We didn't really have a lot in common, I guess. I can see that now, but it didn't bother us when we were little. I was always geeky. He had athletic talent even before he had his first big growth spurt. He played basketball and football and soccer. He'd get picked for these youth teams. People could tell he was going to turn into something special. But he stayed pretty loyal to me, at least for longer than he should have. Maybe he just liked having a friend who was so loyal to him. Maybe he liked having a friend who wasn't on any of his teams." He rolled his eyes a little. "My home life is kind of flooded up. Maybe he just felt sorry for me."

He batted that away with the back of his hand like it was a fly and continued. "Anyway, when Ken was in seventh grade, he got his first concussion. It wasn't in football, like you'd expect. It was in soccer. He and another guy went up for a header at the same time and...." He clapped his hands really loudly. The sound made me flinch. Then it echoed down the parking garage. "Bam. So they did the full medical work-up, and they said he could keep playing, but he couldn't keep getting concussions or he'd have to stop."

"He had his next two in the fall of eighth grade during football. Then his fourth during basketball. He still hadn't shot up yet, but he was quick and had a great handle, so they had him playing point guard. Cracked heads with another guy when reaching in to steal the ball. They said he couldn't play soccer that spring. Not if he wanted to play football when he got to the high school."

"But why...?" I started.

"Exactly. Why let him play at all. Because somebody at the high school needed him. Needed him to win games. So he's played all four years. Wearing Corporation helmets. They're garbage, you know. Made with the cheapest possible materials, flawed aluminum made by the lowest bidder and valued most for being light weight because they have to be shipped across the ocean. They crack during games all the time. If any other player got hit in the head as much as Ken has, they wouldn't be able to get medical clearance to let him play again. It would be embarrassing for the company if some kid died on the field.

"But, like I said, Ken is special. He could win us a national high school championship. He could go to a big name university. He could probably go pro. Or, at least, he could have. So a certain somebody saw Ken as a way to get the attention of corporate headquarters. He made sure there was always another doctor who would clear Ken to play."

"Senior Manager Robb," I guessed.

"Right. Highest ranking company employee in town. Higher than any of the company doctors. So they say what he wants them to say. And Ken goes on playing.

"By ninth grade, Ken and I weren't hanging out anymore. He had his football friends. My athletic ability basically ends at putting on the Abominable suit. Plus, I got really into...some work I do online. So we stopped hanging out. It wasn't ever official. We just didn't have time. Then he was dating Kim, so he had even less time.

"Then, earlier this year, Kim came up to me at school. 'You used to be Ken's best friend,' she said. Not a question. She knew because Ken had told her. 'He needs you right now. He needs somebody who can tell him not to play anymore. He's in trouble.'

"And he was. But so was she. He'd started having these horrible mood swings. Sometimes he'd get violent, even. He never punched her. Nothing anybody else could see. But he'd push her and shake her. She had bruises. They just weren't visible. And then he'd feel terrible and cry. Weep, really. And then he'd fly into another rage, this time at himself. Sometimes he'd even hit himself in the head, even though that was the last thing he needed. Kim begged him to go back to the doctors, to try to get a real diagnosis and get some help.

"I tried to talk to him. Right here, in fact." Graham pointed up at the mall. Then he grabbed the long handle that ran the length of the door, and he pulled.

We both expected it to be locked. It opened. He looked up at me, and I guess I had just as much of a surprised look on my face as he did, because we both laughed a little. It was a tiny, gallows laugh because of the conversation, but I guess we needed to break the tension.

"The electronic doors are off, but they must have let the employees come in to clean up or stock shelves or something," I said.

"I guess. Want to go in?"

"Think we can?"

"Until they tell us to leave."

I shrugged, then followed him into the mall. The lights in the main courtyard were on, filling the space all the way up to the ceiling four stories above with light. We could see the rain smacking into the Plexiglas skylight above. The lights inside the individual shops were out, though. The fountains that decorated the four corners of the courtyard, normally shooting thin geysers of water up two stories into the air, were silent and still, just pools with copper tubes sticking up out of them at different heights. The muzac that always played just beneath the sound of people chattering: Gone. A guy up on the third floor was waxing the imitation marble, so the only sound was a distant, whirring buzz. It felt deeply weird.

"We can talk in here," Graham said. But he wasn't talking to me. He'd was realizing something and talking to himself.

"What?"

He was looking up toward the ceiling, then around at all the closed Corporation subsidiaries. "With the network down, the security department at corporate headquarters can't listen to us. They don't know what we're saying. We can say anything." Then he turned and looked at me, suddenly urgent. "The Corporation is killing Ken. Not on purpose. That's not how they operate, not most of the time, anyway. They kill people in some countries. You know that, right?"

"People who try to start unions. Or talk to reporters about working conditions."

"Yeah. Or who interfere with The Corporation's relationship with foreign governments. Politicians who aren't Corporation friendly have a habit of committing suicide. But most of the time, they kill people like they're killing Ken. They sell dangerous products. They sell poisoned food. Somebody who is trying to climb the corporate ladder figures out a way to shave off a few cents here or there. The Corporation doesn't even know, most of the time. They aren't trying to be malicious. They are just focused on making money. And they are too big, like a giant steamroller that accidentally squashes bugs on the asphalt in front of it. Ken is the perfect example of what The Corporation does. And what the government doesn't stop, because they are too weak now. Anything they did to protect people became 'burdensome regulation,' or 'anti-capitalist.' Then, when Russia wouldn't let The Corporation in and we went to war, all that anti-capitalist stuff became 'communist.'"

"Again," I said.

"Huh?"

"It became communist again," I explained. "'The Red Scare.' It happened before. They just brought it back. Maybe it never really went away. That fear, just hiding under the surface, waiting for The Corporation to wake it up."

Graham nodded. "Right. I read about that online. Some historian. He lost his job for writing about it, I think."

I made a mental note to ask my dad about that.

Graham sighed. "Anyway, I tried to get Ken to quit football. No luck. He nearly beat the stuffing out of me. Then he apologized by email. But he kept on playing.

"When he broke up with Kim, I knew he was in real trouble. She's been his rock, keeping him sane even though he mistreats her. I knew it was just a matter of time until he lost control again, but with somebody different who didn't know him and couldn't see it coming. So Kim and I have been keeping an eye out. She tried to warn you, but..."

"I thought it was just jealous girlfriend talk. I'm so stupid."

"You couldn't have known. So I left you a note in Sky's guitar case."

"You're 'A stranger who is on your side'?"

He nodded.

"You know, there isn't a character limit in notes. You could have explained everything."

"Maybe. But I hoped you wouldn't need a warning. I thought maybe everything would be fine between you two."

"Pretty big risk," I said.

"Yeah. I came to that conclusion, too. So I decided to talk to Lucas, another guy I know a little. I told him I was worried."

"That explains why he was acting weird around Ken."

"Lucas called me when you and Ken left the dance. We guessed he'd take you to the swamp. That's where he used to go with Kim."

"Gross," I said.

Ken shrugged. "Just not very creative. And when I saw you get out of his car, and ran over."

"You were watching Ken and me in his car?"

Graham looked up at the darkened storefronts on the second and third stories. "Um, I guess. Sorry about that, too. Anyway, I ran over, but I didn't know what to do. I could have tackled Ken, but then he probably would have killed me. So I decided to talk him down instead."

"Well," I said, "I think I could have taken care of myself at that point."

Graham put out a hand. "Oh, I'm sure you could have. I didn't think you needed rescuing. But if you'd had to? Imagine if you'd pushed Ken in the dark, he'd hit his head on a rock, and his jelly brain had just given up. Or if you'd had to punch him in the face and he'd just died right there."

"So you were saving him from me?"

Graham looked down this time. "Nah. He's a big guy, Harriet. You might be able to knock over a geek when he isn't looking, but Ken could have really hurt you."

I smiled. "So you were rescuing me?"

"I guess so. In my own geek way."

"Okay," I said, sounding very official, "then I can forgive you for seeming to only care about Ken, and I can forgive you for your sexism (because Ken is a big guy, after all), and I am willing to forgive you for spying on me when I was in a car with my Homecoming date, which is creepy no matter what the motivation, on the condition that you forgive me for pushing you when you weren't looking."

He put out his hand. "Deal."

I shook.

We took another look around the mall, then started back toward our friends.

After we left the mall, as we made our way through the empty first story of the garage, I turned to Graham. "So, what were you doing with *The Complete Works of Shakespeare* when I knocked you over?"

Graham slowed down for a second, then kept walking. "Um, I just realized that the network could come back on any second. We won't know when it does. I think we should talk about that some other time."

"Does that mean we really will talk about it, or that you are just brushing me off so you can keep your weird Shakespeare secret?"

He put a finger to his lips.

"Sorry," I whispered.

We'd reached Sky, Gina, Juan, and Lucas who was back from his smoke break. Graham nodded to Lucas, then the rest of my friends, but he didn't sit down. He turned to me. "I have a feeling we'll talk again, Harriet. I'm the creepy guy who spies on you, remember?"

"You are giving me the heeby-jeebies, Graham," I said.

"I've never heard that expression before," he said. "Is that like cooties? I'm going to go home and look that up right away."

"There's no network, remember?"

"I've got these things called books!" he yelled.

Yeah, so he's a little too much like my dad for my taste.

Once I was back with my friends, they sprayed me with questions about why I'd pushed Graham, then left with him, then come back all buddy-buddy. I did my best to explain.

But while I was talking about it, my frictim became an idea. I realized that the whole situation was caused by people keeping stupid flooding secrets. If someone, Kim or Graham or Lucas, had just told me what they knew, the whole thing could have been avoided. Now Graham had this Shakespeare secret that looked just like my dad's Shakespeare secret.

I was pretty flooding tired of being the girl that learned things too late, the girl that things happened to. And I didn't want to be the girl who kept her own secrets out of spite. I want to be the woman who blows the secrets up, who shines the light on the dark places where the secrets grow like mildew, who solves problems by telling the truth.

Sky likes Juan. She's keeping it a secret. It's tearing her up inside. Maybe some carefully planned truth-telling is just the thing to flip the script. My frictim isn't a plan yet, but now it's an idea!

-24-43-1-10-6-83-67-14-4-
-3-3-43-0-66-0-0-0-6-
-0-7-11-2-1-27-
-5-0-0-80-1-

CHAPTER 13

Thursday, November 1st, 2114

Today, I met with Sky, Gina, Lucas, and Juan at the ice cream place in the mall. I guess that's becoming a pretty normal part of my life now. Sky and I hang out in different places, like in front of the old library, but when we all get together, we generally go to see movies at the theater, we go hang out at Juan's or Lucas' house to watch videos or listen to music, or we come to the mall.

We don't shop much. I get the impression that Lucas and Gina could both afford to do a lot more shopping than the rest of us, but they don't drag us along and make us watch while they try on clothes or look at luxury goods like jewelry or paper books. I appreciate that they don't lord their money over us. In exchange, we don't ask them to buy the ice cream or pay for the movie tickets. It would be nice, but it would also be too weird.

So we were sitting at our normal spot, one of the tables by the railing on the fourth floor where we can watch all the people below us, and we heard shouting. It came from the fourth floor, where we were, but almost directly across from us around the circular mall's central atrium. The mall has very few actual human employees. Checkout counters are automated. Little CorpBots scoot around the floor, picking up most of the trash, polishing the tiles, and leaving a dusty, grimy residue around all the corners. Some of the nicer stores have human workers who schmooze the richer customers and shoo the poorer ones out. And then there are the security guards, the CSGs. Most people call them "Geez." They are invisible most of the time, hiding behind doors with no windows, watching everything coming in from the hundreds of security cameras. But if someone steals something, the WSGs appear like lightning to arrest them. They aren't real police of course. Real police just process and hold criminals for the courts. Geez handle most arrests, and criminals then get turned right back over to corporate private prisons. Real police are much nicer than Geez. That's because real police have to follow the law, but Corporation cops only have to follow company policy, and The Corporation seems to have only one policy for their cops: No one steals from The Corporation.

When we heard the shouting, we all looked over at the source, expecting that someone was about to get caught stealing. There were three kids, two boys and a girl, about our age, yelling at an employee from one of the boutique Corporation subsidiaries that sell the expensive clothes.

The salesperson was yelling at them, too. "Get out of here before I call security!"

"We weren't doing anything wrong!" the girl yelled back.

"Yeah," one of the boys shouted. "It's a free country!"

The employee, a woman in her early 40s, wore a fancy dress that just happened to be Corporation blue. She had gold high heels and a large, gold brooch on her lapel. From our distance it just looked like a blank disc, but I'll bet it had a smiley-face on it. She stood in the doorway of her shop, where she'd chased out the loud kids, and she put her hand on her hip in a dramatic show of her superiority.

"Sorry kid," she said much louder than she needed to if she were just talking to the kids. She was clearly aiming her wisdom at all of us. "Nothing is free. When you figure that out, maybe you'll try to get a job."

The other boy jumped to his friend's defense. "What, so he could be a floodin' corporate slave like you?"

The lady rolled her eyes so dramatically that we could tell from across the mall.

"Yeah," the girl said, "a slave wearing really stupid shoes!"

The lady suddenly stood up very straight. "Oh, that is it!" She stormed back inside the store where she worked. The three kids stood there, making obscene hand gestures and sticking out their tongues.

"Stupid hoodlum trash," Gina said.

I turned toward her, shocked, and before I could even ask what she meant, Sky started to explain for her.

"They go to the public school. It's Mt. Hood High, but everybody calls it Mt. Hoodlum, and they call the kids there hoodlums."

I raised my eyebrows. "And apparently they call them trash, too."

Gina bit down on a spoonful of ice cream, then shrugged. "Most people don't have the guts to say it out loud, but they are. They're too lazy and stupid to get into Alice Louise. They're poor. They're dirty. Most of them are criminals. Their parents are shiftless, unemployed leeches." She shrugged again. "I mean, I'm sure there are exceptions at Mt. Hoodlum. There are probably some very nice people who just had some bad luck. I recognize that. It's not like I'm some kind of bigot. But those three...." She pointed at the kids who were still standing near the doorway of the clothing store. "Those three are not the exceptions. They are the rule."

I wanted to come up with a clever comeback, some sarcastic reply about how she *obviously* wasn't a bigot, but I didn't feel like I knew my friends long enough to say anything like that yet. I looked at the others out of the corners of my eyes. Sky looked down at the ground. Juan was frowning, but he didn't say anything. Lucas caught my eye and shook his head a tiny bit, then smiled and shot a withering glance at Gina.

"What?" she said. "You think—"

But she was cut off by a loud bang. We all swung around to see that the sound came from a steel door swinging into the concrete wall. Four Geez rushed out of the dark room filled with monitors.

The kids hesitated for a second, then began to run. It was a lost cause, and they seemed to know it. As they ran, they tried to shout over their shoulders, things like, "We didn't do anything!" and "We're not breaking any laws!" I could hear the terror in their voices.

The Geez ran them down in a very systematic way. The one in front caught up with one of the boys. He hit him behind the knee with his baton. The boy crumpled, but the first security guard didn't hesitate. He just kept running after the other two kids. Behind him, the Gee who was next in line stopped to beat on the fallen boy with his baton while the third and fourth guard raced past him. Clearly they had trained for this.

The first guard caught up with the girl and hit her in the back of the knee, just like the boy. As she was falling, the third guard, now second in line, yelled out some code word. The first guard understood. He stopped running and started beating on the girl while the third guard raced past him.

The boy in the lead made his way around the atrium toward us. Part of me wanted him to escape, though I wasn't sure where he could go. Another part of me, the most selfish part, wanted the guards to catch him as soon as possible so I wouldn't have to be too close and see what would happen to him. But the boy, panicking, reached out and grabbed the back of a chair, knocking it down in the first guard's path. The Gee tripped over it and he went down hard. I didn't know whether to wince or cheer, so I sat there, my mouth open, staring as the boy rounded the giant room and came toward us.

The fourth guard leapt over the chair and his fallen colleague. Just as the boy was a dozen feet from us, the Gee jumped and crashed into him. Both of them went sprawling onto the hard tile. The boy tried to scramble to get up. He was only six or seven feet from us now. I could see the wild, terrified look in his eyes. His feet slid on the smooth tiles but he managed to squeak out from underneath the guard who'd tackled him. He was on his knees when the third guard, the one who'd tripped over the chair, caught up with him and kicked him hard in the ribs. I could hear the sound of one of his ribs breaking. It sounded like someone biting into an ice cream cone, and even though I was eating my ice cream out of a paper bowl, I lost my appetite.

The boy curled into a ball, his arms wrapped around his broken ribs, but the Geez were both on him now. They raised their batons up over their heads and brought them down on his exposed back. He cried out, a high-pitched scream that tried to turn into a sob but was cut off by the next blow and the next. The Gee who had fallen over the chair wasn't satisfied by the cries, though. He grabbed the boy's hair, lifted him halfway up into a sitting position, and shouted in his ear, "Think you can trip me you flooding hood rat?" Then the Gee slammed the kid's head down against the tile floor.

Blood from the kid's ear and scalp splattered on the floor like someone had stomped on a packet of ketchup. I felt my eyes fill up with tears, but I couldn't look away.

I think the fourth Gee knew that the third had gone too far, because he hit the kid one more time with his baton, a lackluster smack on the kid's back without the rage of his first blows, and then he stood up and took a few steps backwards. The other guy wasn't done, though. He let the boy's hair go, grabbed his baton, and went right back to work on the screaming kid.

"Officer?"

I was shocked to hear anyone talking to the SLGs, and I spun around to see where the voice was coming from. It was Juan.

The Gee seemed just as surprised. "What?"

"Don't you think he's had enough?"

"He's lucky he doesn't get a lot more," the Gee said. But the conversation had gained the attention of the third Gee. He stopped hitting the boy, stood up, and then gave the boy one last vicious kick to the mouth. More blood splattered across the floor, and now it ran out of the boy's split lips and broken teeth, red drool accompanying his sobs.

The third guard stepped toward us, gearing up to join his buddy if we turned out to be the next in line. "They were trespassing on private property and disturbing private businesses. Like he said..." (he motioned to his fellow Gee) "...they're lucky. Castle doctrine says we can use lethal force if we see fit on private property. Any of you got a problem with that?"

Lucas put a hand on Juan's shoulder. "Not at all, officers. We're impressed by your compassionate self-restraint."

The third Gee pointed at Lucas with his baton. "Don't give my any of that fairy attitude, Twinkle-Toes. I can find a place to shove this baton where you *won't* like it."

The other guard thought this was very funny.

The third Gee banged his baton on the tabletop. "Just let us do our jobs and don't give us any lip, okay?"

Juan and Lucas both held up their hands and pressed their lips firmly together.

"Good," the Gee said. Then he turned to the other and motioned to the boy on the ground. I watched, silent but terrified that they would start hitting him again. Instead, they pulled his hands behind his back, zip-tied his wrists, and heaved him to his feet. The boy didn't look at us. His head lolled, and blood kept spilling out of his mouth. He made little whimpering noises as they led him back toward the security room, but he didn't speak.

I scanned around the atrium. The first boy was already being hauled into the dark room, and the girl was on her way, her hands tied behind her back, too.

I jumped when one of the CorpBots beeped loudly behind me. It had discovered the bloodstain, and while it switched from its dry trash collection mode to its mopping mode, it warned pedestrians of a possible slipping hazard with a little flashing orange light and a beeping sound. At first, it just spread the blood around, making little geometric patterns out of its wheel prints. I heard distant beeping and saw that two of the CorpBot's brethren were working on the spots where the other two kids had fallen, though I couldn't see any blood. Just tears and spit, I guessed. When I looked back, the blood was nearly gone, and the CorpBot had switched to a disinfectant mode, spraying a strong smelling bleach chemical onto the tiles and swirling it around with the brushes on its undercarriage.

Sky had been silent for as long as she could manage. "Was he right?" she asked Juan. "Could they have just shot those kids and gotten away with it? I mean, they aren't even real cops, right?"

"Shhh!" Lucas hissed.

"I'm sorry, but..." Sky slid into a whisper. "Is that true? Can they do that?"

Juan shrugged, and Lucas looked back and forth, obviously nervous about what the cameras and microphones were picking up.

"Well," Gina said, almost in a normal voice, "just for the record, I think *that* would have been going too far, even for the hoodlums." Then she took another decisive bite of her ice cream.

I have discovered that it is possible to strongly dislike one of your only friends.

CHAPTER 14

Friday, November 9th, 2114

I haven't talked to Ken in almost two weeks, even though we see each other in a handful of classes. We looked at each other. I think he wanted to apologize. I wanted to tell him I understood. But I know that everybody else was watching us look at each other, too. I just couldn't make myself get up out of my chair, cross the room, and open my stupid mouth. Maybe if I'd told him not to play anymore, he might have listened to me.

Today was the first game of the state playoffs, the first stage of the national high school tournament. It was supposed to be an easy victory. We'd beaten the team before, no problem.

In the first quarter, Ken caught one of those dangerous passes over the middle. He got speared by their safety.

They had to carry Ken off the field on a stretcher.

Oh god, I hope he isn't dead.

-24-43-1-10-6-83-67-14-4-
-3-3-43-0-66-0-0-0-6-
-0-7-11-2-1-27-
-5-0-0-80-1-

CHAPTER 15

Monday, November 11th, 2114

As soon as I got to school, I found some people I barely know, a group of sophomores, talking about Ken. One of them is on the JV football team, but he had heard an update about Ken. Ken is still alive. He did go to the hospital on Friday night, but they sent him home on Saturday. The JV player said Ken wouldn't be in school today, and he wasn't, but I was so relieved to hear that he was okay that I gladly accepted the fact that I wouldn't have a chance to talk to him. I'm still not sure what I would say, anyway. Sorry I didn't know? Sorry I didn't try to stop you from playing once I found out? Glad you're still alive because I heard about how many times you've been hit in the head? None of those sound very good. I will talk to him when he comes back, though. I worried about him all weekend. I need to say something.

I thought about this while I was half paying attention in my Science Test Prep class during 1st period, so I was taken by surprise when Sky turned and looked at me during the lecture. She was frowning and shaking her head, but I couldn't understand why. I started listening more intently. Mr. George, wearing his usual blue shirt and obligatory smile, looked like the fake grin might just fall off and reveal genuine panic.

"Well, that's not really a science question, exactly."

Somebody at one of the other schools spoke. We could hear the audio of his question before the cameras caught up and put him on our screens. "I know it's not going to be on the test, but I think it's the question we'd all like to know the answer to. Why did people let global climate change happen? I mean, the way you explained it, it seems pretty easy to see why it would happen. We're in high school, and we can understand that putting lots of carbon and methane and other garbage into the air would change the whole planet's climate. Were the people back then just really dumb?" The kid was on the screen by the end of his question. He was a white kid with bad skin and long, brown bangs that hung down over half his face. His upper lip was curved into a sneer. My first instinct was to dislike him, but when he flipped the hair out of his way, I could see this intelligence and anger mixing in his eyes that wasn't the product of boredom or rudeness.

"Um, no, they weren't dumb people. But I'm not sure how far back they really understood the way this process worked."

I raised my hand. Actually, my hand shot up and then I discovered that it had done that on its own. I wasn't planning on getting involved in an argument. It was more like those games from early elementary school, where the teachers would drill us with simple math problems and we had to race to answer them first. I felt like Mr. George needed this piece of information that had just popped back to the surface in my brain, so I volunteered it.

"It looks like we have a question in..." Mr. George looked down at his tablet. "Oregon. Um, Miss Washington, what's your question?"

"Well," I hesitated, "it's not really a question. An answer, really. You said you weren't sure when people knew how the process worked. The answer is 1896."

Mr. George frowned. "What?"

"1896. In Stockholm, Sweden. These two scientists, whose names I don't remember, figured out that changing the amount of CO_2 in the atmosphere would change the temperature. At first they thought the level was going down, and they predicted global temperatures would drop down to the temperatures of the last ice age. But then they measured and found that the amount of CO_2 was going up because of the amount of coal that human beings were burning. They figured out that all that CO_2 would raise the world's temperatures by five or six degrees. But they calculated how much coal was being burned in 1896, and they figured out that it would take 3000 years for the world to heat up that much, so nobody thought it was that big a deal."

Silence. Mr. George just stared at me. All the students in my class stared at me. Across the country, 186 classes of students, 50 or 60 a-piece, something like 10,000 people stared at me on the big screens in their classrooms.

"Sorry," I said. "I like history." If anyone wants to do some research on the biggest nerd in the whole world, I think they could make a good argument that it was me at that exact moment.

"Wait a second." It was the guy with the long bangs. When the screen flipped back to him, underneath his face it said, "Donald Trump Corporate High School #2198, Balsam, North Carolina." "Just let me get this straight: People knew that burning fossil fuels would raise the world's temperatures 200 years ago, but they just kept burning more and more until it was too late?"

Mr. George tried to regain some bit of control of his class. "That's not really a science question. I mean, that won't be on the test, so it's not part of this class's curriculum—"

The kid interrupted. "My parents and my little brother are dead. They were killed in a super-storm that caused a flash flood." He shouted the word "flood." I imagined the censorship software trying to figure out if he was talking about the weather phenomenon in his science class (permissible) or swearing (demerit). In my daydreamed version, the software fried its motherboards trying to make up its mind. The student with the bangs continued, "So my question might not be on the test, but it's the question that I want an answer to. And I think I deserve it, whether they put it on the test or not."

More silence, but this time everybody didn't stare at this kid and think, "What a giant geek!" the way they did when I went off on a rant about some scientists in Sweden. Instead, they all stared at Mr. George. Some of us felt sorry for him and wondered how he would escape from the situation. Some of us understood the student's anger, felt our own churning in our guts, and wanted Mr. George to take it on the chin. Some of us felt both things. I'm good at feeling too many things at once.

The tension cracked when a new voice broke in. "Lies. Lies for money."

"This isn't—" Mr. George started to say.

"The coal and oil companies knew, but they lied so they could make more money." The camera cut to the speaker, a guy with red hair and freckles. Underneath the picture, it said, "David H. Koch Corporate High School #3846, North Albuquerque, New Mexico." His face was very pale, and I guessed he was terrified, either of all the other students staring at him or of what Corporation management would do to him, but he plowed ahead anyway. "They hired scientists and paid them lots of money to lie. Then they hired politicians and reporters and paid them lots of money to say there was a lot of scientific controversy, so, since the verdict was still out, nobody would change anything. They bought school boards and textbook companies so students like us wouldn't learn the truth. Even when the storms and the flooding started, corporations fought anything that might cost them money. And when people spoke up, corporations threatened their jobs, threw them in jail, sometimes even killed them. The Corporation was one of them!" There was an audible gasp in my classroom, and I'll

177

bet it was echoed in 185 rooms across the country. "They silenced people who spoke out against—"

The screen went dark for a second.

It cut back to Mr. George. He looked shaken, and his fake smile was gone. "We seem to have lost the feed from David H. Koch Corporate High School #3846," he said, looking down at his tablet. Then he looked up into the camera, staring at all of us. "That's for the best, though. Those...wild speculations you were just hearing have no basis in fact. They are irresponsible. And, most importantly, that whole line of questioning will not be on the test, so we're not going to take any more questions today because we have to get back on schedule. For the rest of this lesson, questions and comments have been disabled." He tapped on his tablet a few more times. "Your messaging and email have also been temporarily disabled, but your note-taking application still functions, and I suggest you use it. Now, when you are asked about global climate change on the test, remember that you will need to be able to explain what a feedback loop is and give some examples of feedback loops. Let's talk about Greenland."

He started talking about Greenland. *We* did not talk about Greenland. *He* did. We did not speak or communicate with anyone else for the rest of the class.

I wonder what happened to that boy in New Mexico. I don't think he'll escape with a trip to his school's senior manager's office and a week of grounding. Will they just kick him out, sending him to the public schools? Will they shuttle him off to do some dangerous job on an oil platform in the middle of the ocean at the North Pole? Will they find some technicality and throw him in jail? Or will they just send some Corporation cops to his house to shoot him and then say he resisted arrest? I don't even know his name. I just know that he's the brave, red-headed boy at David H. Koch Corporate School #3846. And I know that tomorrow, he won't be.

I wondered if I would get in trouble, too. I kept trying to convince myself that I hadn't said anything wrong. Just facts. Just history. But a little voice in my head, a voice that sounded like my dad's, but shrunken down into this high-pitched little annoying voice of reason, kept saying, "There's no such thing as 'Just facts.' Facts are always chosen. They make arguments. And arguments push and pull. Arguments have power. And people who already have power generally don't like arguments, because people in power don't like to share it."

So, no matter how much I assured myself that I was in the clear, I kept glancing sideways for the rest of the morning, expecting the old greeter, Mr. Rorty, to show up to escort me to the senior manager's office. There, Mr. Robb would accuse me of helping "terrorists and terrorist sympathizers" spread "anti-Corporation propaganda." And then he would tell me that I was not a good fit for Alice Louise Walton Corporate High, and that I'd be attending the local public school from now on.

By lunch time, I was pretty freaked out, but Mr. Rorty didn't appear. Instead, I saw my friends sitting together in our usual spot next to the concrete planter box in the courtyard. I waved and started to walk over to them, but someone called my name.

"Hey, Harriet?"

I turned and found Graham. He was holding his tablet, but that copy of *The Complete Works of Shakespeare* was tucked under his arm.

"How's it going?" I asked. "Heard anything from Ken?"

"He's home recovering. No details yet. But that's not what I wanted to tell you. I heard about what happened 1st period."

I dropped my voice, which was stupid, I know; The Corporation can hear everything we say in school, even when we whisper. Their computers are listening through all our tablets, then putting the sound together. They have thousands of microphones in every school. I was probably calling more attention to myself by whispering. But I mumbled, "Yeah. Crazy, huh? That kid in New Mexico?"

He kept his voice even. "I heard about what you said. I wanted you to know, those guys you mentioned? The guys from Sweden? They're gone. Any reference to them has been scrubbed from the Corporation-approved Internet."

"Why?" I asked. But I could guess.

"That information was obviously not helpful in calming down your friend in New Mexico. So now it's gone." He held up his tablet to show me his search results, but I didn't need to see it.

Instead, I looked down at the book tucked under his arm. "You have a way of accessing the non-Corporation-approved web, don't you?"

He followed my gaze, then quickly stuffed the book into his backpack. When he looked back at me, he was frowning, and he shook his head, just one tiny, angry shake. "I don't know what you mean."

I felt like a jerk. "I mean, maybe you and I could go get coffee or something sometime. You know, hangout offline. Somewhere private." It was the best I could come up with. I hoped he didn't think I was really asking him out.

He looked down at his shoes. Then back up at me. "Nowhere is private, Harriet." He suddenly looked really sad. "I'd better go." Now he was the one who was whispering.

"Um, okay. I guess I'll...see you around or something?"

He was shoving his tablet into his backpack and walking away backward. "Sure. Sure." He nodded a bit, then turned and walked off.

I tried to think of something clever to say about his rejection of my appeal for help, but nothing came immediately to mind, and then he was gone. I often wish I could freeze the world around me for, say, 10 minutes so I can think of the right thing to say. Instead, I think of it 10 minutes later anyway, and then I just grind my teeth and grumble because the moment has passed.

Instead of waiting for the quip to arrive and frustrate me, I walked over to my friends.

"Harriet the history-head!" Juan said.

"So you heard."

Sky looked up at me, her mouth still half-full of a big bite of her peanut-butter-and-banana sandwich. "You-ul nee-ul-d to-ul be mor-ul calful."

"This from the person who is about to choke to death on peanut butter."

She smirked, then took another giant bite before saying. "Pealnult bultter uhls a guld way tull die."

I couldn't argue with that.

Though I kept an eye out for Mr. Rorty, lunchtime was mostly normal. We joked around about stupid, insignificant things. Sky got excited and spoke so quickly no one could understand her, then turned as red as a tomato when Lucas made a dirty joke about how all the exercise her mouth got would someday make her life partner a very happy man.

Juan frowned and scolded Lucas, but not too seriously. "Low blow, man."

Lucas smiled. "If he's lucky."

Gina laughed so hard she started snorting, and that's always funny.

I enjoyed lunchtime so much that I nearly forgot about the dust-up during 1st period. Before the bell rang, something flipped that switch in the back of all our minds that told us the bell would sound soon, and we started putting our lunches away. By pure coincidence, Sky, Gina, and Juan left first, giving me a moment with Lucas.

"Hey," I whispered, "I have to tell you something?"

Lucas raised one eyebrow. "A secret? I love secrets. They are divinely sinful."

"Actually, it's the opposite. I realized that everybody has all these secrets, like Ken's whole concussion thing, and I'm sick of waiting to figure out what's going on. I'm going to take matters into my own hands a little."

He nodded. He liked the sound of this so far.

I dropped the bomb. "I've decided I'm going to tell Juan that Sky likes him."

His nodding head made a quick circle and then he was shaking it back and forth slowly. "Nope. Bad idea. Don't do it."

"But why not? Sky deserves him. He deserves her."

"And if it were that simple, that would be great. But you don't know if Juan has feelings for Sky. If he does, he's never mentioned them to me, and he tells me everything."

"Yeah, but maybe if he knew that she liked him—"

He cut me off with his eyebrows and another shake of his head. "And maybe not. And then what? What if somebody told you someone liked you, but you didn't have feelings for them. Would that make you happy?"

"I guess I'd be flattered. It doesn't mean I'd date the person, but it would be nice to know."

"Nope. Not true. You'd be confused. You'd feel awkward around that person. It would not be better."

"I don't know...."

"Really?" He paused and looked conflicted. "I know somebody who likes you. Want to put your money where your mouth is?"

"What?"

He'd finished putting his lunch away, so he stood up and started toward his class. "Never mind. I shouldn't have said anything. Just do me a favor and don't tell Juan."

"Wait!" I followed close behind him as we made our way across the courtyard towards the entrance to Building 3. My class was in Building 1, so I was going the wrong way, but I had to know. "I accept the challenge. Tell me who likes me. We'll see if you're right."

"No. Because I am right. If you don't like the person, it will make your life more complicated."

"But what if I do like him?"

"Do you currently have a crush on anybody?"

"Well, no, but...."

"Then you don't like him. See my point?"

"But I might consider him if you told me he likes me. It does happen that way sometimes. Just tell me who he is."

"No."

"Fine. But I'm telling Juan. That's the only way for me to try to prove my theory unless you tell me who likes me."

Lucas stopped. I almost bumped into him. "I'm not allowed to say. But if I give it away, and you find yourself filled with confusion and doubt, then don't tell Juan about Sky, okay?"

"Deal!"

"He's liked you for a while, but he couldn't say anything because he knew you liked Ken."

I looked around at all the students heading for their classes. "That was public knowledge, so that doesn't really help much."

"Let's just say you had already knocked him over before you knocked him over."

I think I just said, "Oh."

Lucas nodded. "Yeah. Not your type, right? Awkward! So remember that, and don't tell Juan."

"Um, sure," I mumbled, but I wasn't really thinking about Sky and Juan anymore.

"Good," Lucas said, and headed off to his class.

I turned around and zombie-walked to my class. I don't even know how I made it on time, because I wasn't thinking about where I was going at all. In retrospect, I'm surprised I didn't wander into the wrong room. Somehow I stumbled into class, plopped down into a seat, and logged in on my tablet without thinking about class at all.

The English Lit. and Comp. Test Prep. teacher was talking about some poem that might be on the test. Of course, it was The Corporation's test, so when they said it might be on the test, that usually meant it certainly would be on the test. It was some poem by Shakespeare, Sonnet 130. I mindlessly wrote that down while I thought about what Lucas had said.

I'd already knocked him down before I'd knocked him down.

Graham had a crush on me.

Geeky Graham who was always making notes in a book. Geeky Graham who had protected me by protecting his friend, Ken. Graham, who I had just pretended to ask out on a date just so he would tell me his secret to getting around The Corporation's Internet filters. Now I felt terrible about that last part.

I didn't have a crush on Graham. I'd never thought about him that way. Like Lucas said, he wasn't my type at all. I'm the quiet one. I like guys who are loud

185

enough to make up for my shyness. Confident guys. Yes, I admit it, athletic guys.

The teacher was talking about lines of the poem, but they weren't filtering past my confusion. Lucas had been right. My head overflowed with conflicting thoughts.

"My mistress' eyes are nothing like the sun," the teacher said. That just played into my confusion. What the flood did that mean? Of course Shakespeare's girlfriend's eyes weren't like the sun. Who wants eyes that are five million degrees Kelvin and 1,400 kg per cubic meter? They'd be so heavy, they'd fall right through you, but they'd light you on fire on the way down. Gross!

And her lips aren't as red as coral? Good. Those would be freaky lips! And her skin isn't snow white; it's brown. What's wrong with that? So her hairs are like black wires, and her cheeks don't look like red and white roses. I am starting to identify with this girl. Sometimes she has bad breath? Well, that's pretty rude of Shakespeare, but the girl is human. And her voice doesn't sound like music. Neither does mine. My mom's does, and I've always wished I had her voice, so I'm a bit sensitive about that.

"I grant I never saw a goddess go," the teacher read. "My mistress when she walks treads on the ground."

That line was funny. I realized I was paying attention again.

"And yet," the teacher continued, "by heaven I think my love as rare / As any she belied with false compare."

The teacher started into this very slow explanation of the way the poem worked, encouraging us to write down the word "juxtaposition" in our notes and to make sure we used it on the test if we were asked to write about the poem. Personally, I thought the poem was pretty clear. Surprisingly romantic, and romantic because of the surprise.

In our Corporation Lit and Comp. classes, they don't like to talk about bias. Talking about bias makes people think about bias, and thinking about bias makes people question authority. But my parents always talk about bias. Conscious bias and unconscious bias. So I couldn't help but think that Shakespeare not only assumed that his audience was white and would therefore prefer snow white skin to skin that was "dun" colored (not a lot of black people in England in the late 1500s), but also talking about a man's love to a largely male audience. It was his perspective. I get that. But just as he was "juxtaposing" the kinds of stupid things bad poets said about their girlfriends against his truer, deeper love for his girlfriend, I couldn't help but juxtapose my own identification with the girlfriend with my own feelings about guys. I was the girlfriend in the poem. Then, suddenly, I was the one who felt a truer, deeper love.

For Graham? Of course not. I barely know him. He's not super-tall like Ken. He's not made of muscle. He doesn't have Ken's stylish, short hair. His hair is slightly curly and a little on the long side, and it just goes in every direction, like he dries it after he gets out of the shower and then doesn't even bother to comb it before he comes to school. He doesn't have Ken's piercing blue eyes. I'm trying to remember the color of his eyes, and I can't. Hazel? Gray? Light brown? Who knows? Most of the time he's looking away from me, shy as ever (and probably worried that I'll push him down again). He doesn't have that swagger when he walks, the way Ken and all his football friends do. When he walks he...treads on the ground.

And yet....

There is certainly more to Graham than I ever thought about before. Something rare.

Maybe? Maybe he belies all the other guys with false compare.

-24-43-1-10-6-83-67-14-4-
3-3-43-0-66-0-0-0-6-
-0-7-11-2-1-27-
-5-0-0-80-1-

CHAPTER 16

Tuesday, December 11th, 2114

Over the last couple weeks, I've been hanging out with Graham more. He hasn't said anything about having feelings for me, and that's actually made it even more fun. It's like a puzzle. We talk about school, about the stupid drama and the interesting gossip, about the garbage the teachers try to force feed us in classes. We talk about music, about bands no one has heard of, about lyrics that speak to us. Sometimes we talk about his grandma, who he lives with, and about my dad, but never too seriously, never seriously enough for him to ask where my mom is, or for me to ask where his parents are. The conversations are always comfortable. Underneath the conversations, I search his eyes for clues. His eyes are brown, lighter brown than mine, with little flecks of gold. I know this because I try to catch a glimpse of his eyes when he is looking at me, and he always looks away. If I can time it just right, he not only looks away, but he gets tripped up in what he's saying. He hesitates. He stumbles over his words. I get a mischievous thrill out of this every time. Is that terrible of me? Is it vain, to enjoy being liked so much that I look for these little reminders? Maybe. But I really like that he likes me. I really like that *he* likes me. Is that the same as falling for him? I'm not sure. But I'm starting to think so. Here's why:

Yesterday, after school, we met as fast as we could at the front entrance and took the subway across Mt. Hood to the public high school, Mt. Hood High School (which everybody calls Hoodlum High). When we came up the stairs from the subway stop there, we found that somebody had smashed the "M," "T," and the period off of the name attached to the front of the school, and they'd spray-painted the "L," "U," and "M" on in red letters, so it actually says Hoodlum High. I don't know if the graffiti came first and stuck, or if the artist was just making it official. Chicken or egg. But that's what's on the front of the building, and the paint has faded, so I know it's been there for a while. Not like at Alice Louise Corporate High, where the door Ken dented was replaced the next day. At the public school, the damage lingers.

Inside, the halls were filthy. It wasn't just students' trash from lunch left all over the floor, though there was plenty of that. Layers of dirt lined the side of the hall like sediment building up behind a dam, and the dust of crumbling ceiling tiles showed where tiles had fallen and had been kicked into powder by the students walking back and forth to their classes. Instead of monitors on the walls with color advertisements and inspirational quotes printed on nature photographs, the school had these old, beige things Graham called corkboards and bulletin boards. Some were covered with yellow or blue construction paper, but these often had flappy, sagging corners or clung on by the staples that held out-dated announcements.

As we were coming in, their students were leaving. They seemed just like the students at Alice Louise Corporate High, maybe a bit more disheveled but not poorly dressed or dirty like the school. Still, some stared at us with a kind of naive, open wonder that marked them as socially maladjusted or mentally handicapped while others looked at us out of the corners of their eyes in a way that made me feel like keeping a tighter grip on my backpack. That sounds snobby, but I really did feel like a few of the students were sizing us up and deciding if they should jump us.

No one spoke to us, though. There were no guards, no greeters, no metal detectors. We walked right into the office. The secretary barely looked up at us.

"Excuse me," Graham said. "Sorry to bug you, but could you tell us where we might find a friend of ours, Kenneth Ford?"

"School's over," the secretary said. "He's probably on his way home."

"Yeah, we probably missed him. Could you tell us what his last class is? Maybe we could catch him."

The secretary sighed, then tapped his computer a few times. "Ford?"

"M-hmm."

"Special Ed study hall. Room 214. Up the stairs, down the hall, on the right. But he won't be there anymore."

"Thanks," Graham said, turning back toward the door. "We'll see if we can catch him."

I followed Graham. Behind me, I could hear the secretary sigh again.

We ran down the now empty hall, up a flight of stairs, then farther down the hallway on the second floor until we came to room 214. It was locked and we could see that it was dark inside.

"Flood!" Graham cursed.

"Careful," I whispered.

"Naw," he said in a normal voice. "No ears here. The Corporation doesn't want to know what people here have to say. C'mon, let's head back. Maybe we'll run into him on the way."

Neither of us thought that was likely. When we stepped out of the school (which did, at least, have air conditioning), into the mid-day sun and 106 degree air, we noticed someone sitting on a swing on the playground across the street at the public elementary school. That was weird enough. No one plays outside in the middle of the day. We stay indoors and use the subways as much as possible when the sun is shining, because it's too hot to be out. Kids only use playgrounds in the mornings, before it gets too hot, and in the evenings as it's cooling down. Even more strange, the person on the playground was way too big to be an elementary school student. He was well over six feet tall, and even though he was on the thin side, his shoulders were broad. He was....

"Ken?" I said.

"C'mon," Graham said, and pulled me gently by the elbow.

We walked across the street. The pavement shimmered and threatened to melt our shoes. By the time we got to the chain link fence that wrapped around the playground and separated us from Ken, I was already tired, so I made the mistake of leaning on the hot metal. I yanked my hands back when I felt the thick wire burn them. I sucked in a startled breath, and that's when Ken noticed us.

"Oh, hey," he said. He didn't sound as surprised to see us as I felt he should have.

"Hey, Ken," Graham said. "What are you doing out here? It's flooding hot, man."

"I'm used to it. I'm usually out at practice at this time of day. Lot cooler in December than during summer three-a-days."

"Well, yeah, but they have mist machines on the sidelines and people who are keeping you hydrated. It's dangerous to be out in this heat."

"I know. But, what, should I worry about frying my brain? It's beaten to mush, Graham. Who cares if it gets a little cooked, too?"

I expected Graham to push back on that, but he just frowned and nodded. We stood in silence for painful minute.

"So, what's going on back at Alice Louise?"

"Seven classes of Corporation commercials each day," Graham said. "Same as always."

"Yeah."

I couldn't take the long pauses. "How about you? How's the new school?"

"Hoodlum High? There aren't even live teachers on the other sides of the screens. Just videos and worksheets all day. But if you don't do them, no one cares. Nobody expects us to pass the national tests anyway. I'd drop out, but my parents won't let me."

"You know," Graham said, "they used to think charter schools like corporate schools would make the public schools better. That was what they told everybody, anyway. Competition would solve every problem."

Ken shook his head. "People believed that flotsam? What a bunch of idiots." He looked at Graham. "Competition doesn't solve everything. Sometimes it makes things worse. Sometimes it's not fair. Sometimes it's not fair because both sides lose but one loses more. I know."

Graham smiled. It was a bit of a sad smile, but not a mocking one. "They shouldn't have kicked you out. They should have made you Senior Manager. You understand the school system a lot better than Mr. Robb."

Ken laughed at that. "Yeah. Flood that guy."

More silence. "So Ken," Graham said, "seriously, what are you doing out here?"

Ken twisted in the swing, his knees making slow, lazy arcs back and forth. "Sometimes I sit on the swings and think. Sometimes, when I'm mad, I throw dirt clods at the ground as hard as I can and watch them explode. It makes me feel better."

"Okay, I can't deny that the last part sounds pretty cool, but this sitting-in-the-swings part could use some work. Let's go back to your house and play some games. I know you have the newest Sim-NFL. I'll build a team and you can kick my ass a few times."

Ken brightened a bit. "I unlocked a bunch of the best players in history, all in their primes. You won't stand a chance."

"I don't stand a chance out here in this heat. C'mon."

Ken smiled and rose slowly from the swing. He had to duck so he didn't hit his head on the bright red crossbar of the little kids' swing set. But then he just stayed hunched over, like the something might bump into his head again if he wasn't careful. "Okay." Then Ken looked away from Graham and gave me an elevator glance that started at my sneakers and rose to my face. "I'm glad you came, too. You look really pretty, even when you're all sweaty."

Graham and I exchanged a quick look of shared amusement. "Thanks," I said. "You look good, too." That was a lie. He looked terrible, hunched over like that, his skin pink from the sun and the heat.

Ken must have noticed the glance that flashed between Graham and me, but he misinterpreted it. "Oh, I'm sorry, man," he said to Graham. "Are you guys together now?"

Graham blushed. Fast. And his skin color did nothing to hide it. "We..." He stammered, shaking his head a little. "No, we—"

"We're friends," I said. I was careful not to say "just friends," and I purposely filled the word "friends" with the sound of a smile and a little hint of mischief. Maybe Graham will ask about that. If he does, I'll ask him what he meant by "no" just so I can hear him stutter some more.

Ken certainly wasn't sure what to make of my answer. "Um, okay? None of my business, anyway."

"It's okay," I told him, putting a little more meaning into the words to let him know I was talking about more than my friendship with Graham. "We're good."

He smiled, then looked down, nodding. "Good."

"C'mon," Graham said. "Let's get out of here."

I looked for the gate to the playground, but Ken jumped up, pulled himself over the top of the fence, and fell down in between Graham and me. I was relieved to see that his head injuries hadn't diminished his athleticism. Seeing him slumped in that swing made me wonder if he was having trouble moving, too.

Graham and I walked Ken down to the subway. On the train, Ken sat by the window and Graham sat with him. I sat across the aisle. I listened as they talked about video games and which cities NFL teams would be moving to this season. Since The Corporation owns all the teams, it moves them around to boost the economies of cities where it is investing in a lot of new construction. Also, they move them a lot to make fans buy new gear to support their favorite players in new colors and uniforms.

But I paid more attention to the way Ken and Graham acted toward one another. Straight guys are always so scared to talk about feelings or hug each other. I don't know if that's machismo or homophobia or just boys being dumb boys, but it's weird and frustrating to watch them try to show concern for one another, or gratitude, or anything resembling affection. When Graham and Ken wanted to tell each other that they cared, they would make fun of each other, then bump shoulders or elbow each other. One time, Graham threw an arm around Ken's big shoulders, squeezed once and shook his bigger friend, and said, "I've missed you, man." Later, Ken seemed like he was going to do the same thing, but he put Graham in a headlock, just for a second, and just growled like a dog.

When we got to my stop, they offered to walk me back to my apartment, but I told them I was fine and watched them head off down the tunnel toward Ken's house. Even though the boys couldn't say so, I felt a radiating warmth in my chest pushing back against the air conditioned cool of the subway station.

I talked to my mom about it the next day when my dad and I went to visit her. I made Dad leave the room, then quickly tried to fill Mom in on the whole situation.

"Just so I'm hearing you correctly," she said, "you were dating a guy who was very good looking but had brain damage. He tried to get a little hands-on, and this Graham boy rescued you. He's not much to look at, but he's sweet and smart and gentle and everything the other boy wasn't."

"No, no, no," I said. "First of all, no one rescued me. I can take care of myself. Graham rescued Ken from embarrassing himself and maybe from getting a

197

beat-down from my high heels. Second, I never said Graham wasn't much to look at." I looked down at my hands. "He's really cute, actually."

Now, I wrote earlier that I have the ability to blush like a ninja. I should clarify. My ninja powers only seem to work on white people, and only on the ones I don't know. My white friends in Illinois could tell when I was blushing. Of course Selina could tell, too. I'll bet Sky would be able to tell by now.

My mom can not only see me blush: She has super hero mind-reading powers. It would make sense if she could only read *my* mind, but I think she can read all minds, at least to some degree. I'm not the only one who thinks so. Selina thought my mom could read her mind. I once saw my mom look over at a perfectly normal lady on a subway platform, her face expressionless, and Mom walked right over to her, took both of the stranger's hands, and said, "You're going to be okay. Just tell me how I can help." The woman burst into tears, threw her arms around my mother's neck, and just sobbed. Our train came and went, and my mom just let the lady keep on crying while I stood next to them, confused, bored (I was seven or eight — too young to stand still for that long), and amazed by my mother's powers.

Mom turned on her mind reading powers and smiled. "Ah. I see."

"What?"

"So Graham is a keeper."

"Well..." I looked down at my hands in my lap. "I don't.... I mean, I'm not.... I don't...."

"He likes you, too, doesn't he." She wasn't really asking a question.

"Yes. One of his friends told me he did. In kind of a 'Don't-break-his-heart' way."

"Because he thought you didn't like this Graham. But you do."

I looked up at her, searching her eyes. "Do I?"

She smiled even more broadly. My mother has the best smile in the whole world. "Oh, Honey, you do."

"So what do I do, Mom?"

"I guess you need to tell Graham that his friend is wrong, that you aren't planning on breaking his heart." She leaned back in her chair. "You'll probably break a lot of other boys' hearts when you do. That's your burden as the most beautiful girl in the world."

I ninja-blushed again. "Mom, you're the most beautiful woman in the world."

She laughed. "You should see me in my other prison jumpsuit!"

I thought about Mom's advice, and I decided I did need to talk to Graham about us. But first, I had a couple other people I needed to confer with.

That night, I called Juan and told him to meet me at the mall.

"Sure. Who all is coming?"

"It's the CorpMart Mall," I said. "Everybody who is anybody is already there."

Luckily, he didn't press for specifics.

We met at the ice cream place. There are no employees, just self-serve soft ice cream machines, dispensers that pour out toppings, and lots of cameras to make sure you swipe your Corporation card.

Normally, we talk while we wait in line and fill our little, paper bowls, but I didn't know where to start.

"So," Juan asked, "Is something going on? You're quiet, even more than normal. Where's Sky? She normally fills in all the silence."

"I know. Isn't she great?"

"She's a riot. Is she coming?"

I pushed a button and chocolate chips fell onto my vanilla ice cream. "She might, but I haven't called her yet. I wanted to talk to you first."

He frowned. "What's up?"

I motioned to a table over by the balcony. A decent-sized crowd circulated through the various levels below us, in and out of the CorpBucks Coffee, the kiosk selling covers for handcoms and tablets, the boutique subsidiaries selling specialized lines of CorpMart clothing endorsed by reality-streaming celebrities for people who can afford to wear status-enhancing garb, and, far below us, the grocery store where people could most easily carry their big bags back onto the subway.

"So," I started awkwardly, "I know that the whole Homecoming and asking Gina thing was kind of a disaster, and you probably don't want to talk about it, but—"

He shook his head. "Nah, it's fine. That was a lifetime ago. I'm over it."

"I'm glad. You know I was on your side, and I really hoped that would work out for you, but I was skeptical. Your idea was great, very romantic and funny, but Gina...she has issues."

"What do you mean?" He sounded a little defensive, and I didn't want him to be focusing on her.

"I guess I have issues with her taste. Anyway, there's something about that whole...situation that you probably don't know. I mean, you might know it already. I don't know."

"Know what?"

"Lucas doesn't want me to tell you this. He thinks I'm just going to make things weird. And maybe I am. Maybe this is a bad idea. But I had to think to myself, if it was me, would I want to know. And I decided, that's really my job as a friend: to respect you enough to believe you can handle knowing whatever. Does that make sense?"

He smiled. "Absolutely not."

I laughed. "Fine. Here's the thing. Sky poured her heart and soul into helping you ask Gina to homecoming."

"You all did. You were great."

"Well, Sky was the best. And that's what I want to talk to you about. Sky was the most invested in that production because she is the most invested in you. We're all your friends, and we all want to see you happy, but Sky values your happiness more than anyone. Lucas looks out for you, and you know he'd do anything for you. We all would. But Sky? She cares on a whole different level. Do you get what I'm saying?"

"Um, maybe?"

"So that's what made the whole thing like 10 million times more tragic. She was helping you ask out Gina, but she really wanted to be asking you to go with her."

"Oh."

Silence.

A mall can be a horrible place to listen to. Most of the people keep their voices down, trying to be polite to other shoppers and appropriate to the space, but that just means that the background muzac climbs up over their conversations, a humming reminder that says, "Keep moving along, shopping robot. Enjoy yourself, but not too much. Buy. Buy. Buy. You are a consumer drone. Your human interaction is tolerated but not encouraged. Don't let it get in the way of your obligation to purchase. Buy. Buy. Buy."

Plus, when I tried not to look at anything specific, my eyes wandered to the place on the floor where I saw that kid get pounded on. There is no blood there. Nothing left to show there ever was blood there. But I remember the spot.

I didn't want to think about that, so, as the silence between Juan and me lingered, I started to try to identify the original songs that were being diminished and insulted by the muzac. I thought I recognized the song that was playing at that moment. It was one by a singer from New Beach, a resort town in Georgia where The Corporation built the new Disneyland that only the super-rich can afford. They have all these Mouseketeers who become pop stars when they are teenagers, then are quickly forgotten. Dad says that's been happening for over a century, even before The Corporation bought Disney....

Suddenly, Juan stood up. His chair scraped loudly on the tiles, an angry fart sound that might have been funny in different circumstances. "I gotta go."

"Do you want to talk about this at all?" I probably sounded panicky, squeaky even. "I didn't mean to upset you or make you mad." Redundant, I know. I wasn't at the top of my game in that moment.

He motioned with his hand like he was pushing me back into my chair. "No. I just need to think for a while. Thanks...I think. For...I don't know yet."

I leaned back to show him I wasn't pushing the issue. "I get it," I said.

"Well, that makes one of us."

Then he turned on his heel and walked off. A few feet away he stopped, and I thought he would turn back and say something, but he just stood there with his back to me for a second, then kept on going.

So I'm pretty sure I messed things up for Sky. Now, the question is, do I tell her what I did before he does?

-24-43-1-10-6-83-67-14-4-
-3-3-43-0-66-0-0-0-6-
-0-7-11-2-1-27-
-5-0-0-80-1-

CHAPTER 17

Thursday, December 20th, 2114

It's been over a week since I talked to Juan, and I never did confess to Sky.

In one way, that was very hard. She's become my closest friend here, so close I sometimes feel like I'm betraying Selina back in New Rockbridge. But now, every single second I hang out with Sky, I feel like I'm betraying Sky a little more.

On the other hand, Sky makes it easy to keep secrets. She talks most of the time, not because she's annoying, but because she's afraid of silence and she feels like she's being considerate to save other people from it. I genuinely appreciate that. I have no problem butting in when I need to, but there are lots of things I don't feel like talking about, and Sky never makes me feel like I have to. Sure, she makes me a little uncomfortable when she says my dad is cute, but she never expects me to talk about how it feels to see him come home exhausted from a construction job he shouldn't have to do in the first place. Sky never asks about my mom, though she loves to listen when I tell stories about her. We used to talk about Ken, but she doesn't ask about Graham, and that's good because I'm not quite sure what I would say yet. She doesn't talk politics much, even though I know she hates The Corporation. When that slips out, it's mostly in reference to our teachers reading boring propaganda off of their teleprompters. She criticizes the way they read, and only I can tell how much she hates the lies they tell because of that little glint in her eye when she does her impressions of their bored, robotic, artificially cheery voices.

Of course, mostly we talk about other things. We talk about music, about videos everybody is watching and old ones nobody has seen, about celebrities, about places we'd like to travel. Because we're juniors, we talk about colleges sometimes, but not too much. We'll go to the best ones we can get into, and we both like the idea of going to the same one, if we can swing that.

Unfortunately, the other thing we talk about is Juan. Sky didn't even realize she had a crush on him until I guessed it the first day we met, and now she talks about him all the time. She tries not to rip on Gina, so I used to do that for her. I'd remind her how Gina talked about those kids from Mt. Hood High, how she must think about Ken the same way now, how Gina would think about us if we ever got kicked out of Alice Louise.

"No," Sky says. "We're her friends. She'd just think we're the exceptions and we don't deserve to be forced to go to school with *those* people."

"Maybe so. But she wouldn't even reflect on that hypocrisy, on her classist bigotry."

"People who look like Gina are not encouraged to be reflective," Sky says.

At this point in these conversations, I remind Sky that she is much prettier than Gina in my opinion.

Then she strums her guitar and sings,

> "Harriet is the best,
> With her compliments
> And her curls.
>
> She thinks that I'm so pretty
> She makes me wish
> I liked girls.
>
> But I like boys
> And boys like sexy
> And Gina's got their kind of flair
>
> With her bigger boobs
> And swishier hips
> And her legs that go up in the air."

We have had this conversation enough times that Sky has had a chance to play with the lyrics a bit. The song always makes me laugh.

For the last few days, I haven't known what to say when Sky talks about Juan, so I've changed the subject. Am I a coward? Probably. A bad friend? Maybe. I just don't know how to tell her what I did.

The other day, she brought him up in a new, even more uncomfortable way. "So," she said, "have you noticed that Juan isn't talking to me?"

I looked shocked and tried to think of something to say, but she didn't slow down too long. "I mean," she continued, "he talks to me, like when I ask him a direct question. He says hi. But he won't engage like normal, you know what I mean? Like, when we joke around, he'll laugh with Lucas, but he won't really follow up on my jokes. He seems weird about you and Gina, too. Did something happen with those two?"

I only half-lied. "Nothing happened between them that I know about. I'll bet this is just the last stage of him getting over the whole Homecoming thing. I asked him about that the other day, and he said he was over it. Maybe he's finally over her, too, you know?"

"I seriously doubt that," Sky said. "It's like he's in that play by Sartre."

"What play?"

"*No Exit*. Three people in a room in hell. One woman is attracted to another woman, but that woman is attracted to the man, and he isn't into anybody. And they all just get on each other's nerves. That's where that quote is from, "Hell is other people." And they all just stay there and are miserable and at the end you get the sense that they will be in that room forever."

"Sounds like a really enjoyable night at the theater," I said.

"Yeah," she said. "It's not fun." I could tell she wasn't talking about the play.

207

I could have told her right then. It was the perfect opening. Instead, I told her about an old TV show I watched on video that had a depiction of Hell in it. In that show, there was a doorway between Hell and Earth that came up in the suburban town in California. "I'm not sure if it was set in a real town," I admitted. "If so, it would be gone now, anyway." The show, I explained, was about a girl who was about our age who fought demons and vampires. "I know it sounds cheezy, but it was brilliant. There was even an episode where a demon had the power to make everyone sing, so the whole show was a musical. Crazy, but really good."

She agreed to come over to my house after school and watch old episodes with me. So I'd temporarily dodged another bullet.

Then, after school today, I got a text from Sky. "Can't come over today. Going out to ice cream with Juan. He sounds really serious. I'll call you after with the play-by-play."

So, of course, I'm terrified.

I thought about calling Lucas. I expected him to have some insight into Juan's state of mind. But then I realized that there was a good chance Juan was going to try to let Sky down easy, and that meant Lucas would just give me an "I told you so" lecture.

Then I thought about calling Graham. He would listen to me talk about anything. But I played out the conversation in my head, and I couldn't get around they part where Lucas challenged me to consider Graham in a new way. I didn't want to thrust this situation on Graham. Or maybe I did, but, if so, it was because it might be convenient way for me to broach the subject of us. I thought about what it would sound like when Sky called to say Juan had just broken her heart, and I announced that I'd just confessed my feelings to Graham. I may be a bad friend, but I'm not that selfish.

Instead, when I got home, I paced around the small living room, my handcom in my hand, thinking about who to call. I was just about to call Selena in Illinois when my dad came home from work.

He frowned. "What's up?"

"It's that obvious?"

"It's obvious that you're upset. Look, the temperature is getting down into the seventies. It's a good time for us to take a walk." He pointed at the corners of the room, as though he knew where the cameras and listening devices were hidden.

I didn't argue with his paranoia. "Sounds good," I said. I grabbed my sweatshirt because I didn't know how long it would take me to explain everything, and the temperatures have been dropping fast now that winter is here.

When we were out in the hall, I started to talk, but Dad frowned and shushed me by shaking his head a little bit. We went down the elevator in silence, then out through the lobby. We never went out that way. We'd only stop on the first floor because that's where the mailboxes are, and we only get old fashioned mail once every few weeks, tops. Even then, we don't use the door to the outside there. We always go down to the subway platform in the basement. It felt really weird to be going out on the street through the building's front door.

Outside, I saw our apartment building from the same perspective I'd seen it when we first arrived in Dad's rental. It was strange to see it from outside of a car. The smooth exterior, with its storm-resistant Plexiglas shielding on every exterior surface and its rounded top to cut down on its wind resistance, made it look like a taller version of the prison where Mom lives. I looked across the street at another apartment building, then the next, then the next. They were all basically the same, just silver half-eggs in neat rows built along the subway line beneath the street.

"They look like the prison," I said.

"Well, they're mostly above ground and most of the prison is underground, but, basically, yes, they're the same. Permanent storm shelters."

"These are what you build all day?"

"The company is still moving people in from low-lying areas that won't last. There's a continuous need for more housing." He dropped his voice. "I'll tell you a secret most people don't know. They intentionally don't build them fast enough."

"Why not?"

"Lots of reasons. Keep the real estate prices high. Cut down on the riff-raff. They tell people that they are building them housing. They move people out of low-lying areas a family at a time, to prevent panic. They time it out. Then, when the flooding comes, half the people have moved to the new Corporation cities. The other half? Swept away. No more news from those towns."

My eyes were wide. "All dead?"

"Or homeless refugees. Some make it to the cities, find work and eventually housing. But what can they say? 'You owed me a new house'? The Corporation isn't a charity. It's a business. They want to keep the people who can't pay the rent out of their cities. Easiest way is to just let the weather take care of them."

"But shouldn't somebody be helping them? The government?"

"The government is basically broke. Once the corporations bought the politicians, all the politicians were for lowering corporate taxes and the taxes on rich people. Down, down, down. When the corporations consolidated, the politicians always had to be on the side of the winners, or they lost their jobs. And then the 'corporate persons' became the 'corporate person.' So if The Corporation says, 'Jump!' the pols in New DC say 'How high?'"

"And if they say to let Americans drown?"

"The pols say, 'As long as the campaign check doesn't bounce.' After all, who wants to be the anti-business crusader?"

"You do," I said.

He chuckled, but it was a sad laugh. "Maybe once. I was a historian. I wrote about the history of monopolies, trusts, and corporations. I didn't even have to spin the story. Just solid research, as objective as I could make it."

"And so they fired you." I knew the story.

"I should have seen it coming. You can't poke a hornet's nest with a stick and then say to the hornets,

'This stick is just made up of well-researched historical facts.' Telling the truth is an aggressive act. I knew that. I even suspected I would lose my supposedly-tenured position at the university. But I didn't realize they would go after me by attacking your mother."

"It's not your fault," I said.

"No," he said. "It's not. But I should have seen it coming. I had other options. I just didn't know...well, I didn't see it coming. That doesn't make it my fault, but knowing that doesn't make your mother magically appear."

We walked in silence for a while.

"But you were going to tell me something," he said. "Why were you pacing around the living room?"

"I was just making the Corporation spies dizzy."

He laughed, then waited for me to go on.

"Well, it's kind-of a long story."

"Then I'm glad you brought your sweatshirt," he said.

So I started with the backstory about Sky and Juan and Gina and Lucas. I kept apologizing about making him listen to high school drama, but he'd just wave that away and ask me to go on.

Finally, I got to the part where I spilled the beans about Sky's crush on Juan. "Now he's having a big serious talk with her, and if he's letting her down easy, she's going to hate me. Do I deserve it? I feel like I do. I feel terrible."

"Hmm," he said. I expected him to immediately tell me that it wasn't my fault, or it wasn't a big deal. Instead, we walked in silence and I started to gear myself up for a lecture about minding my own business.

Finally he spoke. "I wish your mother could talk to you about this, not because I don't want to, but because it's not my area of expertise. She's the sociologist. Group dynamics and social interaction and that kind of thing. I just study history. But, in this case, I can think of some stories that might be helpful.

"Once upon a time, there was a man you might have heard of, named Samuel Walton—"

"Dad!"

"What, you got somewhere you're supposed to be? Let your old man tell you a story!"

"Fine," I grumbled.

"After the second world war, this guy moved from Salt Lake City, Utah, where he'd been stationed, to Newport, Arkansas, where he bought a department store with a 20 thousand dollar loan from his father-in-law and five thousand dollars of his own money that he'd saved while he was in the army. He bought the store, but not the building. He was renting that. He was so successful that the man who owned the building decided to take it back. He hiked up the rent so high that Walton had to sell him the store and all the inventory inside. So Walton had to start a new store, but he'd learned his lesson. He started a new store in a building with a guaranteed 99 year lease. Walton then saw what a competitor was doing with another chain of department stores, liked the idea of one-stop shopping, and copied it. He focused on putting up new shops in small towns, but always within a short distance of his warehouses so he could buy in bulk. He tried to buy American-made products. He also paid his workers very low wages, admitting that he was, to use his own word, 'chintzy.' He taught his managers that if his employees were so good at their jobs that they could get higher paying ones, the managers shouldn't try to give them raises to retain them; they should just let them go because keeping wages low was the key to expanding his business. He even went so far as to break the law to try to get around paying them a minimum wage. He made a bunch of fake companies and tried to split up the corporation into a bunch of small ones so he could claim the small companies were exempt from the minimum wage law. The courts busted him and he had to pay the employees back wages. Some say he told the managers to spread the word that if anybody cashed the checks, they'd be fired."

"What a jerk," I muttered.

"Yeah, that's pretty bad. Most of the time, when people say a company's wages are criminally low, they are exaggerating, but in Walmart's case, it was true. But the company kept on growing. By the end, Sam Walton had around 400,000 employees.

"Now, let's stipulate that his habit of paying as low a wage as possible is morally repugnant. But think about the man starting that first store with a loan from his father-in-law. Think about the man forced out of his first store by a greedy landlord. Was that Sam Walton setting out to build a corporation that would eventually buy out all the others and essentially take over the world? The courts, remember, hadn't even declared that corporations had the same legal rights as people. They did that after Sam Walton was dead, bit by bit, first giving them freedom of speech, then freedom of religion, then the rest of the rights previously reserved for real people. That can't be blamed on Sam Walton. So, was he a bad guy?"

I thought about it, and I started to formulate an answer. "Well—"

"Okay, now hold that thought and let me tell you another story about another man. He was born into a poor family, the son of a preacher, and he decided to cash in on the do-it-yourself home decorating fad in the 1970s. He took out a loan, too. $600 thousand buck. He built a store that sold craft products. He made it into a company that made billions of dollars every year."

"Sounds a lot like Sam Walton."

"He was, in some ways. But that's not why history remembers him. Hobby Lobby was bought by The Corporation, I don't know, like 75 years ago. Nobody remembers it."

"Except you."

He chuckled. "Right. Except me. Here's why it's important. See, there was this President who made an attempt at universal health care."

"What's that?"

"It's the idea that everyone should be able to get health care paid for by their taxes, as a government service. Lots of countries used to have it, back before the U.N. Universal Declaration of the Rights of Corporations. You know what the U.N. was, right?"

"It was a big not-for-profit NGO dedicated to peaceful conflict resolution. Came out of the League of Nations, right?"

"Sort of. It was more like a diplomatic clearing house, a place where all the countries of the world could theoretically come together and figure out what they could agree on. Basic minimum principles, that kind of thing. They had a Universal Declaration of Human Rights. But nobody paid it too much attention. Then, governments stopped paying their dues to the U.N., so the U.N. turned to the few corporations that were still left. This was during the Era of Mergers and Acquisitions, also known as the Great Consolidation, when all the companies were joining into one. So the U.N. tried to make them all happy by getting all the countries it could to sign onto the Universal Declaration of the Rights of Corporations. It basically said that no government could take markets away from private companies by offering services to its citizens which companies would otherwise be able to profit from. Then the corporations went into all those countries and used that as the legal justification to take over as many of their services as they wanted.

"But I'm getting off topic. Long before that, about a hundred years ago, this president tried to bring universal health care to the United States, but it was a kind of half-assed universal coverage. It was designed to keep the private insurance companies happy, so it just forced everybody into the private market and gave subsidies to people who couldn't afford the insurance. It was better than nothing, a real improvement, but not far enough. Anyway, that's where David Green comes into the picture. He decided that his company shouldn't have to spend any money on birth control for its female employees, because his particular strain of Christianity was against that. The government thought they found a way around that, saying that he didn't have to pay for the birth control. They just had to pay for insurance. Then the private insurance companies had to pay for birth control. The government and the insurance companies wanted to pay for birth control anyway. It saved them both money. Cheaper to pay for that then pregnancy and babies, right? But David Green took this all the way to the Supreme Court, and they decided that if companies were people, those corporate people had the right to a religion. Pretty soon, all the corporations found Jesus or made up new religions, whatever church would say that they didn't have to pay for this or that. Religions that didn't believe in paying for any medical care but the free power of prayer. New religions that didn't believe in paying taxes. New religions that believed that paid overtime and sick leave came from Satan. And the court recognized all these religions.

"Now, is David Green responsible for all that? Do we have him to thank for the Corporation's Church? Not any more than Sam Walton is responsible for the rise of a single corporation. But here's a big difference. David Green had no problem investing his own money in companies that made birth control pills. He was fine with his family and his company making money on contraception, just not spending money to give it to his employees. It wasn't really about his religion, or if it was, it was a religion of convenience."

"What a jerk!" I said again, this time with a bit more vehemence.

"Right," my dad said. "But neither of these men could foresee the long term effects of their choices. That wouldn't be a fair way to judge them. Some people say the road to hell is paved with good intentions. I understand why they think that. A lot of horrible things have come about because people had good intentions. But that's not what created the world we live in. It's made up of good intentions and bad intentions and mostly people wandering down the road, not giving much thought to where they are going. Personally, I'd rather be on the side of the people with the good intentions than the ones with bad intentions or the ones who just don't care.

"Now, I could give you a third story, one about somebody who had good intentions and they worked out and everybody lived happily ever after. There are lots of those stories, too. I'm not trying to compare you to Sam Walton any more than I'm comparing you to David Green. I'm just saying, this situation with Sky and Juan might not turn out how you want it to. They may both end up being mad at you. And maybe the situation with Graham won't work out, either. Who knows? But, at the end of the day, I know I'll be on your side, because your intentions were always good ones."

I love my dad.

-24-43-1-10-6-83-67-14-4-
-3-3-43-0-66-0-0-0-6-
-0-7-11-2-1-27-
-5-0-0-80-1-

CHAPTER 18

Thursday, December 20ᵗʰ, 2114, continued

After I came home, I made my last entry in this journal, then tried to distract myself with some videos on my tablet. I watched a new video, a remake of an old movie and sitcom called *The Odd Couple*. The new one is called *The Worst Roommates*. It's not very good, but the recorded laugh track finds it hilarious. I watched a couple episodes, then paced some more. I kept checking my watch. Three hours since Sky met up with Juan. Still no word.

Then my handcom just blew up. I mean, not literally, but it started to beep and buzz and whine and screech because all my different notifications were going off, one after another. A lot of the notifications I've picked are animal noises because I think it's funny when it sounds like I have an elephant or an eagle screaming in my pocket. My tablet was on the couch, and it started dinging and cawing and roaring, too.

219

Dad had gone back to his Shakespeare project at the dinette table. "Did you bring a zoo into the apartment?"

I ignored him and scanned the texts. Some were directly to me and others were group messages.

Graham to Me: Lucas is pissed at you.
Lucas to Me: What did you do?
Gina to Lucas and Me: Um, what just happened?
Sky to Me: Holy flooding flood! Call me!
Juan to Me: I'll let Sky share the news, but ;)
Lucas to Gina and Me: Harriet played matchmaker.
Graham to Me: Before you call Lucas, you'd better call me.
Gina to Lucas and Me: Harriet, who did you hook up?
Lucas to Me: Call me before you talk to Juan.
Juan to Sky, Lucas, Gina, and Me: Sky and I have some good news to share. Sky, want to do the honors?
Gina to Lucas and Me: Nevermind.
Sky to Juan, Lucas, Gina, and Me: We're dating!!!!!!!!!!!!!!!!!!!!

I shouted to my dad, "Sky and Juan got together!"

"That's great, Honey," he said, not nearly as excited as I was.

I started writing my replies, but the messages kept coming in.

Gina to Juan, Sky, Lucas, and Me: Congrats!!!

Me to Graham: It worked out, so he shouldn't be
pissed. I have to call Sky. Then I'll call
you.
Lucas to Juan, Sky, Gina, and Me: Just what the
world needs: More happy breeders. ;)
Juan to Lucas, Sky, Gina, and Me: Ha! Well, happy,
yes!
Lucas to Me: You still need to call me.
Graham to Me: It's more complicated than you think.
Call me before you talk to Lucas.
Me to Lucas: I need to call Sky, but I'll call you right
after.
Me to Graham: I need to call Sky, but I'll call you right
after.
Lucas to Me: Fine. But don't forget.
Graham to Me: Talk to you soon.

I called Sky. "Hey!" I said. "So, tell me the whole story."

Sky started talking, and she spoke so fast I honestly don't know how she managed to avoid passing out.

"Okay, well, you know that Juan called me right after my last class before I even got to the door, and he wanted to talk, and right away I knew it was a big deal because A) he called instead of just messaging, and B) his voice sounded weird, so I said sure I would go talk and he suggested the ice cream place at the mall so I thought maybe other people would be there too but he said he just wanted to talk to me and right away I thought that was strange. So of course I said yes because I was intensely curious and because it's Juan so of course I wanted to hang out one-on-one. We took the subway over there and he was really quiet and that made me uncomfortable so I just filled the air up with my blabbing because that's what I do when I'm nervous, and I kept right on talking while we got our ice cream and found a place to sit out by the railing, but then he was looking at a place over on the ground like staring off into space and he said that was where that Mt. Hood kid got beat up by the Geez for no reason and I said it was, so he asked if I would mind if we took our ice cream for a walk because he didn't want to be there when he talked about this. I didn't know what "this" was but I liked the idea of taking ice cream for a walk, like taking a dog for a walk but so much better because dogs freak me out ever since I read about those packs of wild dogs that form when people abandon their pets because they are moving to higher ground or whatever, and then the big dogs eat the little dogs and form these horrible packs of vicious mutts that will attack and eat people sometimes."

"I didn't know you were afraid of dogs," I said.

Sky rolled on. "Plus the Geez sometimes use dogs to sniff for explosives and drugs and stuff and after what we saw in the mall and the pictures I've seen of the Geez siccing the dogs on protesters in other countries who try to demand better working conditions in the factories — have you seen those?"

"No," I said. What was Sky doing researching stuff like that, I wondered. And where would she get access to that kind of thing? The Corporation would never

222

knowingly allow those images to pass through their servers.

"Yeah. Really terrible, a person being eaten by dogs. Anyway, Juan and I walked our ice cream around the third floor, then down the escalator, then around the second floor while he talked. Or, really, tried to talk, because he was very nervous and it made him tongue tied which is totally unlike him. It was confusing at the time, but now, in retrospect, it was really cute, because he tried to apologize for the whole fiasco with that play we did so he could ask Gina out in this really creative way. He started with this mumbled apology about the whole thing, then said he had this other play he was thinking about, and he wanted my help with it, and of course I said I would help because, you know, it's Juan. So he explains the plot of his new play to me. He's bringing back the same characters, only it's different. The Brave Knight from the first play is riding through the countryside and he meets up with the Black Knight again. Only this time, instead of fighting with him, the Black Knight tells the Brave Knight (who, Juan says, is not all that brave and certainly not very smart), that the princess he tried to win before is actually an enchantress, and that she took the most beautiful, smart, wonderful woman in all the land and made it so that the Brave Knight couldn't see her for what she really was, and the enchantress tricked the Brave Knight into thinking the Fairest of Them All was a dragon, and he killed her. And now the Brave Knight feels terrible and he wants to revive the Fairest of Them All, so he goes on a quest to find a magic item

223

that will bring her back and lift the curse, only Juan doesn't know what it should be.

"And then he says, 'So, I want you to play the dragon again, because I think you're perfect for the role of Fairest of Them All, but I need your advice. What could the Brave Knight possibly give the Fairest of Them All to make her feel like she's not a second choice, but the first choice that he was just too blind to see?'"

"Wow," I said. "That's pretty good."

"I know! But I was quick on my feet, so I said, "Have you thought about a play within a play, like in Hamlet?' and he says, 'What do you mean?' and I say, 'Maybe the Brave Knight who isn't so brave is really smarter than we think, so he hires some actors and writes a play to perform in front of the dragon, which is weird because the dragon is dead and therefore a tough audience, but the play reveals that the knight doesn't want the dragon to be dead because he thinks she's the Fairest of Them All. And then, when the dragon hears the play (because she can't see it, since she's dead, but in my version she's kind of faking it and listening with her eyes closed), she wakes up.'

"And then Juan said, 'But what does she say when she wakes up?'

"And I said, 'I think she would say that the play is a nice gesture, but the curse won't be lifted until the Brave Knight is really brave and tells the dragon what he really feels."

I nodded even though Sky couldn't see me. "Oh, that was good. Really, really good."

"Thanks!" Sky said. "I thought so. Anyway, then he stops walking for a second, then sees some other chairs and tables outside the CorpBucks, so he leads me over to a little table for two, and he sits across from me and leans across the table and puts his hands around mine. And Harriet, his hands were shaking. Like excited and nervous at the same time, crackling with energy, but not sweaty. And he said, 'Sky, you are the Fairest of Them All. I see that now, and I feel like such an idiot for not seeing it all along. And I know that me being an idiot hurt you, hurt you badly. I just want you to know that I am willing to do whatever it takes, go on whatever quest you want, for me to prove that I do see it, I do feel it, I know it.'"

I was a little breathless, either with excitement for Sky or with relief. Maybe both. "Oh my gosh, Sky. He said that?"

"I know! Oh. My. Flooding. Gawd."

"So what did you say?"

"I said, 'All you have to do for me is tell me I'd the fairest of them all every day until I believe it's true.'"

"And what did he say to that?"

"Nothing at first. He just picked up my hands and kissed my fingers. And then he said, 'And then you'll forgive me? Because it is true. You are the fairest of them all.'"

I flopped down on the couch like a lady swooning in an old movie. "Oh, Sky! So perfect. So...." I struggled for the right word.

"I know! And I was like, 'I forgive you for today, but you'll have to tell me again tomorrow.'"

225

I stared at the ceiling. "It's like a fairy tale, only better. Except for the part about it being in the mall in front of the CorpBucks."

"I know," Sky said. "It's almost so perfect that I forgot the part about the Black Knight flooding spilling the flooding beans to the Brave Knight!"

"I'm sure that was just metaphorical."

She laughed. "Yep. A metaphor for the part where Juan told me about your conversation with him, and then he walked off in a daze, and then he couldn't talk to anybody about it because he was in total shock."

"He could have called me," I said. "I would have helped him write his second play."

"Shut up!" But I could tell she was smiling through the handcom.

"I am so relieved," I said. "Do you forgive me, too?"

"For today. But now you have to tell me I'm the fairest of them all every day, too."

"I don't know. Lucas will be jealous if we don't say he's the prettiest one in the group." Then I sat up on the couch. "Oh, I promised to call Lucas. He's really mad at me because he told me not to say anything to Juan and I did it anyway."

"He knew you said something?"

"He must've found out tonight, but his texts did not sound happy."

"Oh." She sounded very serious. "Do you think he doesn't want Juan and me together?"

"No, it's not that. He didn't know what Juan would say, either. He just didn't want me getting into people's business. Think I should call him and say, 'I told you so'?"

"I would word it more carefully."

"Agreed. But I promised him I'd call. See you tomorrow, bright and early."

"Okay. Maybe I'll forgive you again."

We said our goodbyes and signed off. Then I called Lucas, but he replied with a text.

Lucas to Me: Already on my way over to your place. Meet me at subway platform.

"Dad," I called, "I gotta go meet Lucas down at the subway platform. I guess it's a big emergency."

"Fine. Take your handcom to key back into the door, because I need to go to bed. And don't talk too late because you have school tomorrow."

Like I would ever leave the house without my handcom.

I ran down the stairs, grabbing the railing and swinging around the turns like a little girl because I was so happy for Sky. Also, I admit that I was a little bit excited to tell Lucas the news.

He was already standing on the platform when I got down there, smoking one of his horrible, toxic half-and-half cigarettes.

I was a little afraid of his mood because of his quick appearance at my building, so rather than jumping to "I told you so," I approached with some caution. "So, um, what's up?"

He snorted, blowing smoke out of his nose. "I'm well aware that you want to take a victory lap, Harriet. And I'm very happy for you."

He did not sound happy. I decided it was best to wait for more of an explanation.

He took a deep drag, held it in for a second, and then blew it out of both sides of his mouth simultaneously. "I know you think this is great. They like each other. Now they're together. It seems wonderful. But it's not."

"Why not?"

"There are things I can't tell you, Harriet. That makes this harder than it should be. I could just say you have to trust me, but that's not fair, since I can't tell you why. It's just that..." He paused. "In the near future, I'm not going to be around. Plans have been made. Plans you can't know about. But you've thrown a wrench into those plans. You didn't know you were doing it, but you did. That's why I wish you'd just taken my advice."

I frowned. "What are you talking about, exactly? Did your dad get a promotion? Are you moving or something?"

He shook his head. "No. Not exactly. The world is a really messed up place, Harriet. Really flooding messed up. I don't have to tell you that. Your mom is in jail. We watched a kid get his head beaten in because, what? Because he goes to the wrong school? He was in the wrong place at the wrong time? He wasn't valuable enough to the people who make the rules? And what did we do about it, Harriet? We sat there and watched. There was nothing we could do.

We have accepted this, just like the people before us accepted each little shift, the corporations taking over the government, taking over religious institutions, taking over schools. The corporations could listen to us, record everything about us. They couldn't ever be put in jail, but they could buy the jails, buy the courts, put people like your mom away. People accepted those things, even though they didn't like them. And then all the companies bought each other or merged, and people accepted that. And that gave The Corporation the power to decide who lives and who dies, who gets to escape a flood, who gets to have a job and a place to live and a doctor and food, who gets his head bashed in at a mall. We don't even notice anymore. We don't think it's weird because it's become normal. I just can't take it anymore, Harriet."

He put the cigarette to his lips, then stopped before he inhaled, like he'd remembered something. "You guys get to worry about who likes who, about who is dating who. Your lives go on. That's a luxury. You get to be distracted by love, even in a corporate high school.

"I don't get that luxury. I have to see the world as it is, all the time. We watched a kid get his head bashed in because he wasn't Corporation approved. We watched another get chewed up and spit out by The Corporation when he wasn't useful anymore. Every day we listen to propaganda designed to tell us what The Corporation wants us to hear. And every day we learn a little more about how the higher-ups at The Corporation don't care about us at all."

By this point, I was panicking. "Lucas," I hissed, "they can hear everything you are saying. It's all going in your file. If you aren't careful, the Geez are going to be kicking your door down and taking you away to a corporate jail. Or worse!"

He took another angry drag. "Flood 'em. I won't be here long enough."

"What do you mean, Lucas?"

He shook his head. "Nothing. That's not the point. The point is, your little matchmaking has complicated things in ways you can't understand. When I'm gone, you have to be more careful, and you can't afford to be so naive anymore. Your love life, and the love lives of your friends, are just not going to work in a world ruled by The Corporation. They may not seem to be related, but they are. The company owns everything, and that includes our hearts, Harriet. Trust me. I've learned a lot about not being allowed to love."

"Lucas," I said, "You're really scaring me. What exactly do you mean by 'not going to be here'?"

I could hear the subway coming down the tunnel. Lucas heard it, too. He tossed the butt of his cigarette on the floor and ground it with the toe of his shoe, then looked up at me. "Just, be more careful in the future, okay?"

"Okay, but—" There were tears in my eyes.

"I gotta' go," he said, and got on the subway.

I watched through the car's wide windows. He was the only one inside. He waved at me, then began sliding away down the magnetic track. That was when I realized he'd boarded the train heading away from his house.

He didn't have anything with him, not even a warm coat.

And at that moment, I just had a very strong feeling. I just knew.

I'm pretty sure Lucas is going to kill himself.

CHAPTER 19

Friday, December 21ˢᵗ, 2114

I didn't know who to go to, but I knew I had to tell someone about my fears. If I didn't say anything, and Lucas really did hurt himself, I would never forgive myself. Last night, I lay awake in bed, thinking about telling my dad. He could probably make me feel better, like he did before I knew Juan would get together with Sky. But I didn't want him to make me feel better. I wanted someone who had the ability to help Lucas. What could my dad do? I felt bad for even thinking that, for thinking of my dad as *just* a construction worker, as someone without power in the world. But there wasn't time to deceive myself into thinking Dad could work miracles just because I looked up to him. I knew I had to take action, and fast.

Next I considered telling Juan and Sky. Juan was Lucas' best friend. Maybe he could talk to him, or at least keep a closer eye on him during the Santa Claus break. But if my dad didn't have the power to get Lucas the help he needed, my friends certainly didn't.

And this can't wait until tomorrow. I knew that if I didn't tell somebody today, nobody would intervene for the whole Santa Claus break, and today is the last day of school. My instinct to tell an adult, combined with my acknowledgment that I had to find someone with power, left me with one conclusion, but it made my stomach turn just to think about it. Mr. Rorty had warned me not to trust Lucas' dad, and my last conversation with Lucas had made it clear that his dad was a big part of the problem. Still, I just couldn't believe that any father would be so heartless that he'd learn that his son was possibly suicidal and do anything that might make the situation any worse than it already is. I didn't want to tell him. In fact, I never wanted to see Senior Manager Robb again. But that didn't seem to be optional. Before I fell asleep, I decided I'd go see him before school.

Last night I dreamed that I was walking into a scary cave. Inside, there was someone I couldn't see, a shape cooking something over a fire and talking to himself. And, in the dream, I thought the person might attack me, but for some reason I had to walk farther and farther into the cave to talk to the person.

The walls of the cave were round and mostly smooth, like a cartoon of a cave rather than the real thing, and the light from the little fire silhouetted the figure, sending his shadow back along the roof far behind me. He was swaying as he turned something on a spit over the fire, some meat that sizzled as it dripped fat on the coals. As I got closer, I could hear the person more clearly, but I couldn't make out any of the words he was saying.

Closer. Closer. Now the voice was as loud as any I could hear in normal conversation, but the words still didn't make sense. Then I realized, they were backward. Not like complete words spoken in reverse order, but the words themselves flipped around.

Then the voice stopped. He'd heard me coming. Slowly, he turned his head. I couldn't see his face because the fire was behind him, but I could tell that he'd turned his head way too far without moving his shoulders, like an owl.

"Hello," he said. The voice was perfectly pleasant, even a little too sweet.

Then the shoulders started to move, slowly, following the rotation of the head, and as they turned, he revealed the meat on the spit over the fire. It was a leg, but not a chicken leg or a pig's. It was a human leg, but small, the leg of a small child.

"What can I do for you?" the voice asked.

I woke up, gasping for breath, wrapped up in my sheet and blanket, and I felt trapped. I panicked, desperately kicking them off until they released me and fell over the foot of the bed. I swung my legs over and sat there in the dark, panting like an animal.

It doesn't take Carl Jung or Sigmund Freud to tell me what that dream meant. Still, I had to overcome that fear. There didn't seem to be any other way. It was way too early to get up, but I knew I wouldn't be able to sleep anymore. I took an extra hot shower, got dressed, and tried to watch some videos on the couch in the little living room. But I couldn't even focus on those. When my dad woke up, I told him I had to go in to school early to study for a test. I could tell that he

234

thought that was weird, but maybe he thought I was going to go hang out with Graham, because he told me to have a good day and didn't ask any questions.

I took the subway to the stop under the parking lot, then walked up the stairs to the entrance to Alice Louise Walton Corporate High School #7348. The Corporation smiley face beamed out over the parking lot, clearly ignoring me and facing the cars on the street beyond. I walked up the stairs to the building. They'd retracted the awning from the tunnel to the door because the weather had been okay, but there was talk of another super-storm coming in, and the cold wind stung me as I darted from the heated tunnel towards the heated building. I realized that the building might not even be open that early, that I might have to run back down into the tunnel's warmth, but the door swung open when I yanked on it. Two of the three security guards were there already, old Mr. Rorty and the big Hispanic guy whose name is still a big secret to everybody, and they looked surprised to see a student so early. Mr. Rorty smiled at me like he always does. The big guy looked serious, as usual.

"Miss Washington," Mr. Rorty said, "You are sure here early. I don't think we're technically open for business yet. Gabe, are we even open?"

So the big guy's name is Gabe. He looked at his watch. Then he shrugged and motioned for me to walk through the metal detector, his wand directing me and his eyes saying he didn't really care.

When I picked up my backpack on the other side of the conveyor belt, Mr. Rorty caught my eye again.

"Hey, Miss Washington, I have a joke for you. When is a door not a door?"

"I don't know, Mr. Rorty," I said. "When is a door not a door?"

"When it's ajar. Get it?"

I didn't laugh, but I snorted a little. "Yessir, I get it."

"Not much of a joke, really. More of a riddle and a pun. But worth contemplating, maybe."

"Sure," I said, though I had no idea what he was talking about. It seemed perfectly straightforward to me, the kind of joke my dad might like.

"You have a good day, Miss Washington."

"You too, Mr. Rorty."

"Always a good day at a Alice Louise Corporate High School," he said. I thought I could detect a tiny hint of sarcasm in his voice, but, if it was there, he hid it well.

I walked down the hall, then turned into the office. The school secretary was already there, too. "What can I do for you?" she asked. Her voice was pleasant, maybe a little too sweet, and it echoed of my dream.

"I need to see Mr. Robb."

"If it's about a schedule change, you'll need to use the computer in the hallway. It can print you a new schedule, and there's a form to apply for a change..."

"No, it's about his something else. He said he wanted me to come talk to him about it."

"Oh, okay." She looked down at her tablet, touched it a few times. "I don't see you on his schedule."

"It's not an appointment. He just said that if I heard anything about...his son, Lucas, then I should come to talk to him."

"Well, why don't you go up the elevator, and if his door is open, you can ask if he has time. He normally doesn't see students without an appointment, but he did come in early this morning, so he might see you."

I thanked her and headed onto the elevator where Mr. Rorty had taken me the only other time I'd been called in to the senior manager's office. I walked down the short hall and found his door open. I poked my head in, and I was about to knock on the doorframe, but I saw that he was standing behind his desk, pacing and talking into his handcom. I decided to leave, but he saw me and waved me in with one of those giant hands he has. He pointed to the seat in front of his desk. He wasn't saying anything to the person on the other end of the line, just listening to a voice I couldn't make out. He put his hand over the face of the handcom, an old fashioned gesture from back when they only had one microphone in one place on the device, and he mouthed, "The wife," as though she might hear. Then he rolled his eyes in a way that shocked me. Who does that? People who don't like their wives much, I guess.

"No, Honey, I'm telling you, the meeting went fine....Yes....Yes, I think it will help my chances. Look, here's what happened. We were on the conference call, and there was this senior manager from a tiny school, some little provincial school in a factory town in Alberta or Arizona or something. And he was trying to score points with the regional managers by talking about how he'd done some polling of the kids. He kept calling it 'qualitative data' and talking about the kids' 'feelings' and 'perceptions.' He was driving me crazy. So I tapped in and the guys in Arkansas called on me. I hit them with a ton of their favorite jargon. I mean, both barrels, Honey. I was great. I said, 'My direction has always been, and will continue to be, to examine the quantitative data before leaping to conclusions and creating policy based upon perceptions. That is the way we are going to do business at Alice Louise #7348 because that is what responsible leaders do. They gather the facts, assess the current reality, create a target to achieve, and implement strategic steps to attain it, identifying the resources and supports that they will need along the way.' The guys in Arkansas were all nodding, and you should have seen the face of this little senior manager. He looked like he was going to cry. It was great....Well, they aren't going to announce any promotion right now. They have to wait for the test scores to come in. But if I didn't have a regional manager position locked up already, the conference call had to have helped. Yeah.... Huh? No, not an emergency meeting. Just an early meeting because of the time zone difference. But worth it, right? Get us off this island, maybe to New Minneapolis or Mount Sunflower....Well, not New Little Rock. Not yet. Not with, you know. But maybe after he goes off to college." And then he looked at me, and it was like he realized I was in the room for the first time and was hearing what he was saying. "Look, I've got to go. Someone is here to see me. Yes, I'll call about the maid service. I doubt she stole anything. It's probably misplaced, but I'll make sure there's a complaint in her file so she'll be on her best behavior....Yes, yes, I'll be home by dinner. I've got to go. Bye."

He looked at me again. "Sorry. Early morning meeting. Speaking of which, what has you here so early?"

Before I could say anything, he tapped on the tablet on his big, mostly empty desk. "Says here you want to talk about Lucas? What has he done now? Something weird? Maybe even a little..." He put one of those meaty paws next to his mouth, like he was telling a secret. "...gay? I am aware of that situation, let me tell you."

I felt my stomach drop. "No. Nothing like that. I just wanted to tell you that Lucas and I are friends and I think he's great. I am a little worried about him, though. He seems down lately, and.... You have a wonderful son, Mr. Robb."

His upper lip twitched a tiny bit, but he kept a tight smile plastered on. "That's nice of you to say, Miss Washington. His mother and I have tried to teach him that success is a product of collaboration, and that requires that every individual make an effort to contribute to the betterment of the institution. Sometimes that means we have to sacrifice our feelings and our ...unorthodox perspectives in order to achieve agreed upon targets. That sacrifice can make some people a little mopey sometimes, but that can't be helped. The sacrifices must be made." I decided that's probably what Mr. Robb told himself about Ken, his former golden boy, too. "It's true in any branch of a company, including a school, and it's true in a family as well. Which brings me to something a bit more important, the topic we discussed last time. Have you heard any rumblings from those anti-Corporation people I warned you about? Have they sought you out?"

"No sir, but, if they do, I'll come talk to you immediately."

"Good, good." He was obviously more comfortable talking about anti-Corporation terrorists than about Lucas, and since I didn't have anything to say on the subject, it was clear that our meeting was over. I stood to leave.

"Oh, Miss Washington, just one more thing. What is your feeling when it comes to your peers? Will they all do their best on the next round of testing?"

I tried to look confused. "Of course. Doesn't everybody?"

"Right? Right? Of course they will." He pulled out his chair, mumbling as he sat. "'Qualitative data.' 'Feelings.' 'Perceptions.' So stupid."

I will not be talking to him about Lucas again. Or about anything, if I can help it. That guy gives me the plague-shivers all over. What a sleazebag.

Now I'm in first period, and I don't know who to tell, so I'm writing it down here in this journal, and that just makes me feel even more powerless.

Maybe I'll tell Graham at lunch. He can't do anything for Lucas, either, but misery loves company.

24-43-1-10-6-83-67-14-4-
3-3-43-0-66-0-0-0-6-
0-7-11-2-1-27-
5-0-0-80-1-

CHAPTER 20

Friday, December 21st, 2114, continued

Lucas wasn't in school today. I looked for him all over during lunch. Sky and Juan hadn't seen him. I didn't tell them about our conversation. They looked too happy, just sitting out in the courtyard under the artificial ceiling, the fake sun shining down on them while the real snow fell outside. Sky had her guitar on her lap, and she was strumming lazily and making up silly songs while she leaned back on Juan. He made suggestions about lyrics that made her laugh. Not the fake laugh she used to use to try to make him notice she was there. A real, happy laugh. I just couldn't bring myself to spoil that.

"Um, have you two seen Graham anywhere?"

"Oh, yeah, he's here," Juan said. "He was in P.E. Test Prep and Math Test Prep with me this morning. I think he's in the computer lab on the second floor of Building B."

"Thanks," I said, and took off.

I passed Gina in the hallway on the first floor of Building B.

"Hey," I said.

She smiled. "Hey, Harriet. Want to eat with me? I thought I'd give Juan and Sky some space."

"Yeah, that's probably a good idea. But I can't. I gotta go find somebody. But if they still need space after the break, I'll eat with you."

"Okay. Have a good Santa Claus break."

I headed up the stairs and found Graham in the computer lab, just where Juan said he'd be. He was copying something off the screen into his notebook. Like, onto paper with a pen. That was weird, but I ignored it, I guess because I've seen my dad doing so much note taking lately.

"Hey," he said, barely looking at me. "I'm almost done with this."

I looked at the screen. He had a browser tab opened to a website with a name that was just code, and the page was covered, from top to bottom, margin to margin, in nothing but numbers. "What's that?" I asked.

"Just a little project." He copied the last number down, closed his notebook, and put it in his backpack. "What's up? You didn't, uh.... You didn't call me back last night, so I was wondering what was going on with you."

He was too shy to scold me, even though I deserved it.

"I'm sorry, Graham. I had a talk with Lucas last night, and he kind of freaked me out. After that, it was all I could think about, and I totally forgot. I'm so sorry. Have you seen Lucas? I'm really worried about him."

"Yeah. He crashed at my house. He's fine."

I sighed. "Phew! I was really worried. So worried I actually went to talk to Mr. Robb, and—"

Graham's head snapped up from his backpack so fast he interrupted me without saying a word. The look on his face was pure terror.

I blinked. "What?"

"What, exactly... No, don't tell me anything else about it. Just come with me."

"Wait, what is going on?" I asked, but he just shook his head and beckoned for me to follow him with one hand.

We walked in silence down the stairs, past Gina. She waved and I waved back awkwardly. Graham led me out of Building B, and into the courtyard. I looked over at Sky and Juan. They didn't see me. Then we headed through Building A to the school's front door.

At the security station, Graham leaned in close to Mr. Rorty and said something so short it must have only been two or three words long. I couldn't hear it, but then Mr. Rorty looked at the other two guards, pointed at Graham and me, and pointed us through. They just nodded as I followed Graham out of the building.

The cover for the tunnel had been extended because the snow had started to fall mid-morning, and the weather report said a big storm was coming. Once we got out of the school and started heading down into the tunnel down to the subway station, I said, "Graham, what's going on?"

He just shook his head and made that same beckoning motion with his hand.

"But we'll miss our next class," I whispered.

He nodded. His face said, "It's unfortunate, but it can't be helped." His lips stayed pressed firmly together.

I followed him onto the subway train, and we rode in silence for three stops. Then we got off under an apartment building I've never visited before. We walked inside, but only to the first floor, and then Graham led me out to the street. It was empty except for the occasional car whizzing by through the gently falling snow, and the powder absorbed the normal sounds of the city, so everything was painfully quiet. I pulled my hood up and wrapped my collar tightly around my neck because the wind was so cold. Graham pulled a stocking cap out of his backpack and yanked it onto his head, but the cold didn't seem to be bothering him as much as his agitation. He led me around the building to an alley that housed one of the big recycling dumpsters. There were a few feet on either side of it so that the loader's arms could pick it up, and Graham squeezed between the building and the dumpster, into the darkness. I followed. When my butt brushed against the cold Plexiglas of the building, I felt like I'd sat on a frozen lake, but I was too nervous to complain.

Behind the dumpster, there wasn't as much wind, but it was still cold. There was a recess about four feet deep, and when I got back there, Graham was pacing.

"Okay, I'm sorry about all the cloak and dagger stuff, but I need you to tell me, word for word, exactly what you told Mr. Robb."

"Um, word for word? Okay, I'll try. He was on the phone, talking about trying to get a promotion. Talking to his wife. He didn't seem happy about that. And he made mention of the fact that he wouldn't get a promotion to New Little Rock until Lucas went off to college. That made me nervous about saying anything, so I just said that Lucas was my friend, and that I was worried about him because he seems a little down lately."

"Anything else?"

"He didn't want to talk about Lucas, so he asked me about anti-Corporation forces, and I said I hadn't heard from anybody, but that I would tell him if I did. Oh, and that everybody is going to try their best on the tests. He asked about that, and I said of course we would all do our best. And then I left."

Graham put his hands on his forehead and closed his eyes, and for a second I thought I'd done something terrible. Then he breathed out and smiled. "Oh, Harriet, you don't know what a relief that is."

"Okay, what the flood is going on? Where is Lucas? Is he okay? He said he was not going to be around for very long."

"Yeah, he told me he said that. Which was stupid of him. He admits that now. He thought it was a great idea to keep you from saying anything to anybody. I told him it probably freaked you out and made you more likely to talk to somebody, but I didn't think you'd talk to his dad. Seriously, Harriet? Mr. Robb? That guy?"

"I thought Lucas was going to kill himself! I couldn't think of who else to talk to! But then I heard Mr. Robb talking about Lucas and knew he was not the right person to tell."

"That was a close call, but it's not your fault. It's Lucas' fault. He was trying to keep you out of this because he didn't think you were supposed to know. That's not his part. But his little embellishment nearly wrecked everything."

"Graham," I said, getting frustrated, "I have no idea what you're talking about. Keep me out of what, exactly?"

He paced back and forth, frowning. "Okay, look, I think I can tell you some things, but not everything quite yet. I will tell you everything, though. Better than that. I will show you. No more secrets. You just have to trust me for a little while longer. Do you trust me?"

I frowned. "To be totally honest, I feel like I trust you a little less than I did yesterday, but I'll give you the benefit of the doubt temporarily, if that's what you mean. As long as you start sharing what you can. I'm feeling a little bit jerked around here, to tell you the truth."

He nodded. "Yeah, I get that." He swung his backpack off this back and crouched down, leaning his lower back against the cold building but keeping his butt out of the thin layer of snow that had collected in the alley. "C'mere. I'll show you how I know what I know."

Though I was a little peeved, I liked the idea of leaning against him, not because of any particular romantic motive at that moment, but because I was cold. I mirrored his position, squatting on my own feet and sitting against the building. The Plexiglas was freezing against my butt, the cold biting right through my jacket and jeans, but I could feel some of Graham's warmth against my knee and shoulder.

He pulled out the notebook he's always writing in, then a copy of a book with an old, worn cover.

"Lemme' guess. *The Complete Works of William Shakespeare*," I said.

His head snapped toward mine. "How'd you know?"

"You're not the first person I've seen doing this."

"Oh," he said, sounding a little deflated. "Okay. Well, don't tell me who the other person is. I'm not supposed to know. The fewer of us know each other's identities, the better."

Now it was my turn to be deflated. I thought I'd had some big secret to exchange. Now I didn't have anything. "Oh. Okay. That makes sense. Well, the other person wouldn't show me what he ...or she... was doing with it. How does it work?"

"It's simple, but it's also brilliant. All you need to know is the title of the play and a number. Then, you find the message, and it's just a list of numbers. It's completely meaningless to anybody cracking the code because it actually is meaningless without the key. They could run it through any algorithm they have and they'll never crack the code. But if you know the name of the play and the magic number, you open to that one and count that many letters. That's the first letter of the message. Then, each number of the code just tells you how many letters to count off before the next letter of the message. The message won't be perfect. No spaces or punctuation, so you have to figure it out, and the writers have to tweak their own choice of words to make sure there isn't a letter that's too far away. You wouldn't want to have to count hundreds of letters off to get to a 'z' or something, so they just change the words they use in the messages to make it easier on us."

"Wait," I said. "Who are these 'writers'?"

"Well, I don't really know" he admitted.

"You're taking coded instructions from somebody, and you don't even know who they are?"

He smiled. "Well, when you say it like that, it sounds pretty dumb. But remember, you promised to trust me, or at least to give me the benefit of the doubt. I've been communicating with these writers for years, Harriet. If they were Corporation spies, I think they would have kicked down my door a long, long time ago."

"But you aren't positive. It could all be an elaborate plan to get a whole bunch of conspirators like you to gather in one place and round you up."

"That's always been a possibility. Especially since we don't know who the other members are. Like, I didn't even know Lucas was involved until a couple months ago. He saw me working on decoding the messages, and he figured it out because he's been doing the same thing. But the whole thing is designed so that we don't need to know who the other members are. We have very specific tasks, and there's redundancy built into the plan. If one person chickens out or gets arrested, as long as they don't reveal everything, the plan can move forward. I'm telling you, whoever is in charge of this whole thing is brilliant. They have this all planned out down to the minute."

"What do they have planned?"

"Well, that's the part I can't tell you. I don't know it all, anyway. I only know my part."

"Which you can't tell me."

He flashed me an excited grin. "Nope, but I can show you. Very soon!"

"Okay, fine. What can you tell me? How did you find out about all this, these brilliant evil geniuses you discovered?"

Graham nodded his head slowly, remembering. "They hang out on the deep web, where The Corporation slows everything to a crawl. That's as close to you can get to a place with old-school free speech if you're a human-person and not a corporate-person. Of course, free speech means a lot of gross speech. That's where the drug deals are happening, the sex trade business, the racist and sexist and nationalistic and homophobic jokes that are barely jokes. But it's also where people are criticizing The Corporation, telling the truth about what is happening in places we don't hear about on The Corporation's newsfeeds. It's where workers look for support when they want to form a union or just beg for fair treatment. And it's where they tell the world when the crackdowns happen. You would not believe some of the things I've seen. Corporation flying drones that launch missiles into crowds. Amphibious robotic tanks that come right up out of the water to fire on protesters at docks. Drones that are almost human-shaped that can go house to house, clearing neighborhoods that get out of control. You have no idea how bad it is." He looked at me quickly, revealing a flash of that characteristic nervousness. "I mean, I don't know how bad it is, either. Not completely. No one does. But it's a lot worse other places than it is here. And these writers, wherever they are, they have bigger plans than Mt. Hood or the Pacific Northwest or North America. They want to take on The Corporation all over the world."

He looked at me, shifting enough that our shoulders separated but our knees pressed even more tightly together. "I want to be a part of that, Harriet," he said. There was a confidence in his voice that I hadn't heard before, a voice to match his bold antics that he could normally only pull off when he was disguised in the mascot suit. But now he was right there in front of me, his cheeks pink from cold, his eyes wet from the wind, but bright and just a little bit wild.

And I thought he might kiss me.

And I thought I wanted to kiss him.

Maybe he could read that in my face, because he looked down at the snow in front of him, his normal shyness re-appearing like a gust of cold wind had blown his confidence away. "Um, so, I know you probably have a lot more questions, but I thought we could try the code, and that way you could see how it works and we can send short messages. What do you think?"

"Sure," I said. I tried to hide my disappointment. I thought he was about to say more.

"Okay, so let's use Romeo and Juliet, and we'll start with the nineteenth letter. Don't write that down anywhere. Romeo and Juliet. 19. Oh, and the letter you include in the message doesn't count in the numbers you're counting off. Like, if you have a five and then you come to the next letter, and it's an 'A,' you write that down, and then start counting the numbers off at the next letter. It took me a while to figure that out. Oh, and ignore the stage directions and the names of the speakers. Just the lines they say."

I nodded. "Okay. I get it."

"Good. I'll send you a link as soon as I get home. I have to use a computer with the software to mask my location, but it will be okay if you use your tablet to look at the page."

I could tell he wanted to say more. He hesitated, like he didn't want to break contact with me. He let his shoulder inch away from mine, then his knee as he rose to his feet. "So, yeah, I'll send that to you as soon as I get home, okay?"

"Got it," I said. "Cloak and dagger. Say nothing to no one. If you tell me anymore, you'll have to kill me. I get it."

He looked down at the snow. "I'm sorry about all this. It will all make sense soon. You just have to trust me."

"Mm-hmm."

251

I guess it was mean for me to give him such a hard time, but I resented the whole situation.

He frowned, nodded, and turned. We left the little alley separately and went off in different directions toward our own apartment buildings.

I got home long before my dad would return from work because Graham and I had skipped our afternoon classes. Within a few minutes, I got his email. The subject line was empty, and the text looked like this:

"1-23-24-43-1-10-6-83-67-14-4-1-5-0-3-
3-43-0-66-0-0-0-6-15-12-0-7-11-2-1-27-
19-33-5-0-0-80-1..."

It went on for a while, 159 numbers to be exact. I went over to my dad's little shelf by the kitchen table and found one of his copies of *The Complete Works of Shakespeare*. I flipped through it and saw that the letters in many of the plays, especially in the first few acts, were carefully crossed out. *Romeo and Juliet* was untouched, though. I found a pencil in a drawer in the kitchen along with a small pad of old-fashioned paper, and I set them down on the table next to the open book and the message on my tablet. I crossed off the 19 letters Graham had told me about. The next was a letter "I." Then I counted off the next 23, carefully crossing off letters as I went, and the next letter was a "W." At first, this was tedious and frustrating, but I got faster at it, and pretty soon it was actually fun.

When I got through that first part, the message read:

"IWISHICOULDHAVETOLDYOUTHIS
LONGTIMEAGO"

I thought, Yeah, Graham, I wish you'd told me
"this long time ago," too. But now I was enjoying the
code cracking. I could even see why he'd dropped the
"A." Sometimes letters just weren't where you needed
them to be, and adding one more would have led to
counting off hundreds of letters until the next could
be found. That 80 was tough to get just right, and I
had to count it a couple times to make sure, but then
"G" isn't as common a letter.

His message continued:

"INAFEWDAYSIWILLCOMEGETYOUA
NDSHOWYOUEVERYTHING"

How many days? I wondered.

"IWONTLEAVEYOUBEHIND"

What did that mean? Where was he planning on
going? Was this what Lucas meant when he said he
wouldn't be around for much longer?

"TRUSTMEEVENIFICANTSAYTHISTO
YOURFACEILOVEYOUHARRIETILOV
EYOU"

I know I should have read the message and then burned it. I never understood what my dad was doing before, but now I do, and I see why he burned the things he wrote down after he translated them. That's the responsible thing to do.

But I can't. It's the first time he's told me how he feels. I'm saving the note, tucking it into my journal. If anyone finds this journal, The Corporation will know enough to kill us all, anyway. There's no turning back, even though I have no idea where I'm going.

And now I have to wait to find out.

But I know Graham is waiting, too. He must be desperate for an answer, but I can't say anything about the message.

So I'm sending him this reply:

1-30-2-47-10-11-13-10-3

I think he'll forgive my spelling. It's just too far to the next "Y." It says:

"ILOVEUTOO"

-24-43-1-10-6-83-67-14-4-
3-3-43-0-66-0-0-0-6-
-0-7-11-2-1-27-
-5-0-0-80-1-

CHAPTER 21

Monday, December 24th, 2114

The next two days were a kind of torture. The predicted storm rolled in and trapped us in our apartment. As super-storms go, it wasn't that super. It dumped three or four feet of snow, and then the temperature dropped too low for it to snow anymore and the wind came ripping through town, gusts nearing a hundred miles per hour, trees cracking and tossing branches against the bulletproof windows of buildings hundreds of yards away. But it lasted for only three days, and then it died down as fast as it had arrived.

During those days, I didn't want to send messages to Graham because I wasn't sure if I was allowed to use the code to talk about the kinds of things I wanted to say to him. Plus, I wasn't sure what I really wanted to say, anyway. I wasn't lying in my one message. My feelings had grown to that point. I'd fallen for the shy boy who could barely look me in the eye. In fact, when I thought about him, I had to admit I'd fallen hard.

But I was still mad at him. All these questions swirled around in my head, and I couldn't find any answers without his help. I hate the feeling that I can't do things on my own, and there I was, helpless.

I was pretty angry at my dad, too. Obviously, he was in on this whole thing and he'd kept it from me. That pissed me off. Worse, now that I knew about it, I still couldn't talk to him because he was convinced The Corporation could hear and see anything in our apartment. I tried to write him a note that just said, "Can we at least write about this?"

He took the note from me, scribbled for a few seconds, and handed it back to me. "Better not. Not quite yet."

I rolled my eyes, crumpled up the paper, and threw it at him.

"Sorry, Honey," he said aloud, and he did sound sorry, but that didn't stop me from scowling at him and stomping back into the living room without a word.

The one time I did get out of the house was even wrecked by all the secrets. The evening of the last day of school, I called Sky at home, and her step-mom said she was over at a friend's house. I knew she was at Juan's so I didn't call, but I sent a text, and she didn't reply. On Saturday, I called her in the morning and asked her if she wanted to go to the mall to do some last minute shopping for Santa Claus Day. She was hesitant, and it took me a while to get the truth out of her. She was going over to Juan's again.

"Oh, that's fine," I said. "Maybe another time."

"How about tomorrow?"

"If you want to hang with Juan, that's cool," I said.

"I can take a break from my boyfriend to hang out with my best friend, I think," Sky said. She sounded light and happy, but there was an undertone of defensiveness.

"I'm glad," I said, and then I realized that might have sounded sarcastic. "I mean, I want to hang with you and I'm really sick of this apartment."

"Yeah, I get that. Maybe we could all go out tonight? You and me and Juan and Lucas could meet at the mall? And Graham? How are things with him?"

"That's...hard to explain," I said.

There was a pause while she waited for me to try.

"Oh," she said finally. "Okay, well maybe just the four of us?"

"I don't think Lucas..." I trailed off. "He probably wouldn't be the best idea, either. But Juan would be fine, I think. Except he might wonder why Lucas isn't there, and—"

Sky rescued me. "Sounds like it should just be you and me."

So, the second day of the storm, I met Sky at the mall. We did some shopping, but neither of us has much money, so we mostly window shopped. I did find some cheap knit gloves, gray and made out of some synthetic wool that was warm and fuzzy, and I had cold weather on my mind, so I bought four pairs, two for me and two for my dad for Santa Claus Day. I got each of us a scarf and a hat, too. I thought he'd like the idea that I wanted us to match, even if I couldn't afford an expensive gift. It would be a peace offering, even though I was still mad at him.

The shopping should have been 100% fun, but I could feel all the things I wanted to talk about with Sky pushing at the back of my throat. I could tell there were things she wanted to say, too. For a second, I wondered if she knew about the code and the mysterious plans, but I doubted it. She probably wanted to talk about the Juan situation but couldn't because I wouldn't talk about my relationship with Graham. And, of course, I couldn't ask if she knew about the code anyway. That was very frustrating.

When I got home, my dad silently broke the silence. He came over while I was watching a video on my tablet and handed me a note.

"We need to pack," it said.

He handed me the pencil. I set the note on my tablet and wrote, "For how long?"

He wrote, "Everything." His answer didn't give me the information I was looking for, but, in its own way, it told me even more.

"Moving?" I wrote.

He nodded.

"When?" I wrote.

He shook his head.

I wrote, "Where?" even though I knew he wouldn't tell me that, either.

"Sorry," he said.

I scribbled for a few seconds, then handed him my note. "Can I at least say goodbye to some friends?"

He frowned and shook his head.

I looked up at him and stared into his eyes. "I'm not sure I can do that," I said out loud.

"Trust me," he said.

I got up from the couch. "I've been hearing that a lot, lately."

I went back to my room and started packing. It didn't take long. I haven't bought much since we moved here, and everything still fit in my two bags and my backpack. I didn't pack Dad's two pair of gloves, his scarf, or his knit cap, though. I hadn't wrapped them yet, but I put them in their bag and set them on top of my suitcase. Was that childish, not wanting to pack his stuff, wanting him to find his gifts and feel guilty? Yes, it was. But that was how I was feeling.

When my bags were situated at the foot of my bed, Dad's gift placed carefully on top, I thought about going back to the living room to watch some videos or waste time online, but I just couldn't bring myself to do it. I also thought about writing in this journal. I'd previously thought of it as a kind of therapy, but now I was intensely aware that it was my dad who had originally asked me to do it, to keep a record of my time at Alice Louise Walton Corporate High School #7348, and I started to suspect that it was a part of this big plan, a plan that was conspicuously and intentionally kept a secret from me. I just couldn't bring myself to write another word in it. Call it "Writer's Rage Block." I was too mad to write.

I thought about my friends, about Sky and Juan and Gina. Lucas and Graham obviously knew about the plan, but what about the other three? What would they think when I was suddenly gone? Would Sky forgive me? Would she take comfort in the arms of her new boyfriend and forget all about me? Maybe that was unfair to her and to me, to our friendship, but I wondered it anyway. I admit that I curled up on my bed and cried for a while, then finally fell asleep.

That brings me to this morning, though that was so long ago it feels like days have passed. I woke up feeling ragged. I hadn't slept well, and I still felt like punching a wall. Instead, I took some paper from my dad's notebooks and began writing letters. I wasn't sure if I'd ever get a chance to give them to my friends, but I figured it couldn't hurt to have them ready just in case. After all, no one was telling me the plan, so I might as well be as prepared as possible, right?

I wrote the first letter to Sky. That one was really hard, especially since I couldn't even explain where I was going or why. I didn't want to tell her about Lucas or Graham's involvement, for fear that the letter could be found and their names could lead The Corporation to them or to their families. I made a passing reference to other friends of ours, knowing that if Lucas and Graham were also gone, she'd know who I was talking about. Still, I didn't explain the code or anything. I focused on my friendship with her and how much it was going to hurt me to be apart from her. I hoped she would take some comfort in that. Then I wrote a letter to Juan, thanking him for being such a good friend to me and giving him explicit instructions to take care of Sky. I explained a few inside jokes that he wouldn't know, some of her favorite things to do around town that he could do with her to remember me. It still ended up being a short letter. I tried to write a third to Gina, and I found that I had almost nothing to say, so I scrapped it. I decided it might be easiest for Gina to just dismiss us as anti-Corporation people who'd duped her, and who she was lucky to be rid of.

I exchanged some texts with Selina back in Illinois. I couldn't tell her anything specific, but I explained that I was going through a really rough time and I wished she was here to give me a hug. I told her that I was wearing the necklace she gave me, and that it made me feel better. She called me *Hermanita Negrita*, and that made me feel better, too. She said that all I needed was the guts to go with my brains and looks, and I'd be fine. I said that was very sweet, but that I needed her guts because I wasn't feeling courageous enough.

"There is nothing this rotten world can throw at you that you can't handle, Harriet," she wrote. "If you don't feel that inside, believe it because you believe me and know I wouldn't lie to you."

See? That's what great friends are like.

The weather reports said the storm was dying down, but my dad and I stayed in the apartment. It was Santa Claus Eve, so the mall would be packed with last minute shoppers, the restaurants would be full of families having their big Santa Claus Eve dinners, and everything else would be closed. I thought about asking Dad if we should go to dinner, but I realized that it probably conflicted with some part of the plan, so I didn't bother.

Around ten, I got an email from Graham. It had no subject line and the text was all numbers, so I went into the dinette and grabbed another copy of one of Dad's books of Shakespeare's plays. I started to head back to the living room, but he got up from the table and gave me the spot he always used. My guess is that he thinks there's less chance a camera can see that spot in the apartment, but maybe he was just trying to make amends with a nice gesture.

Graham's message said,

"ILLBEBYTOPICKYOUUPATELEVENT
HIRTYDRESSWARM"

By the time I finished decoding it, I only had a little while to rummage through my bags and get my warmest clothes on, but because I was rushing, I finished about a quarter after eleven.

I wrote a note to my dad. It just said, "I guess I'll be out after curfew tonight."

He smiled, then wrote underneath, "Just this once."

The days of the storm had been bad ones. The last had been worse. And the last fifteen minutes were the worst of all. I imagined the sounds of one of those old-fashioned clocks, the kind you hear in movies that made a ticking. Torture.

Then there was a quiet knock on the door.

When I let Graham in, he looked at my warm clothes and smiled, but he didn't look me in the eye. I wanted to punch him in the face. It was like some perversion of a school dance, and he was satisfied with my dress but too shy to look me in the face. Maybe I would have found that romantic the night of Homecoming or Prom, but, considering the circumstances, I could barely stand it.

Instead, he looked back into the dinette at my dad. I followed his gaze, and I was surprised to see the look on my dad's face. He was genuinely astonished to see Graham.

"Um, hi Graham. Harriet is busy tonight," he said. "We have some Santa Claus Eve plans and she really can't miss them."

Graham nodded. "I'm here to make sure she makes it to the planned events."

"Oh," Dad said. "Okay. Well then, you two be safe."

"We will," Graham said. "I promise." He opened the door and motioned for me to follow him out into the hall.

I looked at my dad and raised an eyebrow.

Dad smiled and nodded tightly. Now he was fine with it. I wanted to punch him in the face, too. What in the flooding hell was going on?

I shrugged. "Fine." I sighed, and I left.

Graham and I didn't talk on the way down to the subway tunnels. We didn't talk on the platform. We didn't talk in the subway, either. We took the same train I took to school each day, but he motioned for us to get off at the stop before the high school, so I followed him. We climbed up out of that tunnel, left that building, and walked around behind it to a field that led up a hill. The snow was about three feet deep with a crunchy layer of ice on top, so it was hard going. Other than the sound of our shins grinding through the ice and our breath huffing and puffing, the field was silent, and the town below played along. Occasionally we would hear the distant hissing of a car's tires on an icy street, but we couldn't even see car lights between the buildings. A generous moon had been revealed by the storm's last winds, and the sky was a rich navy, with the trees up on the hill in front of us looming a stark black between snow and sky.

"Okay," I said. "I think I've waited long enough. What is going on? My dad made me pack my bags. Where are we going? Who is going with us? I want some flooding answers, Graham."

He looked over his shoulder and his teeth flashed. "You're about to get them. Right up here at the top of the hill." Even in the darkness, he could tell by the look on my face that I was not satisfied with that answer, and his smile vanished. "Yes, we will be leaving. I can't tell you everybody who will be going, because I honestly don't know. You saw the look on your dad's face. He didn't know I would be coming to get you. I only knew he was involved because you told me he'd been going through Shakespeare's plays, but I couldn't give him any more information because, like I told you, we all have our parts and we're not supposed to talk about them, even to each other."

The field sloped up onto the hill, and Graham kept talking as we made our way into the trees. "Like I told you before, Lucas and I discovered that we were each involved, but we would have been part of the redundancy in the plan. If I were caught, Lucas would have been the one who picked you up tonight. The planners are so insistent that you be brought here, that, when you told me about your dad working with the plays, I was just sure he was one of the writers. But then he would have known I was the one showing up, because they are the only ones who know who we all are. But he didn't know, so I guess it's not him. You saw his face. He wasn't faking."

I had to concede that. He didn't know. "So my dad isn't the big mastermind of the plan. But what is the plan, Graham? Other than picking me up, what is your part?"

He held some branches so they wouldn't smack me in the face, and he led me into a small clearing, this one near the top of the hill. "I'll show you. Look down there."

He pointed down this new face of the hill, and there at the bottom was our school. We were off to one side of it, but I could make out the four buildings, the ceiling of the fake courtyard between them, the football field stretching off behind them to our left.

"Now, look there, at the front door," Graham said.

Now that I was oriented, I quickly found the front door on the corner closest to us, on our right. The cover that led down to the subway tunnel, which must have been extended during the storm, had been retracted, and a figure was coming up the hill, his legs leaving two deep lines in the snow behind him. He walked slowly but steadily up towards us.

"Who is it?"

"I'm not supposed to know, but I figured that one out, too," Graham said. "'When is a door not a door?'"

I frowned. "Mr. Rorty?"

"Yep."

"The greeter?"

"He wasn't always a greeter. He used to be a teacher. A real one, at a public school, back when they still had some who taught classes. He hates The Corporation."

"Okay, so?"

"Keep watching," Graham said. It was almost a whisper, but it contained so much excitement I couldn't help but feel it.

Mr. Rorty continued coming up the hill, and he was only 30 yards away, now clearly visible, when another figure came running out of the doors. This person was younger, taller, thinner, and wore a trench coat I recognized immediately. He bounded into Mr. Rorty's tracks and then ran up the hill behind him.

When Mr. Rorty got to us, Graham clasped his hand and pulled him into the tree line. The man was obviously winded. "Big...hill.... Darn...snow."

When Lucas caught up, Graham said, "Is it going to work?"

"It better. We've been piling furniture and papers and toilet paper with all the cans Mr. Rorty hid in one of the supply rooms. We've been at it for hours. I don't know how much—"

I interrupted. "Is that fire?" I could see an orange and yellow glow flickering in the windows on the top floor of the administration building.

Lucas and Graham smiled at each other. "I guess it's going to work," Lucas said.

"Watch," Graham told me again.

Seconds later, there was an explosion. It wasn't gigantic like something made with computers in the movies. Just breaking glass and a big Whoomp! as flames shot out of the windows, then curled up and licked around the top of the building.

"What have you done?" I mumbled.

"Just wait," Lucas said.

I couldn't see the second explosion because it came from the far side of Building C, but I could see the flames rise up over Building A and D in front of me. Then the windows blew out in B and D in quick succession. The air from the first two must have fueled the fires that spread to those buildings. Inside, I realized, everything must be on fire.

Mr. Rorty rose from his crouch and put a proud hand on Lucas' shoulder. "Thanks for all your help, Lucas," he said.

"It might be the most beautiful thing I've ever seen," Lucas said.

Graham was bouncing on the balls of his feet. I took a step back and stared at him. The light of the fire barely reached his face, but I could make him out clearly in the moonlight. His smile was wide and pure. All his hesitancy, all his shyness was gone. He was perfectly happy.

"What have you done?" I asked again. "Graham, it's a school! I know you hate The Corporation, but you just set fire to a school. A school!"

He turned to me, his joy not completely faded. "No, Harriet, you don't understand—"

I cut him off. "And you! Mr. Rorty, how could you? A school? Your school? You welcomed kids to that school every day. And now you guys think that you can set it on fire and be... what? Revolutionaries? You're arsonists. Terrorists!" I stepped back into the clearing. "I don't want anything to do with this."

"Wait, Harriet," Graham said. "You'll see. Just hold on a second."

267

"No! This is wrong, and you're all proud of yourselves. I'm not a part of this. I'm out of here!"

I turned around, looking for the place where Graham and I made our way through the trees, scanning for our tracks, and then I heard other crunching footsteps and a clicking noise I'd only ever heard in movies before. I recognized the sound right away, though.

The gun inched into the moonlight first, and then Mr. Robb stepped out of the shadows. "Stop right there," he said. His voice was low, only directed at me, but then he called to the others. "Freeze! Put your hands up and come over here where I can see you."

Graham, Lucas, and Mr. Rorty stepped into the clearing.

"Rorty," Mr. Robb said. "Of course. And Graham. Always on the computers. And Lucas. My own son." Without looking away from us, he tapped a button on his handcom. He must have already dialed the number. "This is Senior Manager Robb from Alice Louise. The building is on fire, and I've caught the culprits. Send fire trucks to the school right away, and send Corporation security officers up to the hill above the school....Yes, I can detain them here until you arrive. If they try to run, I'll shoot them. Get those trucks to the school immediately."

He pressed the button to cancel the call, then dropped the handcom into his pocket.

Then he looked straight at Lucas. "You know, it might go better for me if I just say that you all decided to run."

CHAPTER 22

Monday, December 24th, 2114, continued

"Dad, please, please don't do this," Lucas said. He sounded terrified, and that told me his dad really would pull the trigger.

Mr. Robb's face scrunched into a horrible sneer. "Oh, so now I'm 'Dad'? Now that matters to you? It was never enough to do your part for the family, to hide your personal...issues for the sake of dear old dad before."

Then he pointed the gun at Mr. Rorty. It moved so fast that I thought he was going to pull the trigger, and I jumped a little, moving closer to Graham. Graham stepped toward me and wrapped his arms around me, turning me behind him.

But Mr. Robb didn't pull the trigger. "Rorty. I should have guessed. Greeters are the most useless employees in the whole company. I could replace you in about five seconds and no one would even know the difference."

The barrel of the gun swung toward Graham and me. I wrapped my arms around Graham's ribs and held tightly.

"And you two? Well, it's a shame to lose you two. You were two high sets of test scores. Still, whether you get taken off by the company or die right here on this hill, it makes no difference to me. I don't get your scores either way."

He extended his arm, pointing the gun right at my face. "You, little lady, what was your name again?"

Even in the dim light, I could see the blackness of the barrel. All my attention was focused on that little point, that period, that end of my sentence. I tried to find my voice, but it was cut off by that punctuation mark floating in front of me. The best I could manage was a choked-out 'H' sound that trailed off.

"Harriet, right?" Mr. Robb said. "Yes, I remember. And I told you to stay away from anti-Corporation terrorists, and to come tell me if you heard anything. But you didn't, and now it's too late. You had your chance."

He turned the gun back on Lucas. "So it comes down to you. They don't matter, but I might be better off if you die, and if I kill you, I'll have to kill them, too. I'll bet you wish you'd kept all that flouncy, fairy stuff bottled up now, right? Your friends are going to be the ones who pay for it."

"Dad, please," Lucas repeated. "Please—"

"Step forward, Lucas. You know how this works. It's time to take your medicine."

Graham whispered, "Lucas, don't."

I was looking up at Graham's face when Mr. Robb pointed the gun up into the air and fired. The crack made me jump, and I think I screamed a little.

Mr. Robb pointed the gun right at me, but he looked at Graham. "You interfere again and I'll shoot her first." Then he looked back at Lucas. "I said step forward, Lucas."

Lucas took one slow, short step toward his father, then another.

"Good," Mr. Robb said. "Now get down on your knees."

Tears were running down Lucas' face, but he didn't say anything. He just slowly bent his knees, then fell into the snow.

Mr. Robb stepped toward Lucas and put the gun up against the side of his head.

"Dad," Lucas said. He was choking down a sob, but he managed to repeat the word. "Dad."

"Stop calling me that!" Mr. Robb said. I was sure, 100% sure he was going to pull the trigger, but he raised up his other hand, his fist clenched tightly, and backhanded Lucas across the face, his knuckles crushing Lucas' lips against his teeth.

Lucas reeled, but he didn't fall completely, and then he straightened his spine, putting his head back against the barrel of the gun. He looked straight ahead. When he spoke, I could see the blood running between his teeth, but the crying that had been choking him was gone. "You know what? Maybe you should kill me." Then his eyes flicked up at his father's face. "Even after the company finds you not guilty of any wrongdoing, the investigation into it will still be in your personnel file. Your career will be more ruined by pulling the trigger than it ever was because you have a gay son."

Mr. Robb snorted. "You think there will be an investigation? When I say you tried to run, they won't even ask a single question. That's your problem, Lucas. That's what's wrong with all of you. You think you matter. You think they should care. Well, they don't. You're not on the spreadsheet. You don't affect the profits enough to count."

Lucas nodded very slowly. "You're probably right. But then, when they arrive, if they hear the sound of gunfire and see someone standing there with a gun, they might shoot you before you ever get to tell your side of the story. If I were you, I'd hold that gun up high in the air, because I can hear them coming. You hear them, too, don't you? Sounds like a couple trucks to me."

Mr. Robb glanced quickly in the direction of the sound of the coming vehicles. They were driving up from the side of the hill opposite the one Graham and I had climbed, so I hadn't even seen the road through the trees. I followed Mr. Robb's gaze and saw their headlights blinking between the trunks as they came up. Mr. Robb was still looking at them when Lucas aimed a glance at Graham. Graham nodded back.

"They're almost here," Lucas said, staring forward again. "You really should hold that gun up in the air. I wouldn't want you to get shot just because of me, Dad."

Mr. Robb caught the last word and looked down at his son again. "Flood you, you little brat," he barked, but he didn't shoot. Instead, he pistol-whipped Lucas. This time the barrel hit him in the eye, and he did fall back into the snow.

Mr. Robb pointed the gun at each of us in turn as he stepped away from his son. Then, when he felt he was a safe distance away, he raised his hands up into the air, showing the side of the pistol clearly.

The two trucks burst through the trees and into the clearing. The doors on the far sides flew open and men jumped out, then pointed rifles at us. The drivers' windows came down and they pointed shotguns out.

"Drop the gun and step away from it," a voice boomed.

I couldn't see the men in and around the trucks clearly in the dark, but I thought I recognized the voice.

Mr. Robb did as he was told, dropping the gun and walking a few steps toward the trucks. "Officers, I'm the one who called you. These are the people who started the fire."

The men on the far side of the trucks started to walk around toward us, their rifles still pointed at Mr. Robb.

"Hey, Dad?" Lucas said.

Mr. Robb didn't turn to face his son.

"I said, Dad!" Lucas shouted.

Mr. Robb looked over his shoulder.

Lucas sat up, then pushed himself to his feet. "I said 'they' were coming. I didn't say 'they' were your Corporation geez."

When Mr. Robb turned back to look more closely, four armed men were standing around him, all pointing their guns right at him. Behind him, Lucas walked over, picked up his dad's gun, and joined the circle.

Now that he'd stepped into the moonlight, I recognized the man who'd been driving the second car. "Put your hands behind your back," Manuel said.

I looked at the faces of the other men. They were all my dad's construction buddies. One of them stepped forward and grabbed Mr. Robb's hands, then wrapped a zip-tie around his wrists and pulled it tight.

"Get down on your knees," Manuel said.

Mr. Robb sounded desperate. "I'm a senior manager. Alice Louise Corporate High, right over there. I have some serious pull. I can pay you."

"He said 'Get on your knees,' you sack of plague," one of the other men said, and he kicked Mr. Robb in the back of his leg, knocking him into the snow. Then the burly construction worker grabbed Mr. Robb by the hair while another man grabbed the shoulder of his coat, and together they pulled him up onto his knees.

"He called the Geez a few minutes ago. They're on their way," Lucas said.

Manuel looked at Lucas' face. "He do that to you?"

Lucas nodded.

"Want to kill him?"

Lucas shook his head. "No. He's my dad."

"Want me to do it?"

Lucas shook his head, but Mr. Robb couldn't see that.

Manuel stepped forward. "Well, Mr. Senior Manager, you are having a very, very bad day. Your school is in pretty bad shape. Lucky for you, your son doesn't want me to kill you, and I don't want to shoot a man in front of his own son."

I could see Mr. Robb's shoulders sag in relief.

Then Manuel lifted his shotgun up over his shoulder and brought the butt of it down on Mr. Robb's face. I heard bone crunch. When Mr. Robb sagged to the ground, Manuel stepped forward and kicked him hard in the stomach with the toe of his boot. "And you're really lucky that the Geez are on their way, and that I have places to be, because I would love to mess you up really bad for being one of the most worthless excuses for a father I've ever seen." He looked up at the rest of us. "But we gotta go. C'mon."

Graham still had his arms around my shoulders, and he led me past Mr. Robb toward the vans.

As we neared them, Mr. Robb cried out from the snow, "I know who you all are! I know what you look like!"

Manuel looked at Lucas. "Does that flooding *pendejo* want us to kill him?"

Lucas looked back at his father lying in the snow. "Dad, you don't get it. Your school is burning. Your son is leaving forever. And your wife is leaving you for the desk clerk at the auto parts store. You are the one who doesn't count anymore, no matter what The Corporation says."

Lucas climbed into the back seat, and Graham led me around to the other side while the men laughed at Mr. Robb and got into the trucks. I sat in the middle, between Graham and Lucas. We turned around and headed back through town.

"Lucas, let me see your face," I said.

"I'll be fine."

"C'mere," I said more firmly, and pulled away from Graham. I took Lucas' face gently in my hands, careful not to touch his mouth or eye.

"You're going to have a bad shiner," I said. "But I don't think he broke any bone. Let me see your teeth."

He flashed a Cheshire-cat grin. Blood ran between his teeth still, but the teeth themselves weren't broken.

"Am I still as sexy as ever?" he asked.

"Your face is going to swell up pretty bad. We'll need to get you some ice. Where are we going?"

Manuel turned his head but didn't look away from the road. "Going down to the docks. The boss has us on a strict timeline."

"Who's the boss?" I asked.

"You'll see!"

He sounded excited and happy, but I was sick of the games.

"Harriet," Graham said, "I know you think we shouldn't have—"

"No," I snapped. "I don't want to talk to you right now. You set fire to a school."

"Harriet—" Lucas said.

"Not you either. Shut up or your face will swell up worse. Hell, I'll make it worse. A school? A school?"

Lucas inhaled like he was going to speak again.

"No! Just. Don't. Talk."

Graham put a hand on my shoulder and another on my forearm. I spun on him and shoved his hands away. "Don't even try. Manuel, I want to know what the flood is going on. No more secrets. No more wait and see."

"Well," Manuel said, "I guess I can see where you're coming from on that, but I really hate to ruin the surprise."

"Enough with the flooding surprises, Manuel."

"That's fair. Okay, fine, I'll tell you what you want to know, but it's a little complicated, and I have to keep my eyes on the road, so you're going to have to bear with me here a little bit." He made a turn just a little too fast for my taste, but we didn't lose traction on the salted roads. The tall, bulbous buildings whipped by. The street lights flashed off their shiny surfaces and the deposits of snow lumped up on the sidewalks and leaning against the building's sides. There were no cars on the road with us, but, down a street, I could see the flashing lights of fire trucks racing back toward the high school behind us.

I started to say something, but he raised his voice to let me know he was going to continue. "I am telling you, though. Because you have been kept out of the loop, and that's not fair. I always thought your dad should have told you the whole plan, but he said that we were protecting you by keeping you in the dark, just in case things didn't work out. But they have worked out, I guess. So I can tell you now."

"So? Tell me."

We'd left the urban district of Mt. Hood behind, and now the buildings were shrinking and falling

277

apart on either side of the road, the old, wooden, abandoned houses with their roofs torn off by storms sat filled with snow, the trees reclaiming them into the shrinking forest. The road underneath us was gravel, so it was harder to hear Manuel. "You'd be surprised at how long this has been in the works, Harriet. It started even before you and your dad moved here, but I wasn't part of it then. I was recruited pretty early, though. I got in touch with the writers of the codes, got my books of Shakespeare until all the letters were crossed through in some of the plays. You learned about the code, right?'

"Manuel, quit stalling," I said.

"I guess I'm not as good at it as Lucas, eh? He did a good job of stalling. And nobody's even pointing a gun at me!"

I was really, really pissed. "Do I need a gun? Do I need to jump out of a moving car? Because so far I have nothing to do with this whole thing, and you guys are the ones who just committed like a hundred crimes, and I'm basically being kidnapped and you won't tell me where we're going or who this boss is."

"I said we were going to the docks," Manuel said. He slowed and turned the truck onto another gravel road. "They're right up here. That's where the boats are. We're getting on the boats and we're leaving. Tonight. I don't know where the boats are going to take us, exactly, because they don't tell me and it doesn't matter to me. It will be a place where The Corporation can't find us. And my wife will be on one of those boats. That's what I care about. And I said I'd take you to the boss, but you don't want to be surprised, so, fine, I'll tell you."

The truck took a left and aimed down toward the water. I saw the beams from the headlights pass over four of five boats moored along the docks. It was hard to tell in the darkness. But then the lights fell on a cluster of people loading things onto the boats from some other vehicles parked by the docks. Manuel aimed the truck at the person directing all the others and slowed to a stop. He pointed through the windshield.

"That's the boss right up there."

I saw her, but Manuel couldn't help himself.

"I said I wouldn't surprise you, though, so I'll just come right out and tell you. It's your mom."

-24-43-1-10-6-83-67-14-4-
-3-3-43-0-66-0-0-0-6-
-0-7-11-2-1-27-
-5-0-0-80-1-

CHAPTER 23

Tuesday, December 25ᵗʰ, 2114

Last night, once we arrived at the docks, I ran to my mom and just held on as tightly as I could. My eyes filled up with tears as I pressed my face into the space between her shoulder and neck, and I guess my brain just shorted out or something, then decided to restart using its Little Girl operating system, because my memories of everything get blurry. I don't know how long I held onto her like that, but I'll bet she hugged me back for a few solid minutes before she remembered that she still had a lot of work to do. To me, it felt like seconds, and then she was stiff and talking to people over the top of my head. I didn't care. I just held on.

She said things like, "Harriet, Baby, we're not safe yet. We have to get everyone onto the ships."

I don't think I said anything at first. I just held on.

"Harriet, Honey," she tried again, "we gotta get moving."

"Mom," I mumbled, sniffling, not moving, "they burned down the school. The school is on fire."

"I know, Honey. I know. I'll explain everything once we're safe."

"They said it was a distraction, but it's a school. Why a school, Mom? Why did they choose a school?"

"They didn't choose the school, Honey. I did." Then she spoke over my head again. "Sky? Juan? Can you come help Harriet find her cabin?"

"But why a school?" I kept saying.

"Harriet, Sky and Juan are here. See?"

I turned my head a little, but I wouldn't release my mother from my grip. Sky and Juan were standing together, beaming at me. Sky put her hand on my shoulder.

"I'll explain everything, Harriet," Sky said. Her voice was slower than usual, like she could see that my brain wasn't working.

"They burned down the school," I told her.

"Mm-hmm. C'mon, Harriet. Let's get up on the ship, okay? We really have to get moving."

My mom called out over my head. "Elijah, will you come get Harriet?" I couldn't see him come over, but I could feel him there, and my mom's voice dropped. "I think she's going into shock. Let's get her onto the ship and into her sleeping bag, maybe with some extra blankets."

I still wouldn't let go, so my mom walked up the short gangplank with me still wrapped around her, my dad's hands guiding me by the shoulders, keeping me from falling in the dark water of Lake Willamette.

In the little cabin, they got my shoes off and helped me into a sleeping bag. Then my mother turned to leave and I kinda' freaked out. My dad had to basically restrain me, and my mom came rushing back in to whisper soothingly in my ear until I basically passed out.

I woke up this morning in the tiny room with bunks set into the walls. I was on the bottom bunk. Across from me, Lucas was still asleep. Someone had slept in the bunk above his. There was a sleeping bag still rolled out and half open. I guessed right away that it was Graham's bunk, but he'd come in after I went to bed, and he'd already slipped out. Though Lucas was soundly asleep, and it was hard to tell since one eye was turning a grayish purple and one side of his mouth was all puffed up, he had a bit of a frown on his face and a crinkle between his eyes, like something was bothering him in his dreams. I could only imagine. I guessed that he was still in shock, too, even though he knew most of this was coming.

I found the bags containing most of my possessions on the bunk above mine, next to two other bags. I guess my dad had grabbed them after I left the house yesterday. I wanted to get more answers, to ask him again why he hadn't trusted me with the plan. I changed clothes as quietly as I could, trying not to wake Lucas. It felt weird, knowing that Graham slept in the same room with me. I still couldn't decide if I liked him or hated him. If I hated him, I didn't want to sleep so close to him. If I liked him, I wasn't ready to be sleeping so close to him, with me drooling on my pillow, my face slack in my sleep. I had slept in my clothes, one more sign that I'd stumbled into the sleeping bag and passed out. I wasn't sure if I wished that Graham had seen me in some more flattering pajamas. I was very glad that, in my dazed state, I hadn't chosen to sleep in my underwear.

I squeezed the room's small door, opening it as little as I could, and I shouldered my way through the thin hall to the stairs leading up to the boat's main deck. When I came out, the morning sun was starting to burn through the haze on the water. I looked around for bearings on the horizon, some point of reference. If there was a coastline in any direction, some mountains off in the distance, I couldn't see them through the fog. I couldn't even tell if we were still on Lake Willamette, or if we'd come out into the Pacific Ocean. I'd been on boats in smaller lakes and swamps before, but nothing the size of Lake Willamette. I didn't know the difference between the waves of a tidal lake and the waves out in the world's largest ocean. I had no sense of where I was in the world.

That wasn't my biggest concern, though. I could see the boat behind us, another fishing boat about the same size, and there were two boats ahead of us, one larger and one smaller. None of us seemed to be in much of a hurry, but all four boats were moving through the water in the same direction, their solar engines barely humming. Someone must have known where we were all going, so I didn't worry about that. Instead, I looked around for my parents.

In the front of the boat, I found Sky and Juan holding hands and looking out over the water. I wanted to go talk to them, but, before they saw me, I noticed Graham sitting near them, looking off in a different direction. He saw me, raised his eyebrows, and opened his mouth like he was going to say something, then fell silent. It was the same thing he used to do when I'd flirt just a tiny bit and get him flustered, only it was different now. Everything was different. Because he'd plotted to burn down a school, our school. He wasn't who I thought he was. Now I was the one who didn't know what to say. Before he could break the silence, I turned and headed toward the back of the boat.

There was a raised area in the back where the wheel and all the navigational equipment were housed in this little glass, roofed cabin. I went up the half-flight of stairs to the room, expecting to find one or both my parents there. Instead, I found Mr. Rorty.

"Harriet," he said, "how'd you sleep?"

"Fine, I guess." If I was uncomfortable around Graham now because he'd plotted to burn down a school, I was 10 times as uncomfortable around the ancient greeter who had masterminded the whole thing with my mom over the Internet. Still, I was in the little room. There didn't seem to be an easy way to back out, so I looked for a reason. "Have you seen my mom or dad?"

"They're still down in their cabin. Second one on the left. Not that you could miss it on a boat with only four cabins." He looked up and frowned. "I suppose, between the cabins, the small hold, and the two lifeboats, this is technically a ship and not a boat. But barely a ship."

"Okay," I said, though I don't think he heard me. I turned and started to leave.

"Oh, I wouldn't wake them," he said.

I turned back. "Hmm?"

He looked straight ahead, not meeting my gaze. "They've been apart for quite some time."

"Oh."

Now I really didn't have an escape plan.

He kept looking out ahead. "You seemed angry with Graham last night. In the car. Glad to see your mother, of course, and surprised to see Juan and Sky over there, but before that you were angry with Graham. Can I ask you why?"

"I just...I didn't understand why you burned down the school. Then, when I learned it was a distraction, I understood that part, but I still didn't get the school part. Why not the mall? Or one of the other Corporation stores? The car repair place maybe? And Graham seemed so happy to watch it burn. That scared me a little."

Mr. Rorty nodded slowly. He just kept on nodding for way too long. Finally, he said, "Did they tell you what I did before I became a greeter?"

"Graham said you were a high school teacher. At the public school. Mt. Hood?"

"No, not Mt. Hood High. I'm old, remember? Older than that school by a long shot. But I was a high school teacher. I taught history, like your dad. Only he taught college kids. I think that makes him a bit more idealistic than I am. I taught the same kids he taught.

Eager. Ambitious. Thirsty. But I also taught the ones that never got to him. The ones who were unmotivated. The ones who might have been motivated, but they were too hungry or too scared of what was going on at home to care about college. Some were too full of anger to do much but lash out at the world or hurt themselves. And some were just sociopaths." He shrugged. "It happens. A genetic roll of the dice. Doesn't mean they can't go to college, but the ones your dad taught were the ones who'd learned to hide it so they could go to work for the corporations. I got those. I also got the ones who couldn't stop themselves from torturing small animals. We used to get all kinds in the public schools. Then, slowly but surely, they drained us of funding, reduced the human beings to bits of data, and told us that teachers were the problem. If we could just get those terrible teachers away from any kid with potential, the world would be a paradise, they said. By the end of my career, I was babysitting rooms full of kids filling in bubbles on screens."

Then he did look at me. "Lucas is not the first kid I've taught whose dad liked to hit him," he said. I noticed the slip, the way he considered Lucas his student even though he hadn't been a true teacher at Alice Louise Corporate High. I didn't correct him. Now that I think about it, he was just as much a teacher as any other person in the building. The people who were awarded that title by The Corporation didn't ever meet us. "It's not really because Lucas is gay. If Lucas had been born straight, his dad would have hit him for being too skinny or too fat or some other made-up reason. These kinds of parents do that because they are angry at something else, at a world they can't control, and they find a conveniently small person who lives in their house to make themselves feel bigger, more important. Lucas should be very glad he was born a boy. It could have been a lot worse if Mr. Robb had had a daughter.

"And I might be crossing a line by telling you this, but Graham isn't the first kid I've taught whose parents are absent."

"Did they die in the floods? Or one of the plagues?" Those seemed like statistically safe guesses, and Mr. Rorty didn't seem surprised that I'd asked.

"His father may have. He didn't stick around long enough to see Graham's birth. Graham's mom never wanted to be a mother. She had a habit to feed, one that was more important to her than her child. She headed off to the oil platforms in the Polar Sea to make her fortune. Drug addicts can't get jobs working for The Corporation up there, but there's one profession that's always in demand."

"Oh," I said.

"See, The Corporation didn't take away Graham's parents. And The Corporation didn't make Lucas' father a monster. We all have reason to be angry at what corporations have done, sure." He gestured to the water all around us. "But anger can't be the motivation. Graham's parental neglect might explain his anger, if he'd burned down Alice Louise Corporate High out of anger. But he didn't. And it might explain Lucas' anger, if that's why he'd done it. But he didn't.

And I told you about my story. But I didn't do it out of anger, either. Not really."

"Then why? Why a school?"

"Harriet, I appreciate that you love schools. You've got parents who always taught you that education is important. You're luckier than a lot of kids in that way. But you've attended schools for what, 12 years?"

I counted quickly. "14 if you count pre-school."

"I was a student for 19 years. Then I taught in the public schools for 36 years. Since then, I've worked for The Corporation for the last eight and a half years." He smiled. "Plus two more years in school if you count pre-school." He looked out ahead of the boat again, out at the little waves and the white Vs cut by the boats ahead of us. "Harriet, when is a door not a door?"

"When it's ajar," I said.

"I love that riddle. It's not just a pun. Sure, a jar isn't a door. But also, if a door is open, it's just an entranceway, right? It's the ability to close that makes it a door. So when it's ajar, even if it's not literally a jar, it's also not really a door.

"Harriet, I want you to think about another riddle before you talk to Graham the next time. When is a school not a school?"

I did think about it. I stood there thinking about it for a while. Mr. Rorty would smile at me when I looked at him, but he didn't try to help me anymore. He just let me think. Eventually I got too uncomfortable with the silence, so I nodded to him and left the little room.

But I wasn't nodding because I had figured it out. I just needed to leave. I went down to the main deck and sat in a chair, one that faced out to the sea, was bolted down, and had some mechanism in front where a fishing pole of some kind could be attached. I leaned over the mechanism, with its wheels and gears, lay my forearms on the railing, and looked out at the ocean. And I thought.

When my parents came up onto the main deck and offered everyone breakfast, I ate. But I didn't talk much. Sky was excited to fill me in about everything she hadn't been able to tell me. That's when I learned why Lucas had been so mad when I got Juan and Sky together. Juan had been a part of the plan, though only Lucas knew that, and he was worried Juan wouldn't leave without Sky. Then Juan had told Sky, but she hadn't been allowed to tell me she was leaving. That's why our last trip to the mall had been so weird. Luckily for me, Sky had decided to come along, so Juan still played his part, helping with the prison break, while Sky helped get the boats ready. That way, if the prison break didn't work, she could still have walked away. Like Juan, she had a family she was leaving behind. Lucas thought they were sacrificing too much, but he selfishly wanted his best friend to come along, and so did I. Getting them together had made that happen, so Lucas reluctantly forgave me, but he still felt bad that they were losing so much to join us.

I got to have my family along. Sky and Juan had to leave theirs behind, but they got to have each other. Lucas and Graham had given up everyone in their lives except the people on the ships. I couldn't stay mad at Lucas. Not after what I'd seen last night. But I was still angry with Graham. I knew he wasn't the one who ultimately made the decision. The whole plan was orchestrated by my mom and Mr. Rorty. So why did I still feel so angry with Graham?

I spent most of the morning thinking about Mr. Rorty's riddle. And the riddle of my feelings about Graham. My mom and dad kept coming over to hug me as they bustled around the ship doing whatever they needed to do. I still had to struggle to let my mom out of my sight, but I also held in my anger at her about the burning of the school. Why the school? When is a door not a door?

Lunchtime came and went, though I skipped that meal. I could hear snippets of everyone's conversations. Sky and Juan made up a silly pirate song. Lucas and Graham talked in low tones. Mom and Dad and Mr. Rorty talked about next steps and communications and navigation and the weather. I heard all this, and I let it sink in to my contemplations, to become a part of the equation, to fill in the spaces like silt between stones in a riverbed. But mostly, I focused on the riddle. When is a school not a school? In the evening, Mom made me eat dinner. I think she could tell that I was letting her go more easily, but she didn't press me to find out what I was thinking about.

It started to get cold before sundown, so I went down to my little cabin and put on a long-sleeved shirt and my winter coat. Then I came back up to the top deck. We'd dropped the anchor, and I could see the lights from the other ships floating in front and behind us. They weren't moving, either. Everyone in our little...what? Army? Band of misfits? Escaping criminals? Whatever we were, everyone was going to sleep. On our boat, one by one, people drifted away. Dad and Mom and Mr. Rorty went up to the room with the wheel. On bigger ships they call this room the bridge, but everyone onboard this little ship was calling ours the wheelhouse. Light from the room illuminated the main deck, and the shadows of the three adults stretched out and swayed as they milled about during their conversation. Down on the deck, Lucas went to bed first after making a grand announcement. As he walked by me, he put a gentle hand on my shoulder, but he didn't say anything. Then Sky and Juan announced they were calling it a night, too. They both said goodnight to me, and I said goodnight back. Normally I would have been very interested to see if they were sleeping in the same cabin, but I shook my mild curiosity away.

When it was very dark, the old folks came down the stairs from the wheelhouse. Dad and Mom took turns hugging me, and Mom held me for a long time.

"I know this is a lot to take in," Mom whispered.

"You're here," I said. "So it's worth it." That was 100% true. No matter how conflicted I'd felt about the burning of the school, that fact had never changed.

She kissed me on the forehead. "I love you, Harriet."

"I love you, too, Mom."

And then they were gone, and I was alone with Graham.

Only a minute or two passed, and then he started to head for the stairs, but I stood up and that stopped him. I took his hand and led him up to the front of the boat. We stood there, looking into the darkness. The lights of the two boats ahead of us bobbing in the distance, and the stars turning so slowly they seemed to stand still, separated the night into two kinds of black, one frozen, one liquid. I put my arms around Graham's ribs and pulled him close. He wrapped his arms around my shoulders.

"It's cold," I said.

"Better now," he said.

We stood there, slow dancing to the boat's rhythm. After a long song, I pulled away slightly. "I didn't understand at first."

"I know."

"I thought you were doing it out of spite."

"I wasn't. I promise. I—"

"I see that now. It wasn't a school. Not a real one. I don't think I could forgive you if you'd destroyed a real school. I know you worked very hard to make sure no one was inside, that no one would get hurt, but even then, if it had been a school... People around the world are desperate to get into schools. They walk for miles. They spend everything they have on uniforms for their kids. People with my skin fought and died so I could go to a school with people with your skin. If you'd dishonored that, if you'd desecrated that.... Well, you can see why I was so mad."

"I get it."

"But you didn't burn down a school. Because it wasn't a school. A school is a place where there are teachers who care about students. It's a place where learning is more important than test scores, where what we do every day is more important than what colleges we attend or what corporate jobs we get after we leave. It's a place that cares more about the truth we discover than the beliefs they want us to buy."

"'When is a door not a door?'" Graham said.

"Exactly. A door is a door when it has the ability to close. And a school becomes a school when it has the ability to care about students, not the ability to make money or get the right test scores."

"It was a diversion," Graham admitted, "but we wanted one that had a point. We thought about spray painting anti-corporate propaganda all over town at specific times and places to lead the cops away from the prison, and that might have worked, but the next day? It was just a prison break, and everything would go back to normal. Now, all the students will have to go to Mt. Hood High, at least until they can rebuild Alice Louise. It's not a permanent solution, but, for at least a little while, people will be sending their kids to a building with some real teachers inside. Rich kids and poor kids will be mixed together. Maybe the managers will demand that The Corporation or the government improve Mt. Hood, get more teachers, take better care of it. Maybe they'll even say they are willing to pay taxes to make their kids' school into a worthwhile place. It seemed like a better choice than spray painting stores. I mean, the car repair shop repairs cars. The grocery store gets people their groceries. But the school that's not a school? We decided that had to be our target because it was the thing that most needed to go."

I squeezed him tighter, pushing my head into the crook of his neck, my forehead against his jaw. "I get that now." Then I leaned back and looked at him. I could barely see his face by the light coming from the wheelhouse, but I could see his eyes, and he looked into mine. "Speaking of now," I said, "what happens to us?"

"Do you mean all of us, or us-us?"

I smiled. "I mean all the people in these boats. The students in Mt. Hood might all be going to the same high school when break is over, but where are we all going?"

"First, we're going to run. The Corporation will come after us. I don't know how, exactly, but they will come. If we can get away, well, then we probably come back."

"To burn down more corporate schools?"

"No," he said, quite firmly. "To burn down the whole corporation. To take on the whole idea that a company has more power and more rights than the people it employs. That's what I've signed on for, anyway. The long fight."

"And what about us-us?" I asked.

He smiled. "We're planning on running pretty far away. I'd say we have quite a bit of time."

I couldn't see him very clearly in the darkness, and I wanted to get my aim right, so I reached up and put my hand against the side of his face. Then I leaned in and kissed him, just a quick kiss at first. I pulled away.

"We have more time than you think. Like you said, it's a long fight."

Our next kiss was much, much longer.

-24-43-1-10-6-83-67-14-4-
-3-3-43-0-66-0-0-0-6-
-0-7-11-2-1-27-
-5-0-0-80-1-

EPILOGUE

Sunday, January 6ᵗʰ, 2115

Now this diary isn't a diary anymore. My dad made sure my journal made it onto the boat (obviously), and he convinced me to type it up and have Sky, Juan, Lucas and Graham help me encode it. Again, I guess that's obvious if you're reading this. Dad assures me that my story, even though it's just the story of one high school junior and her day-to-day drama, will actually help people understand what the corporate schools are like and why we're fighting back.

I can't tell you where we are. They've shown me on the maps, taught me how to read them, but I'm not allowed to reveal that information. I know where we're headed, also. I even have some idea of what we'll do when we get there. I can't say what that is yet, just in case The Corporation cracks the code, but as long as this is out there, you know that we still exist. And we're planning to come back.

I wonder what The Corporation will say about us. Will they say we're terrorists or just a bunch of criminals who broke out of jail? Will they say we're dangerous, or will they say they have everything under control? They will probably just try to cover the whole thing up, scrub any mention of the jail break and the burnt-down school from any outgoing email or blog post coming out of Mt. Hood, make sure nobody talks. If so, that will be a big mistake. We won't let them keep us a secret.

If you've gone to all the trouble to decode this, you've been through each of Shakespeare's plays many times. You know that *The Tempest* ends with a request for help. Well, now I'm asking for your help. The corporations took over the world, then conquered one another, and now we're going to be going up against the only one left standing. They have been brainwashing everyone, through their schools, through their commercials, through every pledge of allegiance to every smiley-faced flag, for generations now. And we have to somehow try to convince everyone that what they have been taught is wrong, that people matter more than profits, and that corporations aren't people. We need you.

> "With the help of your good hands:
> Gentle breath of yours my sails
> Must fill, or else my project fails."

Stand with us.

About the Author

Benjamin Gorman is a high school English teacher. He lives in Independence, Oregon, with his son. He's the author of the novels *The Sum of Our Gods*, *Corporate High School*, *The Digital Storm: A Science Fiction Reimagining of William Shakespeare's The Tempest*, and *Don't Read This Book*, and the poetry collection *When She Leaves Me*. He believes in his students and the world they will create if given the chance.

MANY THANKS

Thanks, first and foremost, to my son, Noah Gorman, for generously sharing his dad's time with all this book's readers.

Thanks to my editor, Wendy Hart Beckman, a superhero who swoops in to rescue me from the evil Embarrassing Error.

Thanks to the students who have asked me to come visit their classes to talk about this book. I love your great questions.

Thanks to all the folx who helped with the cover design, including Anna Martin, the artist who designed the second cover to replace the terrible first one, Isaac Mitchell, who gave feedback, VF Libris, the publishing company that produced the translation into Croatian and shared ideas from the third cover, and my co-publisher, Viveca Shearin, who helped with this, the fourth.

And thanks to you, Dear Reader, for giving every word in this novel a reason to exist!

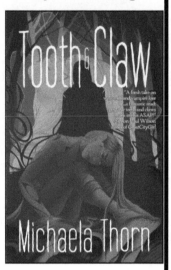

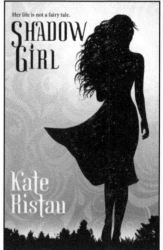

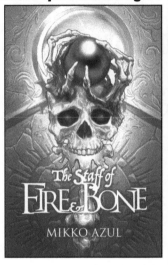

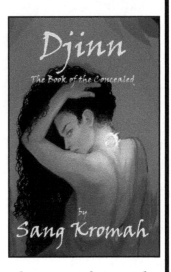

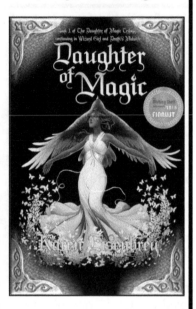

Lightning Source UK Ltd.
Milton Keynes UK
UKHW021933150421
382072UK00010B/522/J

9 780998 388083